the drama of death

dead end witches
book two

Leslie Gail

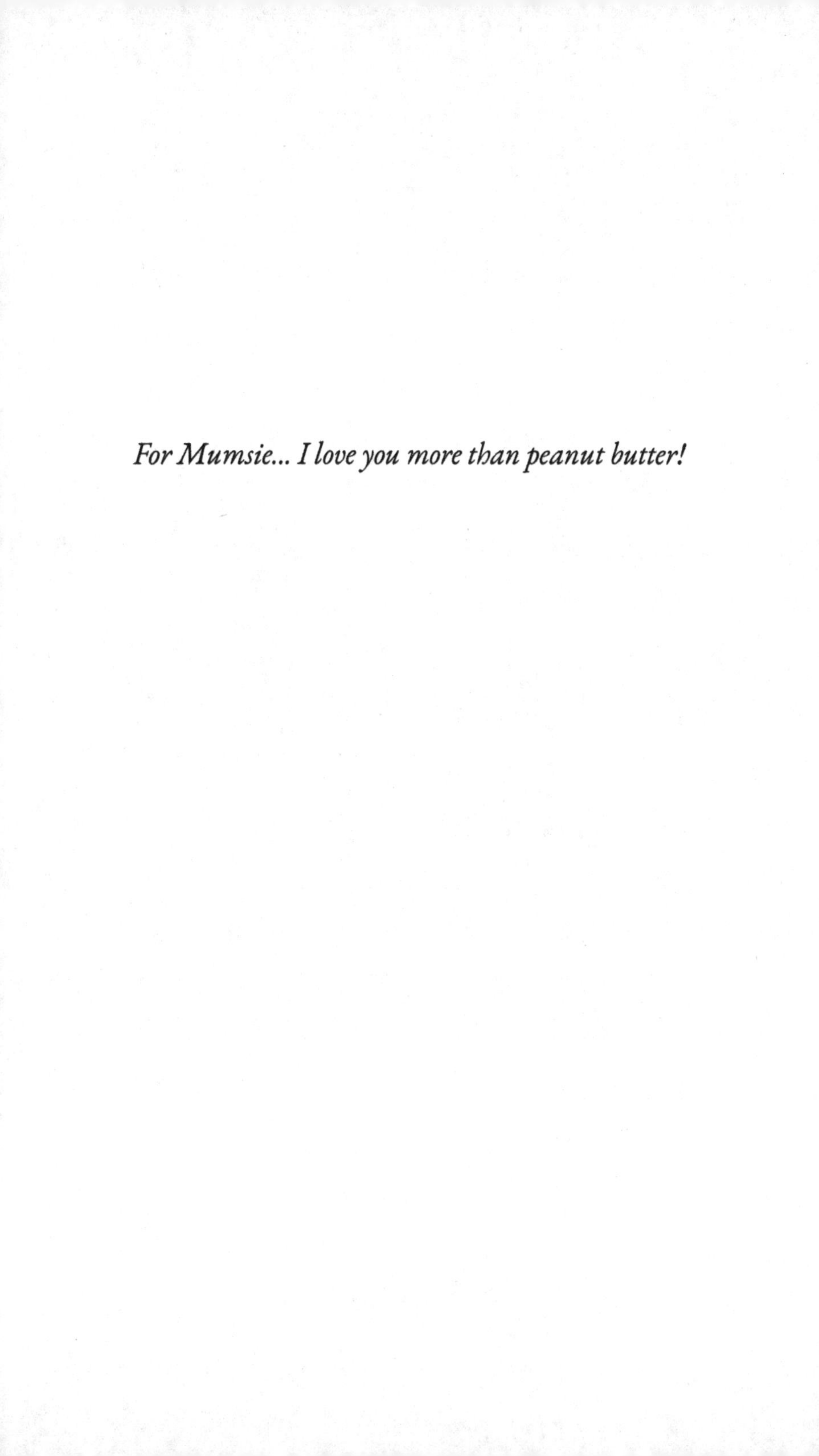

For Mumsie... I love you more than peanut butter!

the bell witches

For those of you who asked for a family tree.

Family Matriarch – **Adelaide Bell/Granny**

   Granny's Daughters:

   Magnolia

   Ruby Dee

   Merilee*

   Willa Jo

Granny's Grandchildren:

   Magnolia's son: **Boone**

   Ruby Dee's daughters: **Star, Astra, and Daisy**

   Willa Jo's children: **Holly, Isaac, Mal, and Fox**

   Granny has one great-grandchild: Astra's daughter, **Teeny**

*Merilee had no children of her own, but has helped to raise Boone, Star, Astra, Daisy, and Teeny at one point or another.

Other important characters and their connection to the Bells:

Aunt Tatty - Granny's sister

Uncle Gavin - Aunt Merilee's on again/off again husband

Carly Davidson - Star's best friend

Grey Miller - Childhood friend of Carly and Star. Carly's current boyfriend

Zeke Fry - Father to Teeny and Kira. Best friend of Boone, runs his bar Pub Dead in his absence.

Kira Fry - Zeke's daughter. Best friend and sister to Teeny

Rock Davidson - Carly's brother, and Star's ex. He is also Daisy's producer.

Former Sheriff Paul Briggs - Godfather to Carly and Rock

Caroline - House ghost. No relation to the Bells.

Acting Sheriff Dusty Palmer - Star's friend, Carly's boss

chapter
one

Black Friday

THE ORANGE JUICE carton careened toward my head, and I barely had time to shield my face with the bacon platter. I waited for the sound of the *thunk* against the ceramic dish, but when it didn't come, I peered over the edge and spotted the carton ensnared in the vines of the pothos plant—vines which had definitely not been long enough to snake across the room a few minutes ago.

With a flick of her wrist, Aunt Merilee gently lowered the carton to the table while retracting the vines into their pot. She glared at Daisy then at me in turn. "We don't use our powers to hurt each other, girls."

Daisy sighed and waved her index finger, righting the salt and pepper shakers I'd knocked over when I'd grabbed the empty platter. I placed the platter back on the counter and didn't bring up the fact that while Aunt Mer could strangle someone with plant vines and Daisy could bean them in the forehead with beverage containers, it wasn't like I could weaponize my ability to talk to the dead. The worst I could do was bore someone to death with ghost stories.

"I didn't orchestrate getting the three of us alone before breakfast just to have you two make a mess in my kitchen. What was today's argument about?" Aunt Mer's voice was level, but Daisy and I both knew that look. She'd had enough.

Ever since my little sister, Daisy, had shimmied her way back into our lives on Halloween, I'd seen that look on Aunt Mer's face almost daily. For years, it had been just me, Aunt Mer, and my teenage niece, Teeny—who I'd helped raise—living in Aunt Mer's farmhouse. So having Daisy and her entourage around constantly was a lot. We'd maintained a semblance of peace for Thanksgiving, but it seemed the truce was broken with the holiday done. Black Friday shoppers had nothing on the post-Thanksgiving Bell-family shenanigans. I hoped Daisy's filming hiatus would end soon. Otherwise, I wasn't sure Aunt Mer's kitchen would survive.

"Sorry, Aunt Mer." I picked up the orange juice carton, checked for leaks, and placed it in the middle of the table. I quickly scanned the spread to see what else we were missing.

Daisy tucked one of her blond locks behind her ear, dusted the spilled salt into her palm, then threw it over her left shoulder. "Me too. Why did you want to get us alone?"

"I think you know, Daisy," Aunt Mer said.

I studied Daisy's face, searching for clues, but she hadn't been the star of her high school drama club for nothing.

Her face was blank when she said, "Do I?"

"Your mamma told me you have something you want to ask Star, and I think you should get it over with. She's not gonna bite."

"Mamma told you?" Daisy's mask dropped. "She promised to keep her mouth shut and give me time to work up my nerve."

I *knew* it! I'd suspected all along that Daisy had ulterior motives for her visit, but I kept that thought to myself out of respect for Aunt Mer and instead took a deep breath. "What do you need to ask me, Daisy?"

She opened her mouth and closed it again—then opened it once more. "Nothing. It's not important."

"Apparently, it is, since Mamma called me about it in October! And now Aunt Mer knows whatever it is."

"Mamma did what now?"

"She called and told me to keep an open mind then guilt-tripped me with, 'She's the only sister you have left, Star,'" I repeated in Mamma's drawl.

"She's right. I am!" Daisy said. "You act like I'm some stranger who's squatting instead of your sister who's come to visit."

"Generally, when people visit, they stay a weekend, or a week at most—"

"This!" Aunt Mer stomped her foot on the kitchen tiles. "This constant bickering is exactly what I need to get away from. Ever since Daisy has been home, you two have either been arguing or ignoring each other. You're acting like children, not like two grown women. I'm tired of being in the middle, and you both need to set a good example for your niece. Especially while I'm gone!"

"Gone? Where are you going?" I asked.

Aunt Mer sighed. "This wasn't the way I meant to tell you, but Gavin and I are going on a cruise. We need time to figure out what we are together—and where we might live."

"So, y'all are thinking about it? Finally?" I asked barely above a whisper.

They'd been dancing around—and in, over, and under—the subject since before I was born. She and Gavin had been married but had split up and gotten back together again so many times, Granny said she might as well just keep the ring on.

Aunt Mer grinned. "Maybe?"

"When are you leaving?" Daisy asked.

"The day after tomorrow."

Daisy and I threw our arms around her at the same time. Aunt Mer let out a long, cleansing breath, and I could almost feel her stress melt away. The three of us stood there for a moment, then Aunt Mer gently pushed us away.

"So, please, can we all just get through today without arguing? Then, once I'm safely away on the *Duchess of the Ocean*, you two can kill each other. Just be sure to mop up all the blood before I get home."

That made us both laugh, and in my relaxed and happy state, I was just about to prompt Daisy to ask me for her favor, but voices outside the window and heavy footsteps on the front porch signaled our guests had arrived.

Daisy and her crew had descended upon us like a swarm of locusts last month—minus the decimated crops, unless I counted us constantly running out of milk. The whole gang, minus one, was staying in Daisy's tour bus in the driveway while eating their meals in the house with us—at Aunt Mer's insistence, of course. The *minus one*, Rock Davidson, who also happened to be Daisy's producer, my best friend Carly's brother, and my ex, had been staying with Carly. I'd managed to avoid him for the most part. However, now he stood in my kitchen along with the rest of the crew. And seemed to be trying not to smile.

"Star, what happened to you?" Teeny stood on the bottom step, gaping at me.

I glanced around to find everyone staring at me with amused expressions. I didn't know what the deal was. It wasn't like they hadn't seen me over the last month in various pajamas—all of them decent—before I'd had a chance to put on my makeup.

"You look like Alice Cooper stuck a fork in an electrical socket," Rock said.

I'd been out late with Carly last night at karaoke—it was an '80s-themed night—and was dead tired, so I'd skipped my nightly shower and my usual skin care routine and had gone to bed in full makeup and hair still teased to kingdom come. I turned and glared at Aunt Mer and Daisy. "And you two didn't think to mention my appearance?"

"I was a bit busy trying to keep you and Daisy from killing each other," Aunt Mer said.

"If there's not at least a half pound of bacon left when I get back, I will hex you all."

That only made them laugh again—probably because I'd spent at least half an hour the previous morning explaining that while we Bells were witches, we didn't hex people. Usually.

. . .

Ten minutes later, my face scrubbed, and hair braided into two pigtails—since it was the only way to tame it without washing it, and I didn't trust the bacon thieves enough to stay away that long—I padded back downstairs and found everyone at the table.

The only empty seat not near Rock was next to Kelsey, Daisy's assistant. I still had no clue how she'd fallen in with Daisy. The contrast between them was stark—Daisy was a strawberry blonde who loved everything pink and sparkly when she wasn't in her goth ghost-hunter Drusilla persona, while Kelsey had dull brown hair and sallow skin. She was usually rather quiet and resembled a lost puppy—an underfed one, at that. I slid in beside her. Thankfully, Rock was all the way on the other end, and I could only see him if I leaned forward a bit past Kelsey and Aunt Mer. So, I pretended I had awesome posture and sat straight in my chair.

It wasn't like I didn't expect to be in the same room as him. Some people might say, "Hey, it's been over a decade since he abandoned you to be your sister's producer. Why are you still awkward around him?" And by people, I meant Carly—last night, at karaoke, which was probably why I'd had too many margaritas.

Daisy's makeup artist, Penny, sat across from me. Her purple hair was shaved on one side and long on the other. She had full sleeves tattooed on both arms and a nose ring. She was quiet in a different way and seemed to speak only when she had something important to say. Not like Daisy, who chattered constantly.

We passed the plates, and the room fell silent as we all dug into the feast.

"Scott, come join us," Aunt Mer insisted.

Scott shook his head. He was handsome in a rugged way, dark hair flopping onto his forehead, intense blue eyes, and a lopsided smile that probably got him out of a lot of trouble—or into more of it.

"There's nowhere to sit." He shoved a forkful of cinnamon chip pancakes into his mouth.

"There's a chair, right there, between Daisy and..." I waved my fork in the general direction. It was still hard to say Rock's name, but I'd promised myself when I almost died in October that I wouldn't be weird about it anymore. I was trying. "Rock."

"Isn't Caroline sitting there?" Scott pushed away from the counter and inspected the chair more closely.

Not that he could see Caroline, or any of the ghosts in Dead End. I was the only one with that particular talent.

"No, Caroline is over here, behind me." I turned my head to give her a smile.

On cue, Caroline waved enthusiastically at Scott and jumped up from the window seat. She braced her hands on the back of Kelsey's chair to the right of me. *"He is such a sweetheart, concerned about little ole me."*

"What made you think Caroline was there?" I asked.

"Daisy said she was." Scott shrugged and pulled out the chair.

I raised my eyebrows at Daisy.

My little sister waved a hand in dismissal. "She moved over to the window seat when Star came downstairs. I was caught up in her debut as the Bride of Frankenstein and forgot to mention it."

A few folks snickered, and soon the conversation turned from the chair to classic horror movies, but Daisy held my gaze. When she'd decided they would be staying a while, we'd had a tense conversation about how none of her crew—except Rock, of course—knew the truth about her. And she'd all but begged me not to reveal her secret that she was a fraud. She was going to tell them—at least Scott and Penny, who'd been with her for years. But she wanted to do so in her own time. This would've been a great conversation opener for that. She could've said, "Oh, hey, about that..." But no, she kept up the farce she'd maintained for well over a decade.

It wasn't that Daisy didn't have *any* special powers— just not the one she'd gotten famous for. She could move objects telekinetically. She used to drive Astra and me nuts with it when we played badminton in the yard, back in the day, because she would maneuver the shuttlecock just out of our reach. But she'd risen to fame as a reality star who saw and spoke to ghosts.

"*I've been on the window seat the whole time,*" Caroline

insisted. *"She just didn't want Scott to sit next to her. I can't imagine why. He's such a nice young man!"*

Chronologically, Caroline could be Scott's great-great-grandmother, but as she died in her late thirties, she was closer to him in biological age than I was.

"Oh, really?" I glanced between Scott and Daisy.

"Oh, really, what?" Daisy colored slightly then seemed to realize I was talking to Caroline, which meant she should've been able to hear what Caroline said as well. At least to her crew.

I couldn't stand watching Daisy falter for words, so I threw her a lifeline. "Caroline, I don't think Daisy heard you. Can you repeat that?"

"I could holler, and the girl wouldn't hear me. What are you...? Oh, I see. You're protecting her. Again. What should I say? Daisy, you need to open your eyes and see that Scott would make a fine husband for you and the two of you would make beautiful babies."

Daisy played her part without a script and nodded enthusiastically. "Oh, that is so interesting!"

It took every ounce of willpower I had not to laugh or even smirk.

"So, what did she say?" Scott asked.

I shoved a piece of bacon into my mouth so Daisy couldn't volley this one to me. But she hadn't won the district drama competition in school for nothing. She launched into a story about how Caroline had seen another spirit outside who'd been a neighbor years ago and had hung herself in a tree after a failed affair. This, in turn, started a conversation among them about some of the other spirits Daisy had "encountered" on her show over the years.

As the conversation continued, I stuffed myself with bacon while sneaking glances at Rock. He seemed to fit in well with this motley crew. And it struck me suddenly that they were a family. It was obvious in the way Scott teased Penny about her snoring and how Rock asked Kelsey if she'd gotten enough to eat, and they all knew the punch-line to Daisy's stories. It reminded me of the years before Astra went away. Perhaps Aunt Mer was thinking the same because she was smiling too.

"Oh, hey, Mer, the trellis beside your bedroom window is down again," Penny said. "I'll grab my tools and put it back up for you after breakfast."

"It fell again?" Rock asked. "We just rebuilt it a couple of weeks ago."

Beside me, Teeny muttered, "If someone would use the front door like a normal person, that wouldn't happen."

"Or maybe not hold the trellis while hoisting himself in through the window," Daisy added.

I wouldn't recommend laughing while drinking orange juice. It hurt.

"Star? You okay over there?" Aunt Mer asked.

All the other heads turned toward me as well.

I gave her a thumbs-up while I continued coughing into my napkin and trying to catch my breath.

Teeny jumped up from the table and brought me a glass of cold water, placing it in my hand. "Sorry."

"Never apologize for great comedic timing." I grinned at her.

As the food dwindled and the conversation died down, Scott's phone rang. He promised to come back and help clean up then excused himself from the table. Aunt Mer tried to shoo us away, insisting she could do the dishes. Before anyone could object, Scott burst back through the kitchen doorway like a puppy escaping from his crate. He picked Daisy up and swung her around, knocking over a dining chair.

"Daisy, it's happening! It's really effing happening!"

chapter
two

"*WHAT* IS HAPPENING?" Aunt Mer asked.

"SupeTV is coming here to Dead End!" Scott put Daisy down and brushed his hair off his face.

"SupeTV?" Aunt Mer took off her apron and laid it on the counter. "That's the network *Spirit Slayer* is on, isn't it? Gavin is so obsessed with that show. Why are they coming here?"

"They want Daisy on *Supernatural Truthbusters*. Well, Drusilla Von Leigh, that is." He turned to Rock. "I told you I'd come through. I knew Cal would love her."

Scott held up a hand for Rock to high-five, which Rock did.

Kelsey squealed. "It's such a fun show, and Daisy will be perfect for them."

"Isn't that the one where they reveal people as

frauds?" Penny looked dubiously at Rock, which made me wonder if she suspected the truth about Daisy.

"It is!" Scott said. "That's why it's so perfect. Daisy's the real deal, so it'll be a killer episode!"

After that, everyone began talking at once—everyone except Daisy, who was suspiciously quiet. The pieces fell into place then.

"Why are they filming here in Dead End specifically?" I narrowed my eyes at Rock. "Couldn't you film anywhere? Why bring a whole production to our little town?"

Rock shifted uncomfortably. "It's how they build their cases, I guess, by talking to people who know her and by seeing her in her natural environment."

I looked from Rock to Daisy. "This? This is the reason you're back in town. For the show?"

Daisy's silence and open mouth told me all I needed to know. I grabbed my bag and headed out the door, my chest tight with disappointment.

As soon as I pulled out of the driveway, I called Zeke. "Hey, I'm gonna need some of your brown butter nachos ASAP."

Zeke managed my cousin's bar but had a bit stronger —and only recently discovered—connection to my family.

"Sounds serious. What's wrong?"

"I don't want to talk about it. I just want to stuff my face with your nachos and maybe a margarita or three." I didn't care that it wasn't even noon. It was five o'clock somewhere and half past family drama time.

"I'm sorry, Star! I'm not at Pub Dead today. I'm in Austin, shopping."

"Shopping. In Austin. Is this like code for you've been kidnapped? If it is, say, 'I'm shopping for a pair of red pumps.'"

He laughed. "You're not far from the truth. But change it to purple suede fuzzy boots with a matching keychain, and you've got it. Do you know people are actually crazy the day after Thanksgiving?"

"I do. Why do you think I stay home and get someone else to cover for me at work on this day every year? Why are *you* out in the madhouse?"

"I'm helping Kira shop for Christmas. Or rather, I guess I'm just the bag holder while she shops for her mom. She invited Teeny to come along, but..."

"But Teeny made an excuse about needing to be close to home?" I wasn't surprised. Ever since Teeny had found out her best friend Kira's dad was her dad as well, she'd been understandably awkward around him.

"Yeah. But I get it. Teeny needs time to process the mother of all plot twists."

"You mean the father of all plot twists?"

He laughed. "I can't believe you out-punned me. But

yeah, and Kira wants this instant family, but she's trying so hard not to pressure Teeny."

"It's hard for them both in different ways—going from best friends to instant sisters with one conversation. Give them time, they'll work it out." My phone buzzed. "Hey, Zeke, Carly's calling. Catch you later?"

"Sure! Swing by tomorrow, and I'll fix you a double batch of nachos," he said.

I clicked over to Carly, and before I could utter more than, "Hey…" she said, "Why in the world are you headed out to the lake in the dead of winter?"

"First, we live in Texas, not Maine. It's not like the lake is frozen over. And second, I'm not!" I insisted, but when I looked at my surroundings to tell her where I was, I found I was indeed on the road to Ingersoll Lake.

"I can see exactly where you are. You're not far from the turnoff up to the cabin."

I pulled over onto the shoulder, flipped on my hazard lights, and turned off the car. "I didn't intend to drive here."

"What do you mean you didn't intend to? You don't accidentally drive somewhere, Star. Especially not back to the cabin where you almost died. What's going on?"

"I was stressed and headed to Pub Dead for nachos and got distracted talking to Zeke about the girls. And now I'm here."

"Why, Star?"

"I don't know," I said, but we both knew the reason, whether it was on purpose or a crazy subconscious accident. It was where my sister's body was hidden. I hadn't been back since the ambulance took Dusty and me to the hospital in October. The fact that I hadn't seen Dusty that much since was also a sore spot.

"Star." Carly's voice grew gentler. "You can't be there. You know I'm on your side, but you have to trust the process."

"It's hard to trust the process when most of the people in charge of it can't be trusted."

We'd found out in October that our local government and police force hadn't been trustworthy. Carly and Dusty were the only cops in Dead End whom I felt I could trust. So yeah, I didn't have a lot of confidence in the powers that be.

"We have to give it time. We will get that warrant."

"Why were you tracking me anyway?" I asked, deliberately changing the subject.

After the events in October, Carly had enabled Find My Friends on my phone so she would know my location at all times.

She sighed. "Rock texted me and said you ran off like a bat out of hell. His words."

"Did he tell you why?"

"He said you and Daisy got into it."

I told her exactly what had transpired, from Daisy

continuing to lie to her crew about her abilities, to freaking SupeTV coming to Dead End to film. That was when I knew why I'd subconsciously driven toward the lake. I used to vent to Astra when Daisy was driving me nuts.

"He mentioned something about a big opportunity coming their way."

I cranked the engine, flipped off the hazard lights, and pulled back onto the road.

"Star?"

"Hey, I gotta go. I'm pulling back into traffic now. You wouldn't want to have to arrest me for distracted driving, would you?"

"You're going to the cabin, aren't you?"

"Nope, I'm headed to the lake to think."

"I know when you're lying, Star."

"Love you! Bye!"

She was right, I was totally about to break the law. But I was almost to the lake turnoff when I realized that wasn't what I needed at all. Being at the lake wouldn't help. What I needed was someone who'd known both me and Daisy all our lives, someone who could give me perspective. I made a U-turn and headed back toward town. Granny would know what to do.

. . .

I spotted a parking space across from my grandmother's eclectic shop downtown, nestled among other small businesses. It was originally called the Mercantile, but we in the family, and most of the locals, just called it the Merc. The hand-painted sign hanging outside called it Toil and Trouble. Granny, my maternal grandmother, called it home since she lived alone in the apartment above the shop.

I opened the door and found a throng of people sniffing candles, examining the tarot cards, and flipping through the books on magical subjects. To my surprise, Granny stood behind the register. I'd come here to vent to her upstairs, where she spent most of her time. While she still had a sharp mind and a young spirit well into her nineties, her body had been failing her.

"What in the world, Granny?" I slid behind the register to help her. "What happened to your help? And why didn't you call me to come in?"

"I am completely capable of ringing up a few customers." She smoothed her white curls and smiled.

"So, you fired her?"

Her eyes sparkled, but instead of arguing with her about it, I bagged the customer's purchase and handed it over while she printed off their receipt. A few months ago, we couldn't get Granny to answer the text messages that popped up on the iPad we'd gifted her. Now, she seemed to be a master of the point-of-sale system we ran on the store tablet.

After we handled a few more customers together and sent them on their way, I made my rounds throughout the sales floor, checking on the customers who were still shopping. Finally, once everyone was helped, I headed back to Granny, who was peering over her glasses at the tablet screen.

"We've sold fifteen copies of that new tarot deck since Daisy posted about it on her Ticker."

"TikTok," I corrected her.

Granny pulled out her notebook and wrote that down. She was fond of collecting phrases and terms of the younger generations. I glanced over her shoulder and noted she'd written "Tick Tock" right below "Tweeter."

"Anyway, that girl is good for business."

"If you say so." I had mixed feelings about Daisy, but Granny didn't like it when her grandkids fought, so I kept that to myself. Personally, I thought business was better because Aunt Tatty—Granny's sister, who was traveling in Europe—wasn't there to overwhelm customers with her dramatic stories. But I would let Granny believe it was Daisy.

We'd just sent our last customer on their way with Daisy's book, the tarot cards, and a few candles when the door's bell jangled again. It never stopped. I took a breath, plastered on a smile, and lifted my head to greet the potential customer but found my aunt Willa Jo standing there instead.

She smiled and enveloped me in one of her famous hugs. "Star! You're supposed to be off today."

I loved that she hugged me every time she saw me, whether we'd been apart mere hours or a few days.

"I am off. I just came by to see Granny and—"

"And got put to work!" She put a hand on her hip, which made the many bracelets on her arm jingle.

Aunt Willa Jo was the youngest of Granny's daughters. At a mere fifty-four, she'd been fourteen when I was born and had always felt more like a big sister to me than an aunt. She was the one who'd taught me to roller skate, had taken me to buy my first bra, and had sat with me while I cried over my first heartbreak.

"Where in the world is your help, Mamma?"

"I fired her."

"Mamma! We just hired her."

"*You* just hired her. I didn't like her. Besides, I am perfectly capable of sitting on a stool, pushing buttons, and taking money."

"And what about the customers on the floor when they need help? You can barely get around!" Aunt Willa Jo insisted.

"They have eyes, don't they? They can find things themselves. Besides, Star is here."

"She needs a day off, once in a while. Like today, for instance."

"It's fine. I'm glad to help. Especially today. It helped distract me from my frustration," I said.

"What's wrong?" Aunt Willa Jo turned her attention from Granny to me.

I tried to hold it together, but the gentle way she touched my arm made it all come out. "I was already at my breaking point with the whole Astra thing without having to deal with Daisy's games!"

Aunt Willa Jo enveloped me in a hug and patted my back.

"I can't do anything about Daisy. That's for you two to work out. But I've been trying to figure out what spell Tatty used so I can create a counterspell," Granny said.

Aunt Willa Jo released me from the hug. "Oh, honey! You've been through a lot these past few months. Mamma will figure this out. Meanwhile, would you like a distraction? Something fun to work on?"

"What did you have in mind?" I asked.

"The annual holiday ball!"

"Oh! I forgot about that. You're carrying on the tradition?" I asked.

It hadn't been something we Bells regularly attended, at least in recent years, because it was a stuffy black-tie affair.

"Please tell me you're changing the name of it. What did they call it? The Duchess's Royal Ball or something?"

"The Mayoress's Grand Christmas Ball, and yes, I am going to change it, especially since I'm the one organizing it and I am the mayor, not the mayor's wife. Plus, that's just a mouthful. How does Midwinter Ball sound?"

"I love it! Much less pretentious."

"The ball wasn't always a stodgy affair," Granny said. "The first one, after the Great War, was held in a barn. The theme was a Christmas Carol."

I quickly did the math. "World War I? You couldn't remember that."

A look passed over her face so quickly I couldn't decipher it before she said, "Did I say I was there? What is your theme going to be, Will?"

"Oh, I thought winter wonderland, but I might steal the Christmas Carol idea."

"I think that's a wonderful idea," I said. "Just let me know what I can do to help."

"Thank you, honey!"

"Okay, now that's settled, the real reason I'm here. Mamma, did you put back what I asked you to?"

Granny nodded, and Aunt Willa Jo squealed like someone who'd scored Taylor Swift concert tickets as she snatched the viral tarot deck Granny held out to her.

chapter
three

I SLEPT LATER than expected on Sunday morning and woke to raised voices outside my window—quite the contrast to the peaceful going-away dinner we'd had the night before with Aunt Mer. I peeked through the curtains to find Daisy and Rock arguing.

After a quick shower, I felt ready to take on the day and whatever "Drusilla" and her crew might throw at me. Downstairs, I grabbed stuff to make cinnamon toast. Caroline wasn't in her usual spot on the window seat. I hoped she wasn't watching Scott sleep. I needed to have a talk with her about personal space.

My thoughts were disturbed by the screen door slamming. Daisy appeared and stopped short when she saw me. "Oh, I thought you'd be sleeping."

"It's kind of hard to sleep when you two are yelling outside my bedroom window."

She opened the refrigerator and retrieved the milk. "You heard that, huh?"

"Aunt Mer probably heard it on the highway." I glanced at the clock. They'd planned to leave around five, so they should be boarding the cruise ship in Galveston by now. "What were you two fighting about? And why is he here so early?"

"He came by to discuss the *Truthbusters* opportunity." Daisy grabbed the cereal from the pantry and poured it into a bowl, then drowned it in milk. "I don't want to do the show."

"Then why did you sign up?"

"I didn't! That's the whole point. I don't blame Scott because he doesn't know, but Rock of all people... That man frustrates the hell out of me sometimes. He's so freaking stubborn. When he gets an idea in his head, he won't let go of it."

I snorted. "He's been your producer for ten years. Surely you're not just now discovering he's stubborn. I figured that out on our first date."

"Yet you dated him for years and almost married him," Daisy pointed out. "So, we're not so different. But I swear on Astra's soul, that's not why I came back."

I gave her a sharp look, but she seemed sincere—on that subject at least. But there was more to it than that. She hadn't come back just to visit. That I knew. And I also knew I wouldn't get the truth out of her.

Daisy shoved a spoon into the bowl and sat at the table. I plated my toast and ambled into the living room. The sofa was covered in sheets, blankets, and pillows. I plopped into the overstuffed chair and reached for the remote, only to find Daisy and her cereal following from the kitchen.

I nodded to the sofa. "Why didn't you sleep on your bus?"

She fiddled with the edge of the blanket. "I needed time away to think."

"About the documentary?"

"What if they find out?"

The words hung suspended in the air between us. *What if they find out Daisy's a fraud?*

While I hated that she pretended to have this power, my power, I didn't wish her any ill will. "Then, like I said before, why do it?"

"Like you care." She huffed a breath, and without giving me a chance to defend myself, she continued, "He's scheduled a video meeting with some of the producers at SupeTV. Today."

I was about to dig into that more, but the screen door slammed, and Teeny burst into the living room, all smiles and chatter. Kelsey stood behind her, less talkative but also smiling.

"What do you think?" Teeny twirled then held out her arms.

Something about her eyes looked different. "Are those fake eyelashes?"

"What? No! These are mine. Kelsey showed me how to make my eyes pop. She plucked my eyebrows too. So? What do you think?" she pressed.

I sat there in shock. She'd never looked so much like Astra.

"Wow, you look just like your mom." Daisy beat me to the punch.

"Really?" Teeny ran to the hallway mirror and examined herself. "But her hair was red, and mine is brown."

"Your eyes are hers," I said softly.

She grinned. "And Kelsey said I could borrow a dress of hers to wear tomorrow too!"

A dress? Teeny had been wearing a moderate amount of makeup, mostly mascara and a bit of eyeliner, for the past few months, but she hadn't worn a dress since she was seven—despite Aunt Mer's best efforts.

"Oh, that's nice of Kelsey. And you look beautiful. Kelsey did a great job!"

"She's the best!" Teeny gave her a squeeze. "I'm going up to my room to try on the dress."

After she ran up the stairs, I said, "I haven't seen her that happy in a while. And over makeup and clothes? Is she turning into a teenager?"

"She's been one for over a year now," Daisy pointed out.

"I know that, but she hasn't acted like one. Not like you. You were a teenager at the age of nine."

"I can't imagine Daisy as a kid," Kelsey said. "What was she like?"

"Precocious. Imaginative. Dramatic." I ticked off the descriptors on my fingers.

"You forgot bratty," Daisy said.

"Believe me, I haven't forgotten. But Kelsey asked what you were like, not what you are."

Daisy rolled her eyes but smiled.

"You two seem to get along a lot better than Daisy led me to believe," Kelsey said.

"Oh, really? And what picture did Daisy paint of me? Evil half sister? Wicked witch?" I smirked.

Color filled Kelsey's face, and she stammered, but Daisy rescued her. "Don't put the girl on the spot. Yeah, maybe I did throw your name around like it was a curse, but you can't say you haven't done the same in my absence."

"Kelsey, do you have any siblings?" I asked.

"I do, and yeah, we don't get along so well. My sister and I were close at one time, but not so much anymore."

"As long as she's still alive, you have a chance of reconciliation. I missed that chance with Astra."

Teeny's footsteps sounded on the stairs. Once she stepped off the bottom step, she gave a twirl. "What do you think?"

I thought it was a bit too mature for her, or perhaps it was just the blinders that would always make me see her as a kid, but Daisy took her hand and twirled her around.

"Absolutely stunning!"

"It's not too late with her, though." Kelsey nodded toward Daisy. "You should probably make peace with her while you still can."

Her words hit deeper than I expected. I watched Daisy spinning Teeny around, both of them laughing, and felt something shift in my chest. Maybe Kelsey was right. Maybe it wasn't too late after all.

A couple of hours later, Daisy and her whole crew crowded around her laptop at the kitchen table.

"What's going on?" I asked.

Just then, a man popped up on screen. He had dark hair styled into a quiff and cheekbones a statue would envy. Thankfully, I was off camera to the side, as were Rock and the rest of the crew, but Scott sat beside Daisy in front of the screen.

Rock whispered to me, "It's the producer for the SupeTV documentary."

"Let me guess, you 'suggested' she at least hear them out?" I whispered back.

He shrugged. "I *asked* her to at least hear his pitch. It's her decision after that."

I probably should've gone upstairs, as I'd intended, but I stayed to see and hear what was going on. Yeah, I was being nosey, but hey, it was my house and my Wi-Fi they were using, after all.

"Hey, Cal!" Scott said. "How's it going?"

"Much better now that I see your smiling face." He looked up through long lashes and lids rimmed in dark eyeliner. "I like the beard. It gives you an edge. How's life on the road?"

"It's pretty great, man." Scott sounded like he really meant it. "Hey, I want you to meet Daisy."

Daisy gave a small wave. She wasn't her usual exuberant self.

"*This* is Drusilla Von Leigh? Who's your makeup artist, and can we steal her out from under you?" Cal laughed, but I wasn't sure he was completely joking.

He also had a good point. Daisy, while at home, never looked like her on-camera persona, Drusilla Von Leigh. No fake tats, fake lashes, wig, fake husky voice, or any of the other accoutrements that made her Dru. Her strawberry blond hair was in a messy bun, and she didn't have on a stitch of makeup.

Scott turned the laptop toward Penny. "Penny Sinclair is the magician who transforms Daisy."

Penny gave a reluctant wave then moved out of range.

Cal examined his black-painted nails then looked up at

Scott through those impossible eyelashes. "I'm thrilled to be working with you again, Scott."

I whispered to Rock, "Did Scott work for SupeTV too?"

"No, I think they worked together on some other series at one time," he whispered back. "I get the feeling they have history, but Scott's connection to Cal is what got us in the door."

"What's all that whispering?" Cal asked. "Who else are you hiding off in the wings?"

Daisy turned the laptop slightly to bring Rock and me into view. "This is my producer, Rock Davidson, and my sister, Star. Oh, and my assistant, Kelsey, is here as well."

Instead of waving, as Rock and I did, Kelsey stood still. I hated to be cliché, but she was like a deer and headlights and all that jazz.

Cal stared at her a beat. "Does this Kelsey move and talk? Or is she a puppet?"

Kelsey's face turned a deep shade of magenta, and she strode out of the camera's range to the sink, where she got a glass of water.

Scott chuckled. "You know, Kelsey is the one who told me about *Supernatural Truthbusters*. She's obsessed with the show and mentioned Daisy would be perfect for it. She got me to watch an episode, and when I saw your name flash across the screen as producer, I knew I had to try."

That explained her reaction to being on camera. She was starstruck.

"Is that so? In that case, thank you, Kelsey, wherever you ran off to, because after watching a few of Drusilla's... or Daisy... which should I call you?"

"Daisy is fine," she said.

"Great, so yeah, after watching some of your webisodes and showing them to Fiona, we're both excited about the potential to work with you."

"Who's Fiona?" I asked Rock.

"The host of the series," he whispered back.

Cal continued, "She sends her apologies for being late. She's trying to wrap up a previous engagement. But while we wait, let's talk about some of the logistics. Full disclosure, we don't hold back. We do our research and get up close and personal. Some people find it uncomfortable to be under such scrutiny and with cameras in the way all the time. I have to know if you're up for that."

It was Daisy's out. *But will she take it without talking to her crew?* We all collectively leaned closer to find out. But just as she opened her mouth to give her answer, another person popped onto the screen.

"Fiona Cameron!" Scott whispered in awe.

Not having watched the show in question, I didn't share in the excitement, but Fiona was a commanding presence. Even on screen, in a seated position, I could tell she was tall. Her blond hair was upswept, her bright eyes framed in long lashes.

"Oh my god! Drusilla Von Leigh in the flesh! I'm so excited to meet you. I have binged some of your episodes, and, girl, you have presence. Please tell me you've agreed to our demands and that we can begin shooting immediately!" Fiona said.

Daisy gave a nervous laugh. "I haven't agreed to anything yet."

"There's a yet! Wonderful. So we have a chance. What are your demands? Is the fee not enough? Cal, darling, let's pay her more!"

"We haven't discussed payment yet," Cal said.

I left them to discuss particulars and went to make more coffee. Whatever Daisy decided, we would need the caffeine.

chapter
four

A WEEK PASSED with no decisions made, as far as I knew, since Daisy didn't actually confide in me. Teeny went to school, I went to work, and Daisy sulked. With all that and everything else going on, I'd completely forgotten Zeke promised me nachos until he called one afternoon while I was at the Merc.

"Hey, you still at work?" he asked. "I thought I saw your car parked out front this morning."

"Yeah, Granny's not feeling great today. Her legs are bothering her, and I've been training our new part-time help."

"Another victim for the Merc, huh?" He chuckled. "Where do you bury all their bodies?"

I glanced up to see horror cross the face of the college student I was training.

I laughed. "He's totally kidding!" Then, to Zeke, I said, "You're on speakerphone."

"Oops! Oh yeah, I was just giving Star a hard time. The Bells are actually really nice people. They only turn you into a toad if you're late to work a second time. So..."

"Zeke!" I suppressed a giggle, took him off speaker, and stepped into the back room. "It's hard enough keeping help around here without you telling them stories!"

"You should go ask those frogs that hang out in the back alley for the truth—"

"You're no longer on speaker," I said.

"You're no fun." He chuckled. "Fine, down to business."

I waited for him to continue, and when he didn't, I said, "And?"

"You're supposed to ask me what business."

"Okay, what business?"

"Nacho business. Get it?"

"I swear, finding out you have another daughter has doubled your number of dad jokes. But hold up, are you telling me you have nachos for me? You better not be joking."

"I do! I intended to bring them over, but if you have help, you could take a break and come here—for a change of scenery."

Within two minutes, I was sitting on a stool at the bar.

"I present to you, the Starlight Special." He placed a platter of brown butter nachos in front of me, along with a glass of soda.

"You're the best, Zeke Fry!" I gave him a hug and a peck on the cheek.

"Well, it's not completely for selfless reasons. I thought you could catch me up on Teeny, since I haven't seen her much." He seemed to be trying to keep his voice light, but I felt the undercurrent.

I told him about the makeup and dress. "It feels like she's growing up so fast."

"Yeah, and I've missed most of it." He sighed.

"But have you?" I cocked my head. "You helped change her diapers. You were there the day she took her first step. You stood in the hall with me on her first day of kindergarten. You've been in her life as long as I have."

A lopsided grin formed on his face. "You got me there."

I squeezed his arm. "And maybe not as her father officially, but you've been a father to her long before any of us knew the truth."

"Maybe that's why this is so hard. I've been in her life, and I thought she enjoyed being around me, but now she's... different. She doesn't seem to want anything to do with me. I don't know what I've done wrong."

"You haven't done anything wrong." I shrugged. "She's young, and her hormones are whackadoodle. She can't think logically. But, Zeke, she'll come around. We just have to give it time. You were her best friend's cool dad. Now, you're the long-lost father she probably always imagined would be a musician with long hair and tattoos."

"I have tattoos," he said. "And I play a mean kazoo."

I laughed and squeezed his hand. "She'll come around. Just give her time."

I didn't know if it was the threat of being turned into a frog or if I'd finally found good help, but the college student was dusting shelves when I returned—without even having been asked. After showing her our closing procedures and checking on Granny one more time, I finally headed home.

On the drive, my mind was busy with the mental checklist of things I needed to do when I got home. I hadn't realized how much extra work there would be with Aunt Mer gone. Scott, thankfully, had continued to cook the meals. I taught Teeny how to do her own laundry, which in truth, should've happened long ago. And thanks to Penny, there wasn't a single creaky door in the house. She'd even painted the chicken coop.

We didn't see much of Kelsey except for meals and in

the laundry room. Apparently, she had been cleaning the tour bus from top to bottom—and doing the crew's laundry.

I pulled up to the house and found Carly's car in the driveway. I'd almost forgotten it was Buffy night. She, Grey Miller—Dead End High School's principal—and I had been doing a rewatch—a rewatch for me and Carly, but it was Grey's first time through. The three of us had been best friends for years, but the dynamic had recently changed when they started dating. It hadn't changed Buffy night, however. Thank the Slayer!

I trailed into the kitchen, my steps a bit lighter, only to find Rock at the kitchen table, once again, head bent over a pad of paper. Carly stood beside him, pointing to things on the page.

"Hey, you're here! Finally!" Grey called from the sofa. "Maybe they'll stop working and come watch the show."

My glance at their still-bent heads told me they hadn't even noticed me come in. Daisy stood at the sink with Scott and Penny while Kelsey folded towels at the end of the table.

"Hollywood business." Grey used air quotes when he said it.

"What does Carly have to do with the production?" I asked, moving farther into the kitchen.

"Crowd control!" Carly said, finally noticing I was there.

"Crowd control?"

"Daisy has managed to lie low while she's been here because the tourists don't really recognize her out of costume, " Rock said, "but once word gets out that a crew is filming her here, I'd feel better if we had Carly and maybe some off-duty officers she trusts helping out. The studio has approved it."

"Police protection?" I asked. "What are you expecting exactly?"

"Hopefully nothing, it's just... we've had some close calls before. Daisy's fans can be a bit overzealous."

"Can we not talk about that?" Daisy shot him a glance.

"You don't want to talk about the girl who said she'd do anything, even your laundry, just to be near you? That's not what it's cracked up to be, is it, Kelsey?" Rock asked.

Kelsey froze in the middle of folding the towels at the end of the table. "What? Sorry, I was lost in thought."

"Doing Daisy's laundry is a shit job, right?" He chuckled.

"No. It's fine," she said, but her knuckles were white on the towel.

That girl had suppressed issues to work out. No one could always be that willing to help. *And, Miss Bell, how many nights have you answered "yes, of course" to Granny when she needed you at the Merc? Shut up, self!*

I snapped out of my thoughts and heard Daisy returning to the original topic, which made no sense since I only heard the last bit.

"...and it was like she was trying to be me but tinted purple. So yeah, Carly, all the security you want to bring is great with me!"

chapter
five

A COUPLE OF DAYS LATER, Cal and his crew arrived in Dead End. I'd expected trucks to roll in with tons of equipment, akin to a circus arriving in town, and was almost disappointed when Cal arrived in a rental van with three other people.

He must have sensed our state of underwhelm and the crew's disappointment that Fiona wasn't with him because, after he released Scott from a rather warm embrace that spoke volumes, he said, "Fiona was detained and will be on a later flight."

Rock stepped forward to shake his hand. "Welcome, Cal. We look forward to working with you and your crew."

Cal held Rock's hand between both of his and made sustained eye contact. I couldn't tell if he was flirting or if that was just a Hollywood thing.

Once he let go, he grasped Daisy's hands and trilled, "Drusilla Von Leigh, in the flesh! You are beautiful with or without the makeup, but I have to say, I do like this farm-fresh version of you."

Daisy wore a long-sleeved cotton tee and overalls that had never been used for farming or anything besides posing for social media, if I had to guess. Her strawberry blond hair lay in two braids, Laura Ingalls style, over her shoulders. "Thank you, and I have to say, I adore your 'the pirate wore Prada' look as well."

Scott guffawed. "She's got you there, man."

"Touché! Or would that be arr, matey?" Cal replied. "Now, this is Bryan. I couldn't do what I do without him. He is my DP."

"Director of photography," Rock explained to me on the side. "He's their Scott."

"I wonder if he's as good a cook," I joked. I didn't catch the names of the other two people or the rest of what he said.

"Then I'm the producer and director." Cal bowed with a flourish.

"So, wow, your crew isn't much bigger than Daisy's," I observed, impressed. "I thought Hollywood crews would be massive."

"Yarr, I made the rest of them walk the plank, ye see?" Cal winked. Then, back in his normal voice, he said, "It depends on the production, but for something like this, we're bare bones. With Fiona's assistant and her hair-and-makeup person, we'll have seven of us."

Once the introductions, fashion commentary, and pirate accents were done, we headed into the kitchen. Or rather, they all did.

I was about to head upstairs and leave them to it when Cal said, "Star, aren't you coming?"

"Me? I'm not part of this." I gave him a friendly smile. "I'm gonna get out of your hair."

"Oh, sweetie, you are definitely part of this!" Cal extended a hand I didn't take.

"How?" I asked. "I'm not part of her show."

"You're Daisy's sister. We want to interview you as well." With an intent gaze, he said, "I'm sure this is a disruption to your life. And it's your choice, but once we get what we need, we'll be gone. So, better to get it over with so you can go back to your life, right?"

Something told me none of our lives would be the same after Cal the Pirate King and his crew left Dead End. I took the hand he offered. *But why do I feel like I'm the one walking the plank?*

I found out quickly that showbiz entailed a ton of sitting around and waiting—or checking lighting, rearranging camera equipment, and powdering faces, but mostly waiting for the talent to arrive. The talent being Fiona Cameron.

Her flight had arrived too late the previous night for us to do anything, so the rest of us just spent time signing the necessary papers and reviewing what to expect.

The next morning, the crew arrived during breakfast, once again without Fiona and her entourage. Scott, being Scott, pulled out more bacon to fry up. Thankfully, he'd bought extra, because I wasn't sure my grocery budget would've stretched to accommodate so many more people.

I stayed behind to do the dishes while the rest of them set up outside. I didn't mind doing them on my own and preferred the quiet to being out there with the group. It wasn't because of the forty-degree temps either. I wasn't looking forward to what was coming.

I was lost in thought when I heard a car door slam, and a voice rose above the rest.

"You know my standing orders for Caribou, Starbucks, Dunkin' Donuts—or whatever they call themselves these days—Dutch Brothers, and Tim Hortons! What is the problem, Madison?"

That had to be Fiona. I placed the dish towel on the rack and watched through the window. She was loud enough—or the old walls of the house were thin enough—that I heard every word.

A harried-looking redhead who had to be Fiona's assistant said, "None of those exist here, Fi."

"Are you kidding me? Do these people not drink coffee?" Fiona said "these people" in a way that told me exactly what she thought of being in small-town Texas.

I glanced at the half-full second pot of coffee sitting on the counter and thought about pouring her a cup.

"Where did you get that swill I threw out the window a few miles back?" Fiona asked.

Maybe not. Litterbugs don't get coffee.

"The hotel lobby," the assistant squeaked.

Fiona looked like she was about to explode. This was a problem I could solve. I grabbed a clean cup and poured the coffee, which was from freshly ground beans—my cousin Holly's own blend from her breakfast-only restaurant, Mourning Brew. I added a splash of cream, the way I liked it, but grabbed the sugar bowl, too, just in case Fiona liked it on the sweet side.

I threw on a sweater and headed outside with the cup just as Fiona was finishing her tirade. I let the coffee's aroma, which could raise the dead, drift toward her nose. "We do drink coffee around here, and those who apologize to their assistants could probably get a fresh cup."

I swore I heard a few gasps around me. I might have insulted the Queen Mother herself from the looks on their faces. Cal scurried over like he was about to pull me out of harm's way but stopped when Fiona burst out laughing—not biting, sarcastic laughter, but genuine mirth.

Then she straightened her pantsuit jacket and glanced at the cup, then back at Madison. "No, I'm good."

"Suit yourself." I took a big whiff and sighed. "Just the way I like it, no sugar and a bit of cream."

"Full cream? Not half-and-half?" Fiona asked.

I nodded.

"Madison, I apologize if my lack of coffee and nearly choking to death on mud water from the hotel upset you."

"And?" I asked when Fiona turned back to me expectantly.

"I'm sorry." She said it as if it were new to her tongue, but it was good enough.

I handed her the cup.

She took a sip, moaned, and instead of thanking me, said, "Madison, get with this coffee person later to find out where she purchased this so you can have it ready for me each morning. And make a note to talk to the hotel staff about the poison they serve, and..."

I tuned out the rest of it as I headed back inside to finish the dishes. It was funny how Fiona seemed to command a room, while making someone like me—and probably poor Madison—disappear into the background.

As soon as I closed the door, the outside noise dampened. I took off my shoes and thought about how our quiet family farm had been turned into a circus with

Fiona as the ringleader. I didn't want a ticket to that show. I knew prima donnas like her. I'd been raised by one until she'd dropped me at Aunt Mer's doorstep. Those thoughts were interrupted by the sound of the front door opening and closing once again.

Madison stepped into my kitchen. "Thank you so much! You really saved me out there!" she gushed.

"No worries! I know what it's like to deal with someone like her."

"Oh, no, Fiona is normally great. Everyone loves her! She's just not been herself lately. She's—"

"You don't have to defend her. I recognize a diva when I see one. Just because the whole world loves them doesn't mean they get to treat you like a piece of trash when nobody is watching." I gave a final swipe to the plate I'd been drying and put it with the rest.

Madison pulled out her phone and tapped the screen. "Can you get me the name of that coffee place so I can swing by there in the morning?"

I placed the dish towel on the drying rack and turned to her. "Oh. Yes, it's Mourning Brew. They open at seven a.m."

"That's when Cal wants us here."

"My cousin Holly owns it and is there super early to make biscuits. I can run over and get some in the morning for the whole crew."

"I can't ask you to do that," Madison said.

"It's not a bother. It will help Holly's sales, and if coffee makes Fiona bearable, then I'll drown her in it," I said.

chapter
six

THE NEXT MORNING, I left and returned—by 6:30
—with two thermoses of Holly's coffee and a box of fresh
cinnamon rolls and biscuits.

Madison rushed toward me. "You're a lifesaver! Fiona
isn't here yet, but she will be so happy when I have a
steaming mug waiting for her. Just get me a receipt, and I
will reimburse you."

She helped me unload and took me to their setup for
craft services, which was basically just a folding table
under a canopy with an assortment of utensils, plates,
napkins, cups, and a small but yummy-looking spread of
food that seemed like it had come from the H-E-B deli.

"This is Greta."

Madison gestured toward an older woman, probably
around Aunt Mer's age. Her hair was completely gray and
cut short. Glasses hung on a chain around her neck. And

she wore very sensible and comfy-looking shoes. I didn't recognize her from the people who'd arrived yesterday.

As if reading those thoughts, Greta stuck out her hand to shake mine. "I flew in late last night, and I feel so behind. So, please, do excuse me if I don't make small talk."

"I completely understand. I'll let you get to work. I just wanted to drop these off." I held up one of the carafes.

She put her glasses on and examined me. "What are those?"

"It's coffee from a local place Fiona loves," Madison said. "And pastries!"

"I know about the coffee. Madison told me to expect it, but I don't know if I have room for the rest." She sighed. "Put them wherever you can find space."

Madison placed her items on the table then took mine from me. She lowered her voice. "She's a bit stressed because she missed her original flight, and—"

"It's not my fault I missed that flight," Greta snapped.

Madison took my arm and led me away. "Let's let her work."

As we walked away, I asked, "So, there's only one craft services person? Greta has to handle all that by herself?"

"Oh, Greta isn't craft services." She took a beat to talk into her headset. "On our way."

"Who is she filling in for?"

"No one, we don't have craft services with a crew this

small. We eat breakfast at our hotel, break for lunch and dinner, and we might send someone for coffee once in a while, but there's no dedicated craft services."

"Why not?" I asked.

"We're a documentary crew, not a movie set. We tend to move quickly. Greta is Fiona's assistant, so she's probably acting on Fiona's orders. Fiona was mad at the hotel breakfast this morning, saying their fruit selection was abysmal."

"I thought you were the PA."

"No, I'm the production assistant. Greta is a personal assistant. Yeah, I know it gets confusing since they're abbreviated the same. But I handle everything for the production crew, including the talent. Greta manages only Fiona."

Sounded to me like a full-time job and more.

"Huddle up!" Cal called.

We all gathered around. A glance told me Fiona wasn't present. But Daisy and her crew were.

Cal said, "We have a tight schedule before we break for the holidays, so we need to stay on track. I'll interview Drusilla's crew on their tour bus while Bryan goes with Fiona and Drusilla up to the graveyard. Star, I'd like you to go with them. Where is Fiona?"

"I'm taking her coffee and breakfast now!" Greta hollered over her shoulder as she scurried toward the trailer with a tray.

Cal let out an expletive. "Okay, change of plans. Once again, we're waiting for Fiona."

It was another twenty minutes before she finally appeared. She stepped out of her trailer looking refreshed and ready to go with a coffee cup in hand. "Well, what are you all standing around for? Let's get this show on the road!"

As if *we* hadn't been waiting on *her* the entire time. But no one balked. They all just picked up their gear and got to work.

Even the walk up the hill had to be filmed, it appeared. Bryan stayed in front of us, walking backward with some type of camera contraption strapped to his body. Fiona took her place beside Daisy, who was dressed as Drusilla with the black wig, dark makeup, and tattoos. Jasmine, their makeup person, and Greta had gone ahead to the cemetery in the golf cart. I realized then that I hadn't been up there since shortly after Halloween. We'd made a day of it, cleaning up the gravestones. But though Astra had a headstone here, her body was still in the well at the lake property where she'd died. So it didn't hold the same significance to me as if we were actually visiting her grave.

Fiona looped her arm through Daisy's. "This gift of talking to the dead, when did you first discover you had it?"

"I was backstage with Mamma, and—"

"Mamma being country-music sweetheart Ruby Dee Bell?" Fiona prompted.

"Yeah." Daisy's face lit up. "I grew up on the road with her and my father before I moved to Dead End."

"Geoffrey Dale Faulkner?" Fiona asked.

I hadn't heard that name in a while.

Fiona continued after Daisy nodded. "Your mother's drummer and husband of one of her backup singers."

Daisy stopped. "It wasn't like that, and you said you wouldn't bring that up."

"You're the one who brought him up, my dear," Fiona purred. "I was just clarifying who he was. But just so that our viewers don't misunderstand, why don't you tell them the truth of it?"

Oh boy. Daisy's forehead line suddenly appeared. Trouble was brewing.

"He divorced his wife long before he and my mom started dating, and he married her before I was born."

"Of course. I'm sure it was completely innocent. So, you were saying about discovering your powers?" Fiona prompted.

She would, of course, have already known all that. But it had served its intended purpose, to rattle Daisy.

Daisy continued. "So, I was backstage, and a couple of men nearby were talking about Mamma and how she was trash, so I screamed at them, not realizing they were ghosts."

Rock had coached her to stick as close to the truth as possible. I just hadn't known she would stick to *my* truth.

"Oh really? It happened the same way, in the same situation as it happened to Star?" Fiona asked. "I've done my research, sweetheart. Your mother talked about the Grand Ole Opry incident in *People* magazine once. But the funny thing is, she's never once mentioned your origin story. Why is that?"

"I, uh..." Daisy stopped in her tracks.

By then, we'd reached the cemetery gates.

Daisy flipped a lock of her dark wig over her shoulder. "My story is so boring. That's why I borrowed Star's."

"Let's take a break." Fiona nodded to Bryan, who stepped away with the camera, then took Daisy's hands. "Look, I don't like asking these hard questions. It's not who I am, but it's what the show is. You have no reason to embellish. I am sure your story isn't so boring. Just stick to the truth, and we'll get through this. Okay?"

Her voice was so genuine, I almost believed her.

Daisy took a deep breath. "I was four, and I met a little girl named Steffie Mae who I thought was real, but..."

She was stealing another of my stories—one Mamma had never heard and couldn't talk about in a magazine article. It dawned on me then that Daisy knew all my stories, but I didn't know anything about how she'd discovered her telekinetic powers. When she came to live with us, she'd already had them. I'd never asked. Something coiled in my gut. *Guilt? Regret?* I pushed it away. Daisy could've told me at any time, and she chose not to. She'd certainly never held back on telling me anything else back then. Like how Mamma had taken her to Disney World. She'd never taken Astra or me.

"Is he still filming?" Daisy glared toward Bryan.

My gaze followed hers, and the camera was pointed right at us.

"Of course he is. You're in the business. You know the cameras never go off or you might miss something," Fiona said. "Jasmine, I need a touch-up."

Jasmine scurried over and pulled different implements from a tool-belt-type accessory around her hips. I'd seen Penny with the same, but she was back at the house with the rest of the crew being interviewed. That was why Fiona had separated Daisy from her crew. To get her alone with the sharks. *Does she consider me a shark? Her own sister?* Once again, unpleasant feelings snaked in my stomach.

"Then why tell me they were off?" Daisy insisted. "And why act like you give a shit about me? Maybe someone needs to turn the camera on you and show the world you're the fraud. You acted all nice on the video call to get me to do this show, but then you arrive and turn into this."

"You naïve little girl." The real Fiona came out. "I don't know how you've managed to keep making money with your little reality show, but this is how we do it in a professional production." Fiona looked down at Daisy.

Jasmine whacked Fiona on the nose with a brush.

"What the hell?" Fiona took a step back.

"Sorry, Fi, I don't know what happened. My hand must have slipped." Jasmine's face colored. "I promise."

I believed her, especially when I saw the slight smirk on Daisy's face. Her powers had gotten stronger if she could move someone's hand.

Fiona pushed Jasmine away. "Get out of my sight!"

"But I'm not finished."

"You are done, Jasmine. Go back down to the house and send up the other one. And start looking for a new job." Fiona glared at her then hollered, "Greta! Get her out of here!"

Greta drove Jasmine out of the graveyard, and Daisy took a walk among the headstones. I followed her, but she was too angry to speak. She tapped furiously on her phone, and I kept her company.

A few minutes later, Penny returned on the golf cart with someone else.

"Is that Rock?"

"Yeah, I texted him to come up here." She turned back toward the fence between the cemetery and the woods. So, she didn't see who the *other one* was. I'd assumed it was Madison when Fiona asked for her.

"Penny is with him," I said.

"What?" Daisy whirled and squinted into the distance.

"Looks like she's working on Fiona."

By the time we reached them, Fiona was sitting in a director's chair with her name on the back while Penny spritzed something on her face.

Penny gave Fiona one last look then turned her attention back to Daisy as if to survey a masterpiece she'd just signed. She smoothed a few strands of the wig then said, "Gorgeous as usual. You don't need any touch-ups."

Fiona shot them a look that could've exploded them if she'd had powers of her own. Then she took out her phone and held it up. "Time for a social media teaser. Hello, Truth Seekers! We are here in Dead End, Texas, with the infamous Drusilla Von Leigh to determine if she's a fraud. I won't give anything away, but..."

She droned on, and I waited for Daisy's reaction. Daisy didn't move. She glared at Fiona. Then I saw what Daisy was focused on. The bolts holding the chair together were unscrewing.

"Daisy!" I shouted.

Fiona's chair collapsed, and she tumbled to the ground. She screeched, but it didn't seem like she was bleeding anywhere. However, her head landed very close to a marble gravestone. A few more inches, and we would've been calling an ambulance.

While Penny and Bryan helped Fiona up, Fiona berated Bryan for the chair falling apart.

I pulled Daisy away from the scene. "What are you doing?" I whisper-shouted.

"Whatever do you mean?" She didn't even try to sound convincing or look innocent.

I glared at her.

She shrugged. "She had it coming."

Fiona stalked toward us, yelling at the crew. "Do you have your shit together now, Barry?"

Bryan gave a thumbs-up and mumbled, "The name is Bryan. Just as it has been for the five years I've worked with you."

Fiona said, "Okay, let's get this going. And I swear to god, Greta, if I don't have a fresh cup of coffee in my hands soon, I'll have a heart attack!"

Rock put on his best snake charmer smile and asked to speak to Fiona privately. He stepped away with her. Greta hurried over with an insulated cup and handed it to Fiona. I turned back, trying to listen to the conversation between Rock and Fiona, but I couldn't make out much. Fiona didn't yell any further, so I supposed the man still had it.

The rest of the cemetery scene went without incident. When we were done, Greta took Fiona down the hill on the golf cart, and the rest of us walked down. Daisy dropped back to talk to Rock, and they spoke in low tones, so the trip down was mostly silent, except for the sound of feet crunching on dead leaves.

Fiona was nowhere to be seen when we reached the yard. I assumed she'd gone back to her trailer. Cal was missing as well, but a few moments later, he stepped out of Fiona's trailer, slamming the door behind him and almost knocking Greta over on her way into it. If that was what Hollywood was like, I would be happy to never deal with them again.

We spent another half hour milling about until finally Cal approached us. "Okay, Star, you're up next! I think I'd like you sitting at the kitchen table," Cal said. "I'll be there for this one. We aren't splitting up the rest of the day."

Thank heavens. I was freezing. It had been a milder December day, but I was still chilly. I nodded and stepped onto the porch.

"Madison, get Fiona, please, so we can start!"

Rock called my name from a few feet away just as Fiona stalked toward Daisy.

"Dude, you have to stay with Daisy and protect her from Fiona," I said.

He turned to look where I was staring then back at me. "Fiona hasn't come out of her trailer yet. I'll be back by Daisy's side before she comes out, but I wanted to ask you—"

I opened my mouth to argue just as Madison's scream

cut through the air. At the same moment, Fiona walked through Daisy like she wasn't even there.

Well, crap.

chapter
seven

LIFE WAS CRAZY FRAGILE. One minute, a person could be standing there screaming at people, and the next, everyone might be whispering over their body. Well, maybe not directly over Fiona's body. Cal had tried CPR, but the appearance of her ghost would indicate she was already gone before Madison found her. I'd called 911 from the house while the rest of them—except Daisy, who sat in a chair at the kitchen table with me—huddled near the trailer.

Sirens wailed in the distance, and Carly's cruiser scattered gravel across the grass as she came to an abrupt halt. Rock approached her, and I saw her cast a glance toward the house before she spoke into her radio and headed toward the trailer.

An ambulance arrived, seconds later. Two EMTs

stepped out and made their way through the small crowd gathered in front of the trailer.

I turned my back on the scene, thankful Teeny was at school, and pulled out a chair next to Daisy. "You okay?"

It was funny how death—even the death of someone I didn't like—could make old feuds feel like a silly spat. It didn't mean all was forgiven. It meant we were human.

She nodded.

I didn't buy it, but the sound of tires crunching on gravel once more caught my attention. Two more vehicles parked in the driveway—Dusty's Mustang and Daisy's Mini Cooper. Kelsey stepped out of the latter.

"Where has Kelsey been?" I asked.

"I sent her to the store to pick up tampons for me. She back?"

I nodded as she dashed to the crowd. Dusty followed at a steady but less frantic pace. I had a feeling we would need a lot more coffee. And if they didn't, I sure did, so I started a pot. It was the first time I'd seen Dusty in weeks.

Dusty Palmer, Ingersoll County sheriff's detective and now acting sheriff, and I had been held hostage together in October, and I'd thought we'd had a connection. But since my birthday party on Halloween, it had been crickets.

By the time I made it back outside with the fresh coffee, the paramedics had taken Fiona's body and left.

Fiona was currently giving Daisy an earful—or it would be an earful if Daisy could hear or see ghosts.

"I knew you were a fraud! You lying little witch! You can't see me anymore than I can see Jesus."

Fiona continued to yell and call Daisy every name in the book. Including the C word. I'd had enough. I was about to tell her where she could go, but before I made eye contact, I stopped myself. I was still pissed at Fiona for the way she'd treated everyone.

Fiona then turned to me. *"Are you a fraud too?"*

I ignored her.

"Of course you are! I mean, I knew you had to be, but the one time I needed one of you freaks to not be a fraud, you let me down. I'm dead. I saw my body. What the hell am I supposed to do now?" She stalked off to her trailer, walking right through the walls of it.

Everyone else seemed to be in shock. But Dusty snapped us all to attention.

"Who's in charge now that Fiona is... out of commission?"

Dead. And he probably knew it. But for some reason, he didn't say it to the crew.

"I am." Cal raised his hand as if volunteering in class, his formerly confident demeanor gone.

"With me." Dusty motioned.

Cal strode over to him.

"Star, can we use your kitchen, please?"

He hadn't said anything else to me. Not even a "Hello, Star, how are you? I'm sorry I haven't called, even though I made you think there might be something between us."

I had a mind to ignore him like he'd been ignoring me, but the sooner we got this over with, the sooner we could send the production crew on their way back to Hollywood—since there couldn't possibly be a show without the host—and get back to normal. I gave him a curt nod.

He must have read my expression because he said, "Could you come along, too, so we can talk?"

I followed them, and once inside, Dusty asked Cal to take a seat at the kitchen table, then he pulled me aside in the hallway. "Hey, I'm so sorry..."

Good! An apology!

"...to have to ask this but..."

Not so good.

"Have you seen Fiona... anywhere? Could you maybe talk to her?"

For crying out loud!

"No," I said. "I don't see her."

He nodded and strode back to Cal.

It wasn't a lie. I didn't see Fiona anywhere in my current line of vision. She could be outside. Or maybe, if I was lucky, she had already popped away to some other location. Ghosts tended to gravitate toward wherever they felt most whole. So, Fiona was probably off kidnapping

Dalmatian puppies and dreaming of making a coat from their fur.

"I don't want to cause pandemonium out there, so I wanted to talk to you privately first, Cal," Dusty began.

"Will Fiona be all right?" Cal paced.

"*No! I won't be all right!*" Fiona shouted as she charged toward us through the kitchen wall.

I flinched slightly but tried not to show it.

"*I'm dead!*" she hollered again.

"I don't think they'll be able to revive her," Dusty said. "But I need to ask you some questions."

"Okay." Cal's voice shook.

"Did Fiona have any medical conditions that you know of? Anything that would cause her to collapse like that."

"*Of course I don't! I'm healthier than any of you.*"

I focused my gaze on Cal instead of Fiona raising Cain in my peripheral vision.

"I don't know. She took a lot of pills, so maybe?"

"*Those are all supplements! B complex, collagen, vitamin C...*"

I ignored her while she continued to rattle off what sounded like the inventory of a health food store.

"Where did she keep these pills?" Dusty asked.

"Probably in her purse? Or in her hotel room?" He shrugged. "Greta or Jasmine would know."

"Who are they?" Dusty asked.

"Greta is Fiona's personal assistant, and Jasmine does her hair and makeup."

Dusty jotted that down then picked up his phone like he was texting someone. "Thank you. Do you know anyone who'd want to cause her harm?"

Cal snorted. "Lately? Anyone who met her."

"*You little twit!*" Fiona yelled in his face. "*The secrets I know about you, I could spill to the world and wipe that smug look off your face!*"

Cal, of course, didn't hear a word. But his expression changed as he seemed to realize the gravity of the situation. "You think someone hurt Fiona?"

"*Her sister!*" Fiona's arm shot out and pointed at me. "*The fraud! I bet she did this.*"

Her finger was centimeters from my nose, and I tried hard not to flinch.

"I don't know, Mr. Roberts. I hoped you could tell me." Dusty gazed at Cal expectantly.

However, at that moment, Fiona chose to stalk out of the room—and straight through me. I didn't have time to dodge and braced for the usual intense vision of her death. But instead, I was only slightly lightheaded, as if I'd stood up too quickly. I swayed and tasted coffee, but it didn't taste right, like something had been added to Holly's blend. And that was the extent of the vision. I didn't black out, but it caused me to stumble into Cal.

"Are you okay?" Cal asked.

"Yeah, I just lost my footing a bit."

Dusty gave me a sharp look, but I glanced away. Just in time to see Fiona rushing back toward us. This time, I moved out of the way, which, to someone who couldn't see Fiona, probably looked like I was doing the Electric Slide.

Fiona stopped and turned. "*You saw me, didn't you?*"

I ignored her and tried to think of something to say to Dusty and Cal so I could tune her out.

"She had a fight with Jasmine when we were up in the graveyard!" I blurted.

"A physical altercation?" Dusty asked.

"No, an argument. And Fiona fired her."

"Fi's been arguing with everyone," Cal said. "That doesn't mean Jasmine did anything."

Dusty nodded. "Still, I'd like to speak to each of the crew. Cal, you can go for now, but stay close."

When Cal left, Dusty looked at me. "She's dead, isn't she?"

Fiona had followed Cal out but stopped with Dusty's words.

I said, "I hope not. The paramedics were working on her, so maybe they revived her on the way to the hospital."

Fiona threw her head back and let out an exasperated screech, then went through the wall into the yard. Once Fiona was gone, I slumped into a chair.

"As a doornail," I said. "I mean, if doornails yelled at people and walked through walls."

Dusty gave a half smile at my attempt to lighten the mood then said, "I thought so. Even before I saw you have the vision."

"You noticed?"

"It was much quicker this time than the ones I've seen before, more like just a fluttering of your eyes, but yeah. Tell me exactly what you saw."

"There wasn't much, actually." I explained how I'd tasted the coffee.

"Coffee that was served here?" he asked.

"I don't remember her surroundings. So, it may not have even been today."

"Why are you hiding your gift from her?"

"Mostly because I don't want to deal with her. And partly because I'm being petty. You should've heard how she talked to my sister and her crew. She wasn't a great person. And just because she croaked doesn't mean I have to be her therapist." It felt mean, but it was also true, and it felt good to say it.

The corners of his mouth twitched, but he didn't let them turn into the smile I knew had almost come out.

"You've told me before that your visions seem to indicate some decision the victim made that led to their death. What are your thoughts about the coffee?"

"Based on that alone, I would think someone poisoned her coffee."

"But?" he prompted.

"But we also know the visions aren't always clear-cut."

Just then, Carly came into the kitchen, holding up a very expensive-looking handbag. "I found several pill bottles in her purse."

Fiona was close on her heels, yelling at her for violating her personal rights.

Dusty donned the gloves Carly handed him, identical to the ones she wore, and took the bag from her. He pulled out several bottles and read the labels. "These are all over-the-counter vitamins and minerals."

"*Like I told you before!*" Fiona put her hands on her hips and gave him a disgusted look. "*You people are useless! Now, return my personal items immediately!*"

She grabbed at the purse but naturally grasped air, then gave a frustrated scream and disappeared.

Dusty continued to pull items out of the bag—a compact, a couple of lipsticks, a wallet, keys, and other assorted items from the main part. He unzipped the many pockets and pulled out things like a manicure set, gum, and receipts. Then, when it seemed as if the contents had been exhausted, he pulled out one final item. A small amber bottle with a screw top lid. "Nitroglycerin."

"Isn't that for heart issues?" I asked.

He nodded and opened the bottle. "It's empty."

"Are you thinking that's what killed her? A heart attack?"

"Fiona's dead?" someone asked in a small voice.

I turned to find Kelsey looking up at me with Daisy not far behind her. Both looked only a few shades less pale than the fluffy white clouds sailing by in the sky.

"We haven't received confirmation from the hospital," Dusty said quickly.

"Actually, we have," Cal said from the doorway, holding up his phone. "Greta just called. They pronounced Fiona at the hospital."

It always humbled me that the world just kept on moving after people stopped. After Astra died, the sun still rose and set. And birds still sang as if they weren't the least bit affected that a beautiful soul had left this plane. And though the person who'd died this time wasn't someone I wanted to share space with, much less someone I loved, it was still shocking that her life was over. She was there one moment and gone the next.

In my peripheral vision, I caught a glimpse of Fiona pacing back and forth on the gravel driveway. Okay, not so much gone, but she would never change, never achieve her goals. Whatever they might be. *Did she have a family? Someone waiting for her back in California?*

"Holy crap!" Daisy said. "For real?"

Cal nodded.

Kelsey hugged herself tightly. Daisy put an arm

around her and squeezed as tears rolled down Kelsey's cheeks. It was probably the first time she'd been anywhere close to death.

"I need to tell the crew," Cal said.

"I would like to address them if you can gather them," Dusty said. "I need to call the hospital first and get official confirmation, but I will join you all outside in a moment."

Cal nodded, and we all shuffled outside.

A few minutes later, Dusty spoke to the crowd. "As I'm sure you've heard by now, Fiona Cameron is dead. I am sorry for your loss, and I understand this is a difficult time. But if anyone has knowledge of Fiona's medical history or anything you think I should know, please come talk to me."

The crew talked among themselves while Dusty motioned me over. "The hospital confirmed Fiona's death and gave me a few more details. Very few. For now, all they can tell us is that her heart stopped. Travis County will come get her for an autopsy, of course, as well as toxicology, but until we get anything from that, we'll have to go on your visions and statements we get from the crew."

"Is this a murder investigation?" I asked.

"I'm not calling it murder until we know more."

"Right, it's an unattended death." I smiled at him. It might seem like an odd thing to smile about, but it had been one subject of our several arguments back in October. *Has he only been in my life for two months?*

"You know, there is one person who could shed a lot of light on this." Dusty ran a hand through his tightly cropped curls.

I knew what was coming, and I really didn't want to. "Fiona?"

"Yeah, think about it at least?"

"I will." *Thinking* couldn't hurt.

"Oh, and Star, could you keep your eyes open and let me know if you think we should take a closer look at anyone?"

Feeling sassy, I said, "Sure, but I mean, how do I contact you, since your phone is broken?"

Dusty pulled his phone out of his pocket and examined it, then gave me a quizzical look. "Broken?"

"I assumed it was since you haven't texted me in a month. But if you say it's working, then..." I shrugged innocently and walked off.

"Star... I—"

"Sheriff, I want to talk to you about something." Cal approached us. "Is now a good time?"

chapter
eight

OF COURSE, Cal had to walk up just as I'd gotten up my nerve to confront Dusty about his radio silence. Typical. I left Dusty to his interviews to go pick up Teeny from school.

Since school wasn't quite out, I pulled into a visitor's space and headed straight to the office. I passed a group of students decorating a Christmas tree and made a mental note to get on that at home. We usually decorated the day after Thanksgiving, but I kept putting it off, waiting for Daisy and crew to leave. Still, it didn't feel like the holidays without our tree.

The front office was empty, and I half expected Sadie, the former school secretary, to be standing there, but since she'd died in the fire that had almost killed Dusty and me, they'd had to find a replacement.

Grey's office door stood slightly ajar, and I knocked lightly.

"Come in."

I poked my head through the open door. "Mr. Miller, I've been sent here for detention."

Grey's face broke into a huge smile. "My knight in shining armor here to save me."

I laughed. "What do you need to be saved from?"

He held up a stack of papers. "These."

"Homework?"

"Pretty much. Resumes."

"You still haven't found anyone?"

He shook his head then shoved away the papers. "But that's not what you came here to talk about. How's the documentary going?"

"You haven't spoken to Carly today?" I asked.

"No, I texted her a couple of times, but I assumed she was busy since she didn't respond." He raised his eyebrows. "Spill."

"Fiona Cameron died on set today."

He leaned back in his chair and laced his hands behind his head. "Oh, wow! What happened?"

I shrugged. "She collapsed in her trailer."

"Whoa."

"Yeah, but there's more." I told him about the vision.

"Have you been able to talk to her? Or is she like some

of the other ghosts, where they're pretty disoriented after death?"

"She seems coherent, but I ignored her. I don't want to talk to her."

He leaned forward and steepled his fingers underneath his chin. "Why not?"

"Why do I have to?" I knew exactly why, but Grey always seemed to say what I needed to hear. Even if I didn't want to hear it.

"You have a gift. You don't get to choose who you share it with. She was an awful person, but if she was murdered, she deserves justice, and a killer is out there who could strike again."

"I hate when you're right."

"Hey, that's my gift. Always being right."

"Except on trivia night! But thank you. I needed to hear that. Can I ask a favor?" I glanced at the clock. "Can you let Teeny out of class a bit early so I can take her home? You know, with all that's happened."

He laced his fingers together and extended his arms. "That's another of my gifts. The ability to let small teens out of class in a single bound. Besides, it's Friday."

While he used the intercom to call Teeny's fifth-period classroom, I stepped out into the front office and dialed Dusty. He answered after one ring. He must have been looking at his phone.

"Hey, I've changed my mind. I'll come back out and talk to Fiona. Will you be there for a while?"

Teeny and I arrived home to find the SupeTV crew had gone back to their hotel for the day. They'd left the trailer there, whether at Dusty's insistence or because there was no other place to put it, I didn't know. But the van was gone, as was the rental car the others had come in. Only Dusty's Mustang and Carly's cruiser remained beside my car and Daisy's.

Carly was placing a box of what looked like bags of used coffee cups in the back seat.

Evidence?

"Hey, you okay?" she asked as she approached the open window of my car. She waved to Teeny, who waved back less enthusiastically.

"Yeah, I just wanted to go get Teeny and bring her home."

Teeny, who'd not been happy to be pulled out of art class, slammed the car door and went into the house. I could almost hear her stomping up the stairs to her bedroom.

"I talked to Grey while I was there, and he convinced me that talking to Fiona was the right thing to do."

"You would've come to that conclusion on your own

eventually." She straightened and stepped back so I could open the car door.

"Maybe. What's in the box?"

She echoed my question with a poor imitation of Brad Pitt in the movie *Seven*.

I gave her a pity laugh for her attempt.

"Trash, actually. We bagged all the coffee cups we could find to test for any residue. Because of your vision."

Dusty stepped out onto the porch then with another box, and after he gave further instructions to Carly, she left.

To me, he said, "You ready for this?"

"Yeah." *Not a bit.*

We made our way to Fiona's trailer, and it wasn't until then that I wondered if she would still be there. Maybe she'd popped over to another location. And yeah, to be honest, I half hoped she had so I wouldn't have to do this right now after all. But I found her face down on her small sofa, her long legs hanging off the end.

"Fiona?" I said softly. I didn't want to freak her out and make her disappear. I'd made a ghost sad in October, and he'd disappeared back to his own farm. If Fiona disappeared, she might go all the way back to Hollywood. *There's hope yet!*

She sat up and scrubbed her eyes, but her makeup remained perfect. I hated ghosts sometimes. *"You can see me?"*

I nodded.

"*You aren't a fake. What about your sister?*"

Dead men tell no tales after all, I thought. "No, Daisy can't see you."

"*I knew she was a fraud. And damn, I would've loved the ratings proving that one.*" The rage seemed to have left her.

"She's not a fraud. She has her own talent, just not the same one I do." I wasn't sure why I was defending Daisy, but I also didn't want to antagonize Fiona, so I softened my voice. "What's the last thing you remember?"

She touched the bridge of her nose. "*I was yelling at Jasmine because she swatted me with the makeup brush, then I asked for Penny. What happened next?*"

"You and Rock talked, and we came back down the hill. You went into your trailer. Then, later, they found you dead. What else do you remember?"

She sat still for so long, I was convinced she was done talking. But then, she said, "*The coffee tasted off. Did someone poison it?*"

"Let's not jump to conclusions." But I thought of the vision I'd had. She was right. It had tasted almost medicinal.

"*I don't understand why I can't remember anything after I yelled at Jasmine.*" Fiona's voice grew smaller and more desperate. Then she reached out and grabbed my wrist.

With that, I was plunged into another of her memories.

"Where is it?" I dug through my purse. My chest was tight, and sweat soaked me. I finally found the amber-colored bottle and opened it just as my trailer door swung wide. I shoved the bottle back into the pocket and slammed my purse on the table. "What do you want?"

I glared at Greta.

Then the brightness of the room brought me back to my reality.

Dusty stood beside me, rubbing my back. "Are you okay?"

I nodded and glanced around for Fiona to ask her about the vision, but she was gone. "She was having chest pain, and I think she was about to take the nitroglycerin, but she was interrupted, so she shoved it back into her purse. I think she was hiding her heart condition from her crew."

nine

AFTER I TOLD Dusty what I saw in the vision, we agreed Greta was next on his list to question. My job was to ask Fiona about the pills when I saw her again—and get her side of what had happened with Greta. But that was the last time I saw Fiona for a while. Filming was shut down over the weekend while the studio reassessed the project's safety. Without the host, they didn't have a show. And if Fiona's death had been due to anything but natural causes, they would have other things to consider. At least that was how Cal explained it. Knowing Hollywood, they were likely trying to figure out how to profit from it.

The trailer continued to sit out front, but Fiona was nowhere to be found. It was a bit weird having the RV where she'd died hanging out in our driveway, but they were paying us rent by the day, so I'd allowed it.

With the time off, we did manage to decorate for

Christmas. It felt weird doing it without Aunt Mer, but it wasn't so bad, since Daisy was there to help.

On Tuesday morning, my phone rang as I was about to get into the shower. I answered and put it on speakerphone. "Hey, Holls!"

"Hey! How are things over there with the murder and everything?"

"We don't know that it's a murder," I said. "They're doing an autopsy, though."

"One of my regulars asked me today if my coffee killed Fiona because they'd heard she'd dropped dead after drinking local coffee." Holly's voice held a bit of excitement.

"The rumors are already flying around Dead End like crows in a cornfield. Why am I not surprised?"

"Yeah, well, I'm kind of hoping she was poisoned. I mean, I am not happy she's dead, but if she had to die, and Mourning Brew's Death Knell blend was the vessel for the poison, then that will do wonders for internet sales. I can do a whole *Killer Coffee* campaign."

"Holly!" I admonished her. But sadly, she was right. A celebrity getting murdered in Dead End would probably double the tourism—because the world had way too many weirdos.

"But that's not why I called. Do you remember what day it is?"

"Tuesday? Are you checking me for a concussion?"

"No, silly!" Holly laughed. "It's the second Tuesday of the month! Game night!"

Family—and friends—game night was an institution in the Bell family. Pub Dead closed to the public once a month, and we spent the evening stuffing our faces and playing games of all kinds. I'd never missed a month. Well, except for November, because we'd had so much rain the day before, it had washed out the bridge at the end of our road, so those of us on the farm had missed it. Holly had suggested postponing, but no one could agree on a day to get together. So, they'd done it without us.

"It is! I'll be there."

"And Daisy and her crew? You will invite them, won't you?"

"Must I?"

"Star! Be nice. Yes, you must. Everyone is welcome at family game night. Especially since we're down three people. Oh, and invite Dusty too. He seems sweet!"

"Sure, I'll ask, but I can't guarantee he'll show up. He's pretty busy with the case." I had a feeling that might be why she wanted him there—to ask questions.

"And you'll ask Daisy, right?"

"Sure."

"Promise?"

"Cross my heart." I would ask, but hopefully, Daisy and crew would have other plans.

. . .

As it turned out, Daisy and crew were absolutely giddy about game night. I texted Dusty with the details, as I'd promised Holly, but didn't hear back. *Color me shocked.*

I supposed the good thing about inviting more people was more snacks. Scott brought an elaborate pepperoni and three-cheese-stuffed bread. The rest of the crew brought packaged snacks, but they didn't do like Aunt Tatty used to and pick up the cheapest generic-brand chips. They got the good stuff. From H-E-B.

Teeny, Daisy, and I were among the first to arrive. Aunt Mer would've fainted dead at seeing me show up on time for an event.

Kira skipped over to us and took the tray of my infamous peanut butter cookies from me. Then she grabbed Daisy's arm. "Daisy, I have a question for you. Since Teeny is my sister, does that kind of make you my famous aunt?"

"No, she's not your aunt, silly," Teeny said before Daisy could open her mouth. "It doesn't work like that. She's not related to you."

"But if your mom had lived and married my dad, she'd be my step-aunt. And I'm sharing my dad with you, so you could share one of your aunts with me."

Daisy rested a hand on each of them. "Family isn't just blood. If you want me to be your aunt, Kira, I can be."

Teeny shrugged out from under her grasp and stalked off. Kira shoved the cookies back at me and ran after Teeny, but I couldn't hear their conversation.

"What was that all about?" Daisy asked.

"It's complicated."

Zeke took the cookies—which felt like they were playing musical chairs—from me and stepped over to the food table, where he placed them next to a two-layer cake that looked like it might be German chocolate. Then, over his shoulder, he said in a lowered voice, "It may not look like it, but Teeny is making progress. She actually smiled at me earlier."

"That's something, at least." I patted his arm.

Carly and Grey arrived just then with Rock in tow. I'd almost decided—hoped—he wouldn't come after all. Rock carried a dish of pigs in a blanket covered with plastic wrap in one hand and a shopping bag in the other. I would bet good money on what was in that bag.

I wondered if it was appropriate to have a party when a woman had just died. There wasn't much love lost between Fiona and anyone here, but still, we'd all been there.

The most surprising guest was Cal. He looked uncertain about being there, but then Scott grabbed him in a bear hug. "Hey, buddy, glad you came! I wasn't sure you'd be up for it."

"Thank you. Are you sure it's okay for me to crash a family event?" He glanced my way.

Because I was raised by my aunts and Granny, who instilled in me that everyone was welcome, I strode over to him. "We're glad to have you, Cal. Grab a plate and dig in!"

Just then, Kira hollered, "Everyone, finish filling your plates and pick a game!"

Rock nudged my arm. "You're gonna want to be at my table."

"Am I?"

He shook the bag. "Trust me."

I didn't feel like putting up a fight just then, so I followed him to his table, which already had two other players, Carly and Grey.

"What is this mystery game you said we have to play?" Carly asked.

Rock sat and paused dramatically, then whipped out Hungry Hungry Hippos.

I cackled but took a seat.

"That's why you wanted to go through the boxes in the attic," Carly said.

"It's a classic," he insisted.

"A classic that always caused massive arguments," Grey said.

The four of us had played this so many times in junior high. Yeah, maybe we were already too old for it then, but we'd made it even more fun by making up our own rules.

"Fine, we'll play," Carly said, "on one condition, big brother. You join us for karaoke next time."

"Deal!" Rock shook Carly's hand.

I frowned. Karaoke was mine, Carly's, and Grey's thing. We never invited anyone else. I mean, the whole pub was full of people we knew, but that wasn't the point. Also, the next karaoke would be after Christmas. "Won't you and Daisy be long gone before our next karaoke night?"

"Star!" Carly scowled.

"I just mean, it's in January. The show will have moved on by then. Won't it?" I asked.

Rock shrugged but didn't meet my eyes. Instead, he dumped the marbles onto the red platform in the middle of the plastic hippos. "One arm behind your back and go!"

Rock and I fell into our old rhythm, which meant Carly and Grey beat us, not once, but twice. Just like the old days. I left them to it and moved on to another table. Dusty had shown up while I was in the bathroom, apparently, and had gotten into a game of Canasta with Granny, Aunt Willa Jo, and Holly.

Nice of him to answer my text and also greet me when he arrived.

I pulled up a chair where Teeny and Kira were teaching Cal, Kelsey, and Scott our family's favorite cutthroat game, Nerts. Any awkwardness between the sisters seemed to have disappeared, as they were both on rather familiar turf.

Kira turned to Cal. "So, you and Daisy's crew know each other from before?"

"Not me. He doesn't know me," Kelsey said. "He worked with Scott on the *Barbarians of Mars* movie franchise years ago."

Cal shot Kelsey an amused look, as if he were just noticing she was around. He seemed a bit more with it than when he'd first arrived. Then, to Kira, he said, "Scott and I go way back. Even before that. Did you ever see the kids' show *Hetty the Happy Hippo*?"

I laughed. "Daisy loved that show. I think she still has her stuffed Hetty and maybe even some old tapes in the attic."

"Hetty's in the attic? I thought you threw her away," Daisy said.

I turned to find her standing above me.

"Got room for one more? I haven't played Nerts in forever!"

We scooted and made room for her and the chair she'd brought over.

I turned back to Cal. "So, you worked on the show? Aren't you a bit young?"

Daisy had loved Hetty when she was six or seven years old.

"You're now my new best friend!" Cal exclaimed. "And while I was fairly young when it began, it had quite a long run before me. Scott and I got in during the unfortunate last season. We were both interns in film school." Cal picked up the cards I'd dealt him. "How about your crew? How did you all hook up?"

"I've known Rock practically my whole life. He came on the road with me when no one else would." Daisy avoided looking at me. "It was just the two of us for a while. He was the camera operator, director, producer, and shoulder to cry on for years. Then we grew big enough to have some cash flow, so I hired Penny and Scott. I was a fan of the documentary they were working on at the time."

"Oh yes, *Haunted Hollywood*," Cal said. "The one they both got fired from."

A look that told me Daisy hadn't known that passed briefly over her face. I wondered if Cal saw it, too, but he didn't seem to.

Instead, he leaned back and looked at Kelsey. "And this one? Where did you find her? Does she ever talk?"

"Do you ever stop talking?" she retorted then seemed to catch herself and looked properly abashed.

"Oh, the kitty bites." Cal bared his teeth and winked. "So, tell us, Kelsey, how did you hook up with Drusilla, Mistress of the Dark, and her ragtag band of ruffians?"

"Oh, that's a cool story," Daisy interjected. "I was in Austin at a comic con for an appearance a few months ago, and—"

"You were in Austin?" I asked. "When was this?"

"August, I think? Anyway, the line was super long, but Kelsey was toward the front. She suggested a way of making it go more quickly and offered to help."

Daisy had been that close and didn't come by for a visit? Not even to see Granny? She hadn't come when I was in the hospital either but then suddenly showed up on my birthday. *What's her angle?*

"You good?" Teeny shoulder bumped me and brought me out of my head.

"So, I asked her if she wanted a job and hired her on the spot," Daisy finished.

I nodded to Teeny and gave her a smile that didn't at all reflect what I felt inside. Daisy and I needed to have a serious talk once all this was over.

It did me good to kick all their butts. To be fair, three of them were newbies, and Daisy hadn't played in so long, she may as well have been. But Kira and Teeny had been improving lately, and they put up a good fight. It was nice to have new people to beat. I'd forgotten how much fun Daisy could be at game night.

I was at the table getting more food when Dusty sidled up beside me. I zoomed in on a huge tray of mostly untouched fruits and veggies and took a huge scoop. I bumped him with my hip, trying to keep the tone casual.

"Nice of you to show up. Did you get my text, or are you just psychic when it comes to free food?"

"I got it about an hour ago. Sorry, I was working. I did text back. Are you sure your phone isn't the broken one?" The one corner of his mouth turned up. "And I brought my own contribution." He pointed to the tray of fruits and veggies.

I pulled my phone out of my pocket. Indeed, I had a missed message from him. I wanted to crawl into a hole but instead said, "Oh. Yeah. I see it now. I'd forgotten I turned my sound off when we started playing. Thank you for the tray."

"No worries. I figured it might at least provide something for the adults to eat after the twins finished ravaging the table," he said, reminding me of my birthday party.

He had a healthy portion of fruits and veggies on his plate but also a couple of my cookies. He bit into a cookie and moaned.

"I'm glad you approve."

"You made these? These are dangerously delicious."

I laughed. "Well, when I take them on the road, you can be my hype man."

"Dusty, stop flirting with my cousin, and get back over here so you can put us out of our misery!" Isaac called from a table in the corner.

Dusty chuckled, but his face colored slightly.

"What are y'all playing?" I squinted toward the table but couldn't identify the game. It had many small parts.

"Quacks of Quedlingburg. Isaac's potion is about to explode, but I needed sustenance. I think I missed lunch."

"Sounds serious." I picked up a couple of Aunt Willa Jo's triangle-cut chicken salad sandwiches and placed them on his plate, plus a few cheese sticks. "You'll need more than cookies and fruit."

He thanked me then turned to go but stopped. "Can we talk? I mean tonight, after the games are over?"

"Sure!" I said, probably a bit too brightly. Then I realized he probably just wanted to ask me to look harder for Fiona. But before I could clarify, he was already back at his table.

The rest of the night was fairly uneventful, but as we packed up, I overheard Kira ask Teeny if she wanted to spend the night.

"Dad said he could make his famous waffles in the morning. Remember how we'd gorge on them and sometimes get him to add peanut butter cups? We can do that again."

"No, I can't. Star wants me up early in the morning to help with chores before school. Now that Aunt Mer is gone, she needs me more."

Total lie.

Teeny caught me watching them and shot me a pleading look while Kira glanced at Zeke.

"Why don't you come home with us?" Teeny suggested. "Now that Aunt Mer is traveling, we can raid her good candy stashes. I know where they are."

"I don't want to leave Dad alone. Some other time."

It was the second time Kira had referred to him as Dad instead of my dad. She was trying so hard to include Teeny. Kira ran upstairs, and Teeny joined me.

I slung an arm around her. "You don't have to find excuses. You could just tell her no if you don't want to."

Teeny shrugged. "I don't want to hurt her feelings. She wants this instant family, and I just don't know how to be what she wants."

I kissed her forehead. "Honey, no one expects you to be anyone but who you are."

chapter
ten

WHILE TEENY HELPED PUT the chairs on the table, I ran out to warm up the car. I nearly jumped out of my skin as someone rapped on the window, then I rolled it down when I saw who it was.

"You scared the bejesus out of me!" I gasped.

"Sorry," Dusty said. "Our game ran long. Are you leaving?"

"No, just warming up the car. You're letting warm air out. Hop in."

He crossed around to the passenger side and climbed in, then turned to me, rubbing his hands together. "Hi!"

"Hey, yourself! How was your game, Sheriff Palmer?" I grinned. He had been Detective Palmer up until a few months ago. But because the elected sheriff was in jail and most of his deputies had been fired, he was acting sheriff.

"Long. But fun. I won!" he said. "But mostly, it was good to get my mind off things for a bit."

"Yeah, you and Carly both," I said. "It was good to see you two relax. I've hardly seen her recently. She's been so busy."

I didn't mention that I hadn't seen him either, but it hung in the air between us.

"Sorry about that. That's my fault. She's been getting a lot of overtime since we're shorthanded right now."

"She's mentioned you lost a ton of people."

"Yeah, since the investigation into Briggs and the mayor, they've fired over half the department. That's why I haven't been in touch. I know it might seem like I've been avoiding you since your birthday..." He trailed off.

I'd known all that. But one could text a hello from the toilet or while in bed. And he hadn't played a single game with me tonight. Maybe he'd only come to observe the crew and see if anything was amiss. "Sure! I get it, and it's not like we were dating or anything."

He was silent for a beat, opened his mouth, closed it again, then said, "The truth is that I don't know what to do with how I feel. We shared something in that cabin. Two people don't survive that and not remain connected in some way. Then your birthday happened."

Yeah, my birthday. Halloween.

"But then the investigation into the department

began, and they grilled me about everything that happened in the cabin. And I've been working eighteen-hour days trying to keep the department going since half the deputies got fired or arrested after the investigation. I kept thinking I'd reach out, but then time passed, and—"

"I get it. You don't owe me an explanation. Like I said, Carly has been absent a lot too. I know the stress you're both under. It's fine." The words were true, but the snakes coiling in my gut told a different story. If he'd cared enough, he would have made time, which meant I'd misjudged the way he looked at me Halloween night.

"Then the first time I do see you, it's in the middle of another crime scene."

"Hey, it's not my fault! I didn't ask them to invade the farm, and I certainly didn't ask Fiona to drop dead and dump another load of problems into my lap."

He held up a hand. "No, that's not what I meant. It's just... knowing your skills, I should've asked you immediately for help. But I hesitated because my feelings for Star, the woman I spent a rather enjoyable Halloween night with, got in the way of my feelings for Miss Bell, the woman I knew could help me on this case."

"I enjoyed Halloween night, too, which is why it hurt so much that I've not heard a word from you since then, and now it feels like you're breaking up with me when we never even got a chance to be more than friends."

"I'm so sorry. Again, I should've at least texted. I know that now. I didn't mean to hurt you. That's what I'm getting at." He laid his head back on the headrest. "I think that's why I didn't contact you. I was stuck and couldn't figure out a way to make this work."

"I don't see the issue."

"The way I see it, I have two choices. I can either give in to my feelings and take you out on a proper date, or I can continue to ask for your help so I can find justice for the victim. But I can't do both."

I knew which I would choose. Every nerve ending in my body voted for choice number one. But I got it. It was the reason I'd come back to find Fiona after talking to Grey. It was the right thing to do. "I don't like it, but I do understand. We have to do what's right for the greater good. Not what felt right under the stars."

He released a breath. "I'm not saying never. I'm just saying we need to get through this case first."

"Sure, let's just figure out who murdered a celebrity in my yard, then we'll get back to figuring out us."

He gazed at me for a beat then smiled. "So, are we good?"

"Yeah." I supposed *good* would have to do. For now.

His shoulders seemed to relax. "In that case, would you mind coming with me to Fiona's hotel room tomorrow morning to see if she's there?"

I sighed. But the sooner we solved this case, the sooner we could see what we could be, so I said, "I'll be there."

I didn't sleep well at all that night. My dreams were plagued with Astra, Teeny, Dusty—pretty much everyone who was important to me. So, when my alarm went off at 6 a.m., I felt like I hadn't slept at all. But after a quick shower, minor makeup, and sweats, I drove straight to Mourning Brew and grabbed coffee for me and Dusty and made it to the hotel by 7 a.m.

My hair was still damp, since I usually let it air-dry, and in the winter, that took longer. Dusty, of course, looked like he'd stepped off the cover of a magazine. I didn't know how he could be so put together that early in the morning.

Dusty laughed when he saw me, and for a split second, I thought it was because of my appearance, but then I saw what he held. Two cups of coffee.

"Great minds and all that, right?" He nodded to the cups.

Or should it be "twisted minds," since Fiona might have died from poisoned coffee?

I took a sip. "Thank you for this. I appreciate it. So, what did you find out from Greta?"

"Not a whole lot. She said she brought Fiona some herbal coffee and they talked and, when she left, Fiona was still alive. She also claims she didn't know anything about nitroglycerin or a heart condition."

"I guess we'll see now if Fiona corroborates that."

He nodded and sipped his coffee. "I've already spoken to the manager, and since her room was reserved up until the day before Christmas, all her stuff is still there. The manager was rather compliant, so I also got the key without needing a warrant."

I wondered if the front desk manager's compliance had less to do with her being a good citizen and more to do with Dusty's attractiveness.

"Now, let's just hope Fiona is drawn to moderately priced chain hotel rooms," I said.

I was completely joking, so when we got to the room and I saw a figure at the window, I whispered to Dusty, "She's here."

As I passed the en suite bathroom, he stepped into it so as not to spook her—or maybe to search for possible evidence. I couldn't tell which.

Fiona still had her back to me, so I approached her and said gently, "Fiona? Can we talk?"

She whirled around.

Before she could open her mouth, I held up my hands. "I'm here to help."

"*Help? How can you help? I'm dead! There's no help for that.*"

"I want to find out what happened to you."

"Shouldn't you leave that to the forensics team?"

"That takes time—their tests, I mean. And if someone harmed you, then they could dispose of evidence or leave town before we get answers."

"Harmed me? You think I was murdered?"

Ugh. I felt like I was doing an abysmal job. "We don't know. I had a couple of visions and—"

"Visions?" Fiona narrowed her eyes. *"What in the hell are you talking about?"*

I explained exactly how my gift worked then told her about the visions. "So, in the second one, you were looking for your nitroglycerin pills. You were about to take one when Greta came in, but it looked like you tucked them away again. Were you hiding a heart condition?"

"I don't remember any of that. As I told you before, the last thing I remember was Jasmine whacking me on the nose with her makeup brush." She crossed her arms over her chest.

"But the heart condition?"

"It's angina, and it's a bitch! But it didn't kill me. I had a check-up with my doctor a couple of weeks ago, and he said I'm doing well as long as I stay calm."

Inside, I cackled because the Fiona I'd met had been anything but calm. But to her, I said, "And firing your makeup artist in the middle of a production and yelling at the crew is your idea of calm?"

"I know I lost my temper with Jasmine, but you don't know the pressure I was under. And that wasn't her first offense. If you really think I was murdered, you should probably start with her."

"So... about that. Jasmine didn't hit you."

"Of course she did. That I do remember! She whacked me hard. On the nose. I bet I have a bruise." She studied herself in the mirror.

I mused that ghosts weren't like vampires in that way, at least—if vampires were real.

"Daisy is the one who popped you with Jasmine's makeup brush."

"Are you trying to gaslight me right now? I might be dead, but I'm not stupid. I remember what I remember!"

"Of course, because that's the way everyone saw it. Daisy isn't a fraud. She can't see ghosts, but she has an ability. She can move objects—and now, apparently, people. You were being rude to her, so she moved Jasmine's hand to whack you on the nose."

Fiona stared at me, her mouth open. *"You. Are. Kidding. Me."*

"And when you fell out of your chair—oh wait, you don't remember that. Shortly after the makeup-brush incident, you were in your director's chair, and Daisy loosened the screws, so it collapsed."

Dusty stepped out of the bathroom then and locked eyes with me, but Fiona's squeal snapped the connection.

"Your sister is Carrie?" Fiona clapped her hands together in glee for some reason.

"No! Daisy is not a horror movie." That movie scared me as a kid. I wasn't sure what adult had let me watch it, but no, my sister was not a villain. "And why do you look so happy about that?"

"Because of the story we can tell with this! The ratings!" She beamed when she said it. Then her face fell as the realization hit her like a stone. She sat on the side of the bed. *"But I'll never get to tell that story."*

"I'm sorry. I mean, I'm not sorry you won't get a chance to exploit my sister, but I'm sorry you're dead." It wasn't the first time I'd felt useless trying to comfort a ghost. Nothing I said could bring her back from the dead. I was completely helpless to make the situation better for her—except to get her justice. No matter how awful she'd been to work with, I didn't believe she was a bad person. And the next thing she said reinforced that.

"I'm sorry too. I was a beast on set. I just haven't felt myself lately. Perimenopause is the worst. I guess that's one benefit of being dead. No more hot flashes." She peered up at me.

"That's helpful, since I'm pretty sure death is one of the contraindications for estrogen."

A laugh bubbled up from Fiona, and I joined in. After a few moments, Dusty cleared his throat, reminding me why we were there.

"Right, so, I know you don't remember anything after the makeup-brush incident, but here's the thing. In my experience, the visions usually have something to do with how the person died or the events leading up to their death. The visions don't always make sense at first, but eventually the pieces come together."

"And the visions you had of me were of me drinking coffee then looking for my pills?" Fiona asked.

"The coffee one was very brief because you barely touched me. The other was a bit longer, but—"

"You need me to touch you so you can find my killer?"

"It's not as creepy as it sounds, but pretty much."

Before I could explain the conditions, Fiona's hands shot out, grasping my arms, then I was spinning.

"Fiona, when I tell you to back off. Back. Off." Cal's eyes were angry and close to mine. *"Or I swear to god, I will cancel this whole production and head back to California before you can blink."*

"Sheesh, Cal, simmer down. I'm not going to make waves for the girl. I just want to know the truth."

"Why is it always about the truth with you, Fi? Can't you let some secrets go?"

"I mean, I am literally the award-winning host of a little show—maybe you've heard of it—called Supernatural Truthbusters."

"I swear, Fi, it's like I don't know you anymore. The old Fiona would never—"

"Umm, hey." Kelsey stood outside the doorway. "I'm sorry, but uh, Scott is looking for you, Mr. Roberts."

I scoffed. "Well then, Mr. Roberts, you'd better run along to your boyfriend."

Kelsey closed the door again, and Cal stormed toward me with rage in his eyes.

THEN I WAS NO LONGER in the trailer. Instead, I was floating in the hotel room—or it felt like it at first, until I realized I was cradled in Dusty's arms.

I scrambled out of his embrace.

At the same time he asked, "What did you see?" Fiona asked, "*What in the hell was that? I thought I'd killed you! Why didn't you warn me?*"

I addressed her first, ignoring the last part of her comment. "If you'd waited before you grabbed me, I would have explained that, sometimes, I lose control of my body and—"

"*Ew!*" she said.

"Not like that. I get dizzy. So I have to be somewhere safe. Like sitting or lying down."

"*Oh. Sorry about that. What did you see?*"

I turned to Dusty and relayed the events then back to Fiona. "So, what were y'all talking about?"

"*The hell if I know!*" she said. "*I don't remember that conversation at all.*"

"It sounds to me like you were talking about Daisy. Did you find out her secret?" I asked.

"*No, I had no idea. I mean, I always suspect everyone is a fraud, but I didn't know for a fact. But you say Cal was coming toward me in a violent way? That doesn't sound like him at all.*" Fiona paced the already-worn carpet.

I had to agree. "And as the producer, why would he be protective of Daisy?"

"*Because of Scott, maybe? He and Scott...*" She hesitated then. "*They go way back.*"

"I know, they worked on *Hetty the Hippo*. He told us."

"*Yeah, and well, they were close. Once you orbit into Cal's world, you never leave. He'll do anything for those he loves. And if Daisy was important to Scott and Cal felt like whatever I found out could hurt her, then yeah, I could see him acting like that. He didn't kill me, though, if that's what you're thinking. I'd bet my collection of vintage Barbies that he didn't lay a finger on me.*" She glanced down at her arms and once again into the mirror, searching her neck.

I relayed all that to Dusty while she examined herself.

"I think she's right. Her body showed no signs of

physical trauma. I'll question him about it." He jotted something in his notebook.

"Like I said, start with Jasmine. She had the most reason to want me dead."

I relayed that to Dusty.

"But here's something else you might consider," Fiona said. *"Your sister tried to hurt me twice. If I found out she was a fraud, what might she do to protect that secret?"*

That part, I didn't relay to Dusty. I knew my sister wasn't a murderer, and Dusty and I had enough going on without adding Daisy as a suspect.

We left Fiona in her room after turning on the TV so she could watch a marathon of her old episodes on SupeTV. I'd never thought about ghosts getting bored before. And while they couldn't interact with things on our plane of existence like the remote control of a hotel TV, they could sometimes use items from their plane, like how Caroline, our house ghost, usually sat on the porch crocheting. My last view of Fiona before closing her door was her on the bed, buffing her nails. But the nail buffer that had lain on the bedside table before was still there.

We walked down the hallway without a word until we got to the elevator.

"The crew is staying at this hotel. Should we ask the front desk which room Jasmine is in?" I asked.

"I already know. But I will be questioning her alone." Dusty sipped his coffee.

"Why can't I go?"

"Star. You know why you can't go. I can't take you along on every interrogation. I needed you for this one since I can't see Fiona."

The elevator doors opened then, and I considered not getting in but rather going back to Fiona's room to question her more on my own. But Dusty had the room key, and Fiona couldn't actually unlock her door. I could yell at her to come out, but that would probably get me kicked out and not welcomed back. So in the end, I got on the elevator.

The smell of bacon filled the lobby. I briefly wondered if I was having a stroke. *No, dummy, that's burnt toast. Or is it burnt almonds?* My stomach rumbled, interrupting those thoughts, reminding me that, even though the two cups of coffee had temporarily tricked my brain into thinking I'd broken my fast that morning, I had skipped breakfast.

"Breakfast is complimentary for guests if you're hungry!" a perky front desk clerk—different from the one who'd been on duty when we came in—called from the lobby.

"Oh, I'm not—" I was about to reveal that I wasn't actually a guest, but then my stomach once more made its presence known. This time, loud enough that she heard it as well, as evidenced by her giggle. She couldn't be much older than Teeny and Kira. "Sure! Why not? Show me the way."

"Just a short walk down the hall on your left. Follow your nose." She smiled. "We have a waffle bar with over twenty toppings."

"Thanks"—I glanced down at her name tag—"Xena!"

I made my way to the breakfast room and was ready to cook some waffles when another hotel employee said, "Good morning! Last name and room number, please?"

I stared at the tablet she held and the finger poised above it. *Shit!* I was trying to judge whether or not she watched *Truthbusters* and would know I wasn't the celebrity staying in room 318 when Greta appeared by my side.

"Robinson, room 514. She's with me."

The employee tapped the tablet. "Thank you, this way."

Greta and I didn't speak while we were being led through the dining room to a table near the windows, mostly because the hostess was making small talk about the weather and if we were enjoying our stay. We gave our drink order, and she instructed us to help ourselves to the massive buffet, and as soon as we were left alone, I blurted, "Thank you!"

"What are you doing here? Is there news about Fiona?" Greta stood and headed toward the food.

I followed.

"No, we came to talk to Fiona," I told her.

"You and Daisy?"

"No, just Sheriff Palmer and me. I'm a consultant for the department," I lied. "That's why I can accompany him but Daisy can't."

It was kind of true. I wasn't an official consultant, but he'd been consulting with me on the case.

She gazed at me dubiously as she piled a scoop of rehydrated eggs onto her plate. "Where is the sheriff now?"

"He's upstairs interviewing Jasmine." He might not have wanted me to tell Greta that, but Jasmine would likely tell the group herself as soon as he left. They seemed like a close-knit team.

"And why aren't you with him if you're consulting?"

"Because I only consult on the dead, not the living," I said as if I hadn't just argued the point with Dusty. I dumped half a pig's worth of bacon onto my plate.

"What did Fiona say?"

I popped a piece of bacon into my mouth to give me time to think about how to answer that. I definitely wasn't going to tell her about my ability to live their memories. Dusty and I had agreed that it was better to keep that to ourselves until we figured out who had killed her.

I swallowed. "She doesn't remember much, and she was quite frustrated."

I wasn't sure if I imagined it, or maybe she was just shifting her position, but it looked like Greta's posture relaxed—like she was relieved.

"How are you doing with everything? With Fiona?" I asked. "Were you two close?"

"I've known Fiona since she was a PA," Greta said.

"How long ago was that?"

"Twenty years, possibly? Can it really have been that long? We were both PAs on the show *Trauma Drama*."

"I'm not familiar with that one."

"It debuted at the same time as *Grey's Anatomy*, but *Grey's* took off, and *TD* did not. We only lasted a season."

"Were you two friends?"

"Not really. I mostly kept to myself. She worked her way up to production manager, and when she needed a production assistant on her first film, she called me. She said she remembered how laid back I was." Greta shrugged. "I was that way because I was just there to absorb the atmosphere. I had no desire to move up in the ranks and become a director or producer someday or, like Fiona, transition to being in front of the camera instead of behind it. I just love movies and TV and organizing things, so it seemed like the perfect job."

"So, when did you go from being a production assistant to her personal assistant?"

"Several years ago when she became the host of *Truth-busters*. I had been working with Cal on a different project, and he asked me to work for him on *Truthbusters*. I was at the studio for a meeting and ran into her after her audition."

"Audition?"

"For host. We hadn't seen each other in a few years, and we grabbed lunch. She poached me from his team. I know what you must think of her after experiencing her tirades over the past few days, but that's not the normal Fiona. She can be a handful, but she's loyal. If you do a good job on her team, she fights to keep you."

"And if you don't do a good job?" I thought of Jasmine.

"Then you're out." She shrugged.

"Has anyone ever been angry with her for getting fired?"

"You're thinking about Jasmine, aren't you?"

"Yes," I admitted.

"Fiona wouldn't really have fired her. She just needed to cool off."

"Is that what you were helping her do when you brought her coffee in her trailer?" I asked.

She paled. "I just wanted to help calm her. Is this an interrogation?"

"No, I'm just a witch who talks to the dead. I don't know

anything about investigating." I sipped my coffee, realizing this was my third cup of the day. I probably wouldn't sleep that night. Or I might crash hard if it wired me up all day.

"I heard you solved your other sister's murder and a couple of other murders a few months ago."

"And almost got killed in the process."

She gulped her own coffee and pushed her plate away. "I don't know what happened to Fiona, but I can tell you no one on *our* crew did it."

She put the emphasis on the word "our." "So, what are you saying? Someone on Daisy's crew?"

"All I know is the mousy one, Kelly—"

"Kelsey," I corrected her.

"Always seemed to be lurking where she wasn't supposed to be. You might want to talk to her."

"What about Cal? Would he have any reason to hurt Fiona?"

"No. As I said, check your sister's team before you come nosing around mine." She pushed her chair away from the table and stood. "Feel free to stay and enjoy your breakfast."

I said thank you, but she was already gone.

I finished my food and left a few dollars on the table as a tip for the employee manning the buffet and clearing plates, then headed out. I'd just reached the lobby when Dusty stepped out of the elevator.

"What are you still doing here?" he asked.

"Just waiting for you. I had a thought about the case." I left out the part about interrogating Greta. For now.

"So you decided to get a free breakfast while you waited?" He gazed at me.

"How did you know?"

He pulled a crumb of something from my hair. "Exhibit A."

"Xena told me to!" I protested.

"The warrior princess?"

"No, the desk clerk, but points for that comment. So, what did you find out from Jasmine?"

"Let's walk and talk."

We headed back to the parking lot.

"Just confirmation of what we already knew. Fiona fired her. She doesn't know how her hand slipped and accidentally hit Fiona, and she's made an appointment with a doctor to check for Parkinson's because her grandfather had it." He stopped at his car, which was parked next to mine.

"Did you tell her the truth?"

"I did not. But I don't think she had anything to do with this. She didn't seem to have any hard feelings for Fiona after being fired."

"Fiona wouldn't have really fired her. She was just blowing off steam."

"How do you know that?" He narrowed his eyes at me. "Did you go back and talk to her?"

"No, I ran into Greta at the buffet."

"You interrogated a suspect?"

"No, Detective, I talked to someone I know over limp bacon and mediocre waffles." I glared at him. "I can handle myself."

"Sheriff," he corrected.

"Fine, *Sheriff*." I rolled my eyes. "I didn't interrogate anyone. I wouldn't really know how. I fumbled my way through the last investigation and only really figured out who did it because they literally trapped me in a room and confessed everything."

"Us," he said.

"What?"

"They trapped us. I was there with you. You came there to save me. And you did. And if I haven't thanked you enough, I'm thanking you now. So, did you learn anything else from Greta that I should know?"

"No, just that she and Fiona go way back. Fiona hasn't been acting like herself. She would've eventually cooled off and apologized to Jasmine, and Greta doesn't think anyone on her crew did it. But she thinks Kelsey should be investigated because she lurks."

He leaned back against his car and examined me.

"Next time I have breakfast with a potential suspect, I'll make sure you're invited."

"There won't be a next time. I got a call after I left Jasmine's hotel room. The autopsy results came in. They found evidence of coronary artery disease and heart damage."

"English, please."

"It means the results are consistent with a heart attack. Also, the preliminary tox screen came back negative."

"YOU COULD'VE LED WITH THAT!" I said. "So, what? There's no more investigation? The case is closed?"

"I'd like to talk to a couple more people just to wrap up a few details, and of course, if the advanced screening comes back with something, that will change, but I can't devote more manpower to this right now with everything else going on in the department."

Something didn't feel right about that. *Why was Fiona's last memory of the makeup-brush incident? How would that lead to a heart attack?* I needed more information, and I knew I wouldn't get it from Dusty.

As I drove home, I considered my approach. I'd missed a text from Daisy saying she would be out all day, filming with her crew. I supposed she still had to create content for her channel, especially if the *Truthbusters* shoot was off. With her out of the house, I could tackle the laundry situation that had been bugging me.

Years living away from home as an adult hadn't changed Daisy's cleanliness. I imagined she was used to Kelsey doing everything for her. The irony hit me just then that I was enabling that behavior, but I told myself it was a matter of survival. I hadn't been able to find a single clean towel that morning and had been forced to pat myself dry with a hand towel and dodge across the hallway to my bedroom.

I'd half-filled a laundry basket when a paper sticking out from between the pages of a book caught my eye. It looked like a ransom note, cut-out letters and all. *What in the world?* My heart fluttered as I drew the paper closer.

WHERE THE DEAD END UP AMONG THE TREE-LINED PATHS. DEAD END WON'T SAVE YOU. YOU'RE NOT SAFE ANYWHERE!

"What are you doing in my room?" Daisy asked, and I jumped.

"Daisy? What is this?" I stood and held up the letter.

She paled, crossed the room, and snatched it from me. "Nothing."

"Is someone threatening you?" Protective big-sister instincts surged through my veins.

She didn't reply at first. Instead, she strode back to the door and closed it, muffling the sounds of her crew raiding the kitchen.

"Is it someone in your crew? Is that why you've moved back into the house?"

"Of course, it's not anyone on my crew. I moved back into the house because the bus is out there in the open. Anyone could access it. The house feels more secure."

"But someone is threatening you? How long has this been going on?"

"I started getting them in October." She sighed and sat on the side of the bed.

"October? When you got here?"

"No, before."

She pulled at least a dozen papers out of a tote bag under the bed.

As I read through the letters, I started shaking. Some were outright death threats, while others seemed like weird riddles that made no sense. This crazed fan was disturbed and seemed serious with their intent.

Fear trickled down my back. "Daisy, we have to take these to Dusty."

"To what end? What's he going to do? Stash me in jail to keep me safe? He can't do anything about this. I reported it to the police in Topeka before we came here. They said their hands were tied until the creep made a move."

My heart ached, and I wrapped my arms around her. "We'll get to the bottom of this. I won't let anything happen to you."

She let me hold her a moment then moved out of my embrace. "Why would you think anyone in my crew was responsible for this?"

I told her about Greta saying Kelsey had been lurking.

"Greta noticed? Huh," Daisy said.

"You're not surprised?"

"Of course not. I'm the one who asked her to spy on the production team to see if they said anything I should know—like if they were onto me. Except I didn't put it to her that way, since..."

"Since your whole crew still thinks you see ghosts."

"Yeah. But seriously, Star, no one on my crew is capable of murder."

"Well, it might not be murder, after all." I told her about the results. "And now, I've knocked Kelsey off my list. I still need to talk to Cal, though."

She studied me a moment. "You really get a kick out of this sleuthing, don't you?"

"No, what I get a kick out of is keeping those I love safe."

"Aw, you just let it slip that you actually love me." She threw a pillow at me, and I dodged.

"I won't make a habit of it." I grinned.

On my way to the laundry room, I realized something.

That was why she'd come back to Dead End. She was seeking safety. I'd just shut the lid of the washer when Daisy once again appeared.

"Hey, you might get your chance to chat with Cal. He just called and asked if he could come out and talk to us."

By the time Cal arrived, Daisy's crew occupied the chairs around the kitchen table.

"The studio is clearing us to resume."

"How do you shoot the show without the host?" Rock asked.

"I'll step into the role of host, for this episode, at least, then the studio will reassess," Cal said.

"How will that work? I mean, I know the logistics of it, but how do you plan to handle the shift cinematically? Will you address Fiona's death? Other than the end credit memorial screen?" Rock asked.

"If you're asking if the focus will be on what happened to Fiona instead of Daisy, then no. Daisy is still our star, and the format will continue as it would have with Fiona," Cal said.

"I don't mean to be callous, but we've put in enough time and resources and would like to wrap it up so we can all enjoy Christmas and what comes after." Rock cast a glance toward Daisy that I didn't think anyone saw but me.

What comes after? What does that mean? What are they up to?

"I understand, and we, too, have put in time and resources. In fact, the studio wanted to cancel it altogether, but I fought to keep going. I have to show them something by the end of the week. So, I'd like to get started today if we can."

"Penny will need time to get me in my Drusilla makeup," Daisy said.

"I thought today we could just have some shots of Daisy, instead of Dru," Cal said. "The small-town girl behind the internet sensation."

"I have an idea."

Kelsey was so quiet I almost didn't hear her.

She held her hand up like she was in kindergarten then quickly put it down. "Never mind, it's dumb."

Bless her heart. No wonder Daisy took her under her wing.

"I'm sure it's not, Kelsey. Go ahead. Please share," Daisy said.

"Sure! Let's hear it." Cal nodded.

Her face lit up, and she glanced gratefully at Daisy. "What if Daisy talks to Fiona? And you can incorporate that into the show. That way, the audience can see how compassionate Daisy is, and you could ask her questions only Fiona could answer, things Daisy wouldn't know. That way, you can prove she's not a fraud."

Holy shit. It would be quite brilliant if Daisy could actually see Fiona. But it would probably end up being Daisy's downfall.

To her credit, Daisy didn't stutter—or pale, or blush, or any of the things I would do if I were put on the spot like that. Instead, she said, "Oh, Kels, I love that. I really wish I could, but Fiona has crossed over."

Liar! Liar! Pants on fire!

"Crossed over?" Cal cocked his head to the side. "When? Because Greta said Star was at the hotel with the police talking to her today."

Everyone's eyes turned toward me. I was careful not to meet Daisy's, but I couldn't open my mouth to speak. I couldn't think of anything to say. Thankfully, Daisy had never had that problem.

"Oh, she was, but then, I thought... Star, didn't you say Fiona disappeared at the end of your conversation?"

Okay, maybe not so thankful for Daisy's improvisation skills.

When I finally found my voice, I unfortunately suffered from verbal diarrhea, because I couldn't stop the words once they started coming, and in an effort to help dig Daisy out of a hole, I buried her even more deeply with "...So yeah, I turned on the TV for her so she could watch herself."

"Excellent!" Cal clapped his hands. "Then that's what we'll do. Head to the hotel tonight."

I wished then that I could disappear in a pop like the spirits sometimes did.

As everyone left the table to prepare for filming, Daisy's eyes met mine. And what I saw there said that I'd just destroyed whatever progress we'd made by not having her back.

chapter
thirteen

I DROVE SEPARATELY to the hotel. Rock had offered to ride with me, but I'd declined. I needed time to think. Surely I could find a way to help Daisy. She couldn't fake her way through this one. These people actually knew Fiona. *What if they ask something only the real Fiona could answer?* I called Dusty to see if he had that equipment they used on cop shows, where they sent in the informant to get the bad guys to confess. Dusty didn't answer, so I had to think of another solution.

By the time I'd parked in the hotel parking lot and reached the lobby, I'd figured out an alternate solution. I grabbed Daisy before everyone was about to get into the elevator. "Hey, can you help me in the bathroom a moment?"

Without waiting for an answer, I pulled her arm into

the lobby bathroom and shoved my noise-canceling earbuds into a puzzled Daisy's hands.

"Put these in, and switch phones with me quickly."

"What? Why?"

"My phone is paired with my earbuds. I'll use your phone to call mine, and you'll tell them Fiona walked through the wall into Greta's room. I'll stay behind in Fiona's and feed her their questions then tell you the answers on the phone." I dialed my number from her phone and tested it.

"This is crazy, Star!" But Daisy looked relieved. "Will this actually work?"

"We can try," I said. "I may not be able to lie on the spot, but give me time and a drive down country roads, and I can think my way into a solution to almost any problem."

She shoved an earbud into her left ear and let her hair fall to cover it, leaving her right ear able to hear the outside world.

We exited the bathroom and strode to the elevator, where everyone waited. Once we were upstairs, Greta let us into Fiona's room with her spare key. Fiona screeched when she saw us. I nearly jumped out of my skin at the sound, but thankfully, I was at the back of the group as we filed in, so no one noticed.

"What in the world are you all doing just barging into my room like that?"

"Do you see her?" Cal asked Daisy.

This first part would have to be total improv on Daisy's part, since we were all in the same room.

Daisy nodded. "She's asleep on the bed."

"Ghosts sleep? How odd," Cal remarked.

"Yes, our house ghost, Caroline, often sits and crochets on the front porch swing," I inserted. "Ghosts can do whatever is on their plane of existence. They just can't physically interact with ours."

"I am not asleep! And what are you all doing in my room?" Fiona repeated.

"Interesting." Cal gestured to the TV, which was still on. Apparently, the marathon had ended because some show about cryptids was playing. "I can see why she fell asleep. Can you wake her?"

Daisy shrugged. "I'll try."

"Oh my god, I wish I hadn't died if for no other reason than so I could expose you. It would've been the pinnacle of my career. You are so fake!" Fiona screeched at Daisy.

"Fiona?" Daisy whispered, bending over the bed.

The real Fiona spotted me then and rushed toward me, but I dodged out of the way. I did not want to have a vision in front of these people. Thankfully, no one noticed since I was near the door, standing next to Rock, who shot me a quizzical look.

"What is going on here? Get these people out of here, and can you please change the channel for me? I abhor

Bigfoot. The idea of a hairy man running through the woods, hiding from people, is ridiculous."

I held up a finger to her, signaling, "Just a moment, please."

Just then, Daisy jumped back from the bed. "Fiona, it's okay. Please, wait." Then she turned back to the camera. "She went through that wall."

Without waiting, she barged toward the door, and Cal and the camera followed. I stepped into the bathroom to get out of the way, as did a couple of others, but I didn't follow when they left.

Instead, I shut the door behind them and whirled to face Fiona. "I need your help!"

"You need my help? After you brought a mob into my room and scared the bejesus out of me while I was napping? Surely, you're kidding."

"I didn't bring them here. This was all Cal's idea." Well, actually, Kelsey's, but Fiona didn't need to know that. And when she continued to glare at me, I used the only ammo I had against her. "Fine, hope you enjoy hanging out with Bigfoot."

She glanced at the TV, then her eyes widened as she realized the power I held. I could change the channel for her and put her out of her misery. Or not. She needed me. *"Fine. What do you want?"*

"I need you to help me help Daisy."

"First, change the channel, please. Find me a nice

cooking show."

I did as she asked, and I put my phone on speaker. On the other end, Daisy said, "Fiona, I'm here to help. Do you know where you are?"

The real Fiona muttered, "*Hell.*"

I explained the situation and how I planned to fix it and ignored her jabs at how it was a weak plan at best.

Then Cal said, "Fiona, I'm so sorry you died. I miss you already."

"*What you miss is sneaking into my dressing room and stealing my stash of peanut butter M&Ms,*" Fiona said.

I spoke quickly into the phone and smiled when Daisy was able to repeat it back in the exact tone Fiona had used. I hadn't put much intonation into it, but Daisy had always been good at voices. Once again, drama club kids had many talents. Her performance was followed by a collective gasp from the room next door.

"She's really here?" someone, possibly Greta, asked.

"*I'd rather be anywhere else. Hell, I'd go back to that campground in Mississippi in a heartbeat before I'd stay another night in this two-star hotel if I had my choice,*" Fiona said, then I repeated.

"Does she remember her death?" someone else asked, possibly Bryan.

I knew the answer to that but threw out a line to see if I could catch anything. "Daisy, pause dramatically then say, 'I know what happened, and you think you got away with it, but you didn't.' Then look each of them in the eyes."

Fiona chuckled behind me. *"Well played."*

Daisy repeated it, and the small group all started talking at once. Someone sobbed from the other room, then another question followed, which I didn't have time to answer because Fiona's hotel room door opened, and Greta rushed in, throwing herself onto the bed.

"Fiona," Daisy said through the phone. "Can you answer the question?"

I disconnected the call, hoping Greta hadn't heard. She sobbed into the pillow and murmured something over and over that sounded like "I'm sorry." I didn't know whether to say anything or leave her to it and sneak out, but then she lifted her head, probably to breathe, and saw me.

"Are you okay?" I asked.

She sniffed loudly and wiped her hand across her face. "How much of that did you hear?"

I was about to tell her I couldn't understand what she'd said into her pillow when I felt Fiona rush through me, and the room shifted.

"Fiona, you have to calm down. You're going to give yourself a heart attack if you keep going on like this. Now drink this." Greta handed me a cup—a real one, not one of those disposable cups. "It's your favorite."

I turned the cup around in my hand and saw the curly

font with the words Boss Bitch on it. Greta had given it to me for my birthday, and I loved the way it felt in my hands. It had just the right heft. "Thank you, Greta."

"You're welcome. Make sure you drink it all. 'It'll cure what ails ya,' as my grandmother used to say." She smiled, and right before she closed the door, she said, "If you start to feel sleepy, don't fight it. I'll make sure no one disturbs you."

I started feeling sleepy almost immediately, then my heart felt like someone was squeezing it in their fist.

Opening my eyes, I clutched my chest as I heard Daisy's voice from far away. "Star, are you okay? Is it your heart?"

I sat up, and the whole crew was back in the room, staring at me. I looked directly at Greta, who was still sitting on the opposite bed. "What did you put in her coffee?"

"I didn't mean to hurt her." She buried her head in her hands and began sobbing again.

Could it be that easy? Could I have gotten a confession and solved the murder already? And I didn't even have to put my life in danger again to do it.

"What are you talking about?" Cal asked.

"It was an herbal concoction, a recipe from my grand-mother that she used to give my mother during the change," Greta said.

"The change?"

"Menopause. My mother had quite the temper. Fiona

hasn't always been as angry as she's been lately. I figured she was going through some hormonal changes and thought it would help. I didn't mean to hurt her," Greta said again and sobbed into her hands.

After Dusty came to take Greta to the police station for questioning, Daisy and I stood beside my car. The rest of her crew waited in her car a few feet away.

"What in the world happened up there?" she asked.

"Greta burst into the room, and I had to hang up. How did you handle that?"

"I told them Fiona had gone back through the wall to her room, and that's when we heard a scream. We all rushed in to find Greta standing over you. I thought she'd hurt you, but then I saw your eyelids fluttering and realized you'd had a vision. How did you get Fiona to cooperate?"

"I threatened to leave the TV on the Bigfoot marathon." I smiled.

I'd rewarded Fiona for her help by sneaking into Greta's room and turning her television onto SupeTV so, once the Bigfoot marathon was over, Fiona could pop in there and watch herself again then pop back to her own room for the cooking channel without requiring anyone's help to change the TV for her.

"Thank you for that. I guess my secret is safe for another day at least." She threw her arms around me.

I returned her embrace. "Aunt Mer would be so proud of us for getting along while she's gone."

"Right? She'll be totally surprised to come back and find us both alive."

chapter
fourteen

I HEADED to the Merc to see how Granny was getting along. That was another duty that fell to me with Aunt Mer out of town. Both she and Aunt Willa Jo usually took turns checking in with Granny, bringing groceries whenever she needed, along with doing other assorted tasks. It didn't feel like a "duty" but a privilege. I knew how lucky I was to have a grandmother living into her nineties.

I found her behind the register in a completely empty store. Rare for a Thursday.

I sidled up beside her. "You fired another one, didn't you?"

"Goodness, child, you scared me to death." She pulled out her earbuds.

"Sorry. What are you listening to?"

She held up the phone we'd recently upgraded her to. "Holly introduced me to audiobooks, and I just started a book about some orphan boy who might be a wizard. What brings you by?"

I smiled. "I just came to check on you. Have you eaten?"

"No, but Zeke popped over earlier and took my order. He should be—"

"Coming in hot with a plate of chicken and mashed potatoes!" Zeke chimed from the stairs.

"Thank you, honey." Granny pecked him on the cheek when he leaned down to place her food on the counter. She opened the cash drawer. "How much do I owe you?"

"We're doing this dance again, Addie?" Then he grabbed my hands and twirled me around, doing a poor impression of the dance from *Pulp Fiction*. "This is the dance I'd rather do."

I laughed and mirrored his motions.

Granny clapped. "Dinner and a show! What a lucky lady I am."

Zeke gave a low, elaborate bow.

That was when I noticed Granny's swollen feet. I sighed then turned to Zeke. "Can you help Granny upstairs? I'm covering the floor the rest of the day."

"You are not!" Granny shot at me.

"If you would quit firing your help, I wouldn't have to," I shot back. "Look at your feet."

"Addie, I can sling you over my shoulder, or I can help

you upstairs with dignity, but Star is right," Zeke said. "Those ankles are swollen, and I know for a fact that you've been sitting on that stool all day."

Granny snorted but stood and took the arm Zeke offered.

I picked up the plate to follow them so Zeke wouldn't have to make two trips, but a gaggle of customers came in just then.

I'd taken care of them and sent them on their way with full bags by the time Zeke returned from his second trip with the plate.

"She's settled now with her feet up on the sofa, a TV tray in her lap, and the remote in her hand."

I threw my arms around him. "I don't know what we'd do without you."

He returned my hug just as my stomach growled. "If I'd known you would be here, I'd have brought you a plate too. I'll fix you one and be back in a second."

"I hadn't planned on staying. Just stopped by on my way home from helping Aunt Willa Jo." I checked my watch. "I'll be closing up the shop in less than an hour and can eat leftovers when I get home."

"Are y'all still busy with the whole Hollywood thing?" Zeke asked.

I caught him up on the latest and ended with, "So Dusty came and took Greta to the station this afternoon."

"Look at you solving another mystery!" he said.

I sighed. "Something about it just doesn't sit right with me. It feels like this was more than an accidental poisoning. Plus, there's something else. You have to swear not to tell anyone."

He mimed zipping his lips shut.

"Daisy has been getting threatening letters," I whispered.

"Threatening? How? Like death threats?"

I nodded solemnly. "She won't go to the police about it. And she won't let me tell Rock, but I had to tell someone. You're like a brother to us, and I know you'll help me keep an eye out for her."

"You know I will, Star, but if she's in danger, you have to tell the police. Can't you talk to Dusty about it? Sure, Daisy might be pissed at you for a bit, but better a mad sister than a dead one, right?"

As soon as the words were out of his mouth, I knew we were both thinking of Astra.

As if on cue, my phone rang. Dusty. "Hey!" I answered. "How did it go with Greta?"

"I let her go. The concoction she described is harmless. It wouldn't cause Fiona's symptoms, according to my lab contact. Plus, the lab report came back on the cups we took in. They were clean. The lab tech did corroborate the presence of the essential oils in the ceramic mug Greta indicated the coffee had been in. We missed it when we swept the trailer."

"Oh, wow. So, it was a heart attack after all?"

"I'm not so sure," he said. "It takes a while to get the full tox screen back, but aconite was present in Fiona's blood."

"Aconite?"

"Yeah, it comes from a flower called monkshood, and it's extremely toxic."

"Is that something y'all routinely test for?"

He chuckled. "No, but the lab tech, Sully, works nights, and he watches a lot of those British mystery shows."

I wasn't following, but I let Dusty continue. Zeke strode to the front of the store, where another customer had just entered, and made conversation.

"According to him, on the most recent episode of *Dr. Terrance*, the killer used aconite they grew in their garden. The symptoms were the same, so on a hunch, he tested for it. It came back positive."

"That's unbelievable."

"That's what I said. He ran it again to prove it to me."

"But the cups were clean."

"Exactly. He said it could be transferred by other methods. Through the skin, for instance—maybe a lotion. I'm on my way out to your house now to search her trailer again. Cal said it was still out there."

"Yeah, they're leaving it until the documentary is done."

"When do you think that will be?"

"No idea. I thought they were done filming completely until Cal said he was taking over for Fiona."

"Cal is meeting me there to search the trailer. Will you be home as well?"

His voice held forced casualness, so I matched his tone. "Would you like me to be?"

He was silent for a beat, which I took as an awkward pause, so I did what I did best and began filling the void with my chatter. "I just mean I'm at work, at the Merc, but I could close a little early if you need me there. Or if you were asking because you'd rather avoid me, I could stay away, or like, if you don't care either way, then—"

"Star. I was asking because you're the property owner, and though Cal will be there for the trailer—"

"Oh yeah, of course, totally. But I mean, no, I'm actually not. Aunt Mer owns the farm. But I understand what you're getting at. I think Daisy is there. I'll check. If not, then I'll run home. Let me just call her. Talk later."

I disconnected and banged my head against the counter.

"That bad, huh?" Zeke asked.

"I forgot you were here."

"I wasn't eavesdropping. I was helping a customer up front." He nodded toward where a lady was perusing the candles. "But if you want to talk about it, I'm getting pretty good at listening to female monologues and nodding in all the right places. I can even cock my head to the side and do a pretty convincing, 'Oh no, he did not!'"

I laughed. "It was Dusty. He's currently headed out to my house to search Fiona's trailer again and asked if I would be there. I wrongly assumed he was asking for other-than-professional reasons and blathered on like a teenage girl gushing to her crush."

"Is he your crush?"

"I thought you were going to nod and stuff, not launch a direct hit between the eyes. False advertisement!"

"So, I take that as a yes."

"I don't know what he is. It's..." I cast a glance at the customer up front and lowered my voice. "Well... okay, we went through a lot in October, when we were trapped in the cabin together, then we had one perfect night under the stars."

"Whoa! Too much info!" He put his hands over his ears.

I swatted him. "Not like that. Nothing happened. We talked. For hours. He brought a thermos of apple cider."

"Oh no, he did not!" Zeke said in a fake high-pitched voice.

I laughed. "But after that, it was pretty much crickets, and I didn't see him again until Fiona died. Then I thought there might be a spark again, but after game night, we sat in my car and talked, and he basically friend zoned me."

"How so?"

"He told me that as long as we were working a case together, he had to be professional."

"That makes sense."

"Hey, what about your 'Oh no, he did not' line?"

"I already used it once. Can't overuse it. How about a good ole 'What the hell, man?'"

"That works. But yeah, I mean, it does make sense. Perfect sense. But that's what's so maddening. When you're falling for someone, you aren't supposed to make sense. You're supposed to be wild and crazy and throw caution to the wind, right? So, to me, that means he doesn't feel about me the same way I feel, or thought I was feeling, about him."

"You did that with Rock, didn't you? The whole throwing-caution-to-the-wind thing?" he asked. "And how'd that work out for you?"

"Ouch."

After tucking Granny in for the night by making sure she had everything she needed in her room and locking up the store, I headed back to the house. I decided not to rush getting there. I would give Dusty the professional relationship he wanted. All I wanted was the leftover lasagna in the fridge, a hot shower, and a bit of quiet. But what I found when I got there was quite the opposite.

As I pulled into the driveway to park, my lights shone on the trailer and Cal. He turned a key in the lock then shoved it into his pocket with one hand while shielding his eyes with the other.

I cut my lights and got out. "Sorry about that."

"Not the worst thing that's happened today. But there's pizza inside, and local beer. I've been invited to stay." He offered me the crook of his arm. "Shall we?"

I accepted it, looping my arm through his. I didn't think he was interested in my type—female—but he was quite alluring. Not in a sexual way, exactly, though he was fairly attractive, but in the way the sun drew sunflowers toward it. I wondered why he was behind the camera instead of in front of it and was about to ask, but just as we stepped onto the porch, I heard both my name and Dusty's coming through the screen door. Everyone stopped talking as we entered.

"Why do you all look guilty?" I scanned the room. "Where's Teeny?"

"Up in her room. Jessi-Lyn dropped her and Kira off earlier, and they've been up there since." Daisy filled a cup with ice, poured in soda, and handed it to me.

"We were talking about you. And Dusty," Rock admitted. "He came by with a warrant and took some things."

"He took all cosmetics and anything that could or would be used on the skin but didn't say why."

"They're testing for poison," Cal offered.

"I don't understand. Didn't they already test the coffee for that?" Kelsey said in a small voice. "How could makeup be poison?"

"And how would they get it into her skin?" Daisy wrapped her arms tightly around herself, no doubt thinking of the threatening letters she'd gotten.

I watched everyone for a reaction. Kelsey shrank in on herself. Rock clenched his jaw. Scott and Cal both stared off into the distance, but Penny paled.

"Makeup," she said. "It would be too risky to put it in any of her personal things. But she would never suspect anything that was put on her by a makeup artist."

"Jasmine?" Cal asked.

"She did seem on edge," Scott said.

"Wasn't everyone? With the mood Fiona was in." Cal paced.

"She hit Fiona with the makeup brush," Kelsey said quietly then shrank back when we all turned to her.

"I've known Jasmine for years. She wouldn't do that," Cal insisted. "Maybe it was just clumsiness."

"Daisy, you saw the incident," Scott began. "Do you think it was intentional?"

I concentrated on the pizza because I didn't dare look at Daisy, since she was the one who'd made Jasmine's brush whack Fiona.

But before Daisy could answer, Kelsey piped up, "Jasmine wasn't the only one who had contact with Fiona and the makeup. Fiona sent her away, remember?"

"What are you implying, Kelsey?" Penny narrowed her eyes at the younger woman.

"Nothing. I didn't mean—I know you wouldn't—I'm just trying to say that anyone could have had access to the products used on Fiona," Kelsey said.

"I didn't poison Fiona." Penny ran a hand through her hair. "This is nuts. I need some air."

After the screen door slammed, Daisy said, "Star, can we talk?"

"Sure." I took my pizza and drink and followed her into her bedroom.

She closed the door and flopped onto her bed, leaving no room for me to sit with my food. I pulled out the chair covered with clothes from the vanity and sat. "What's up?"

"I got another letter."

I set my paper plate and red plastic cup on the desk. "It came in the mail? To the house?"

"No, it was in my jacket pocket." She pulled out a piece of paper and handed it to me. "I had it with me all day."

"How do you know it happened today? Could it have been put in there a while back, and you just noticed it today?"

"No, because my hands were so cold this morning, I

shoved them in there while we were waiting for the car to warm up."

I unfolded the paper. I didn't understand the first part.

SLEEPING IN BED FOR DAYS? BUT YOU'LL SLEEP FOREVER.

P.S. GREAT PERFORMANCE TODAY! YOU HAD THEM CONVINCED. BUT NOT ME. I KNOW WHAT YOU ARE, AND SOON, SO WILL THE WORLD.

I looked up at Daisy, and suddenly, she looked years older. It had been a long, exhausting day.

A single tear escaped down her cheek, and she brushed it away. "I'm scared, Star."

"I never thought I'd say this, Daisy, but I think you should go stay with Mamma."

"What? Why?"

"She and her bodyguards can keep you safe. I can't." I shook the letter. "Whoever sent this has been very close to you. Someone on your crew or Fiona's put this in your pocket."

"Definitely not my crew. If it were any of them, they would have had so many more opportunities to hurt me. We live on a freaking bus together."

"Fiona's crew then."

"But why? Plus, we've been working with them for a few days. Everyone seems so friendly. I can't picture any of them wanting to hurt me."

That was Daisy's fatal flaw. She trusted everyone. Even as a kid. *Especially* as a kid. I sighed, remembering the time we found her almost stepping into a stranger's van after school, and I moved from the chair to the bed to wrap my arms around her. "Honey, at this point, we have to assume everyone is guilty. Including your crew. Isn't that why you moved back in here? Because you didn't feel safe with them in the bus?"

"It wasn't because of them, just the bus, since one of my letters showed up in my bunk."

I squeezed my eyes shut. "Who else besides your crew has access to the bus?"

"No one, legally, but, Star, people can break into busses."

"We need to go to Dusty with this."

"No! He would want to interview everyone, including my crew, and they'd want an explanation for the fraud accusation. I need to tell them the truth myself, first." Her voice was frantic. "Finding out this way would destroy their trust in me. They're family. I can't do it, Star. Just give me time, please."

chapter
fifteen

THE NEXT MORNING, I stumbled into the kitchen for coffee and nodded to Rock sitting at the kitchen table. I ambled past Kira and Teeny, who were at the stove, and over to the coffee pot. All three knew me well enough to know I wouldn't be coherent until I'd had at least a sip or two of my coffee. So no one bothered to say anything more than "Good morning."

My body went through the motions automatically, and when I reached for the pot, I found it already full. "You made coffee?" I asked Teeny.

"Rock did," she said.

I filled one of my favorite mugs, a squat blue-and-white stoneware mug that read *I Smell Snow*, then padded to the fridge and pulled out the cream. I poured in a generous amount, took a sip, then another, and my head shot up. "What are you doing here?"

"You're welcome." A smile spread across Rock's face. When I didn't return it, he said, "I have a meeting with Daisy this morning to discuss our next steps. Sorry, I'm a bit early."

"Don't mind her. She gets cranky when she hasn't had enough sleep." Teeny flipped a pancake.

Next to her, Kira poured batter into a waffle iron.

"No, sorry, thank you for making coffee." I nodded to Rock then the girls. "Pancakes *and* waffles?"

"We couldn't decide which to have, so we made both." Kira smiled.

"I wanted to make my mom's sprinkle-chip pancakes that you make us on our birthdays, and Kira wanted to make her dad's Sunday-morning waffles." Teeny smiled.

"It's neither Sunday nor anyone's birthday." Daisy came into the kitchen, toweling off her hair.

"No, but it's the first day of Christmas break. That's not the only reason we're celebrating, though!" Kira said. "We've figured out what to be for each other. We've always been best friends, and well, I guess we've always been sisters, technically, but since that part is new, and since Teeny feels weird calling us sisters, we've come up with a new word. Teeny, tell them."

"Besters!" Teeny put a platter of pancakes on the table. She smiled but also rolled her eyes.

I couldn't help but smile as well. "I like it."

"Riiiight?" Kira squealed. "And this marriage of my

dad's waffles and Teeny's mom's pancakes is a perfect blend of our families."

"Do you have strawberries and whipped cream for the perfect marriage?" Rock asked.

The five of us stuffed ourselves while Kira excitedly told us about the yearbook her mom had found. "It's my dad's. Teeny and I stayed up late last night looking through it. You have to see this!"

I sipped my orange juice while she ran upstairs like a small horse then took the opportunity to lean over and whisper to Teeny, "You okay with all this?"

"Yeah. I mean, it's just pancakes and waffles. I'm not moving in with them."

My heart constricted at the thought that it could be a possibility. I'd never even considered whether she would want to move. Before I could continue that spiral, the horse came galloping back down the stairs and skidded into the kitchen. She flopped the yearbook onto the table and flipped to a page at the back. On the blank pages they provided for the usual "Have a great summer" type messages was Astra's signature in her beautiful, curly handwriting.

A sketch took up about a fourth of the page, depicting two trees with separate trunks, but from the way they'd grown close to each other, the canopy formed a shape that resembled one tree. The branches were bare, minus a single leaf that hung precariously to one small twig. It was an interesting drawing to leave on her best friend's boyfriend's yearbook page, as this was way before Astra and Zeke had their summer romance. And scrawled around the whole shape were the words "Don't stop be-leafing."

My throat tightened. It was like a message from beyond the grave. I'd almost given up hope that I would ever get to see her again, but something about this drawing made me feel like it was a real possibility. As Carly said, I had to trust the process. We would open that well, and I would see my sister again.

"Aren't her doodles the cutest?" Kira asked.

Daisy dragged the yearbook to her, read it, and smiled. "Your mom was a talented artist. I think I have some of her sketches packed away. I'll try to find them later. I think they're in one of my boxes in the attic."

Kira jumped up. "Oh, a treasure hunt! Can Teeny and I go look?"

Teeny grabbed her sleeve and pulled her back down. "Eat first. Then we can go on a treasure hunt. If it's okay with Daisy."

"Fine by me." Daisy shoved a forkful of pancake into her mouth.

. . .

Once the girls were up in the attic, I turned to Rock. "You two go ahead and have your business meeting. I'll get the dishes."

I watched them with their heads bent together over production notes and envisioned Daisy as a kid, Rock helping her with her homework. He'd always kept an eye on her.

"Rock?" I put down the dish towel.

He lifted his head.

"Daisy needs to show you something."

"Star. We talked about this." She shot me a warning glare.

"I know we did, but he's not Dusty. And he already knows the truth. He should know about this."

"Know what?" Rock asked.

Daisy sighed and stood from the table.

"Daisy has been getting threatening letters," I said as she left the room.

She returned and spread the letters on the table.

Rock bent over them, and his jaw clenched tighter and tighter. When he finally looked up, he seemed unable to speak for a moment. Then, in a low voice, he said, "Who else have you told about these?"

"Only Star."

"Hey, look." I pointed to one of the letters, "That one, 'One plus seven plus eight plus eight equals six. Your time equals zero,' makes no sense. Those numbers add up to twenty-four, not six."

"It's from my scavenger hunt a few years ago," Daisy said.

"All the letters are twisted versions of the clues Daisy gave for them." Rock reached into his pocket, pulled out his phone, and stepped away with it.

I studied the letters with new understanding.

Rock returned after a moment. "Sheriff Palmer is on his way."

"Rock, no! Why did you do that?" Daisy asked.

"These are serious threats, D." He shot me a glance. "The police should've already been involved. How long has this been going on?"

"Since early October."

"Are you kidding me with this, D? Why didn't you tell me? I'm your producer. I'm your friend. I promised your sister I would keep you safe!" His voice rose with every successive sentence and cracked on the last.

"You have kept me safe," Daisy insisted. "I didn't tell you about this because, at first, I didn't think it was different from any of the others."

"The others?" I asked.

"I get all kinds of crazy mail."

Rock's jaw worked back and forth again. "I thought you got rid of that P.O. box after the last time this happened."

"The last time?" I demanded. "This has happened before?"

Before Daisy could answer, the screen door shut, and Kelsey came in with a laundry basket. "Star, you sure it's okay if I wash the bus's bed linens here? They're filthy, and—"

Daisy tried to shield the letters with her body.

"What's going on?" Kelsey asked. "Why does everyone look so tense?"

Daisy gathered them up. "Nothing for you to worry about, Kelsey."

Kelsey grasped for one of the letters before Daisy could collect them all.

"'Sleeping in the bed for days. But you'll sleep forever here.' The red letters spell out *hell*. Daisy! Someone is threatening you?"

"Kelsey, please don't mention this to the others."

"Of course I won't, but you should have confided in me, Daisy. I'm supposed to help protect you."

"That's what I've been saying," Rock muttered.

"What is TVW?" I pointed to the one that seemed to have a signature. "Do those initials mean anything to you?"

"She was a crazy fan. It's a long story," Daisy said.

"But do you know what she looks like? Could it be someone we passed today? At the hotel?"

"Yeah, no, I would definitely recognize her. She's a

bigger girl and has purple hair. Someone like that can't lurk behind a bush without being noticed. Not because of her size, I mean," Daisy added. "But because she was a loud, attention-seeking diva."

Just then, a car roared down the driveway. Dust clouds burst from the ground around it, and Dusty's Mustang screeched to a stop in front of the house.

Before any of us could react, he was on the front porch. Rock met him at the door.

Dusty pushed past him. "Where is she? Is she okay?"

He stopped when he saw me standing by the kitchen table.

"What's going on?" he asked. "I thought you were hurt."

"What in our conversation made you think that?" Rock raised his eyebrows.

"You said you needed me here as soon as possible." Dusty glared at Rock as he walked toward me. "You're really okay?"

My heart skipped a beat at the worry in his eyes. "I'm fine. It's Daisy who Rock called you about."

He glanced at the table and the letters spread there. His jaw worked the same way Rock's had. *What is it with men and those jaw muscles that jump around when they have emotions? Just feel your feelings, my dudes.*

He looked up at Daisy. "Tell me everything."

She told him everything she'd told me, including

finding the most recent letter in her jacket pocket. At her revelation, Rock said a few words I was glad Teeny and Kira weren't around to hear.

Dusty scrubbed his chin. "Where is the rest of your crew?"

"On the bus, I imagine," Daisy said. "Why?"

"Can you get them? I'd like to talk to you all at once."

"No, I don't want them to know about these letters," Daisy insisted. "I've told you, you can file a report or whatever, then let's be done with it. I don't want to talk about it anymore."

"My lab guy found a cosmetic spray containing aconite. It was among the items taken from your personal inventory."

"Mine?" Daisy asked.

"Yes. I want to get everyone's statement again," Dusty said.

"Aconite? Isn't that what could kill Superman?" Kelsey asked.

Rock shook his head. "No, that's kryptonite."

"I'll go get them," Rock said.

Dusty followed him onto the porch.

"Is Penny a suspect?"

Daisy and I turned to look at Kelsey.

"Penny took over for Jasmine. She's the one who finished Fiona's makeup, the last person who touched her before Fiona died." Kelsey's eyes widened.

"You can't seriously think Penny had anything to do with Fiona's death." Daisy placed a palm on her own cheek. "Besides, she did my makeup too. Why am I not dead?"

I put my arms around Daisy.

"Before the others get back, I'm gonna get these stinky sheets and stuff out of here. Star, is it still okay to use your laundry room?"

I nodded, too preoccupied with the recent events to form words.

"I don't understand," Daisy murmured.

I'm beginning to. First the letters, now the makeup containing poison. It was too much to be a coincidence. I thought about the visions again, then it hit me.

Dusty returned, and his eyes met mine.

"Fiona's death was an accident. I think Daisy was the intended target," I said.

"ME? Why do you think that? Because of the letters?"

"Those and the poisoned spray. It was in your makeup artist's kit."

"Penny didn't kill Fiona!" Daisy insisted.

"I'm not saying she did, but we need to find out who has access to her stuff. That's why you want to question the crew, isn't it?" I tried to read Dusty's face, but he wore his Detective Palmer, I-keep-my-cards-close-to-my-chest look.

Footsteps sounded on the porch after a few minutes, and Kelsey came back from the laundry room. With a full kitchen and Kelsey having resumed her watchdog place by Daisy, I retreated to the window seat.

When everyone else was seated at the table, Dusty said, "Penny, I'd like to ask you a few questions."

"Not without a lawyer," Daisy told her.

Penny cast a confused glance at Daisy. "Do I need a lawyer?"

"If you'd like to call one, please feel free, but I only have a couple of questions," he said.

"I have nothing to hide." She sat up in her chair and leaned forward, hands palm down on the table. "Ask your questions."

"Walk me through what happened when you replaced Jasmine and did Fiona's makeup," he said.

"There's not a lot to tell. I was down at the house when they told me I was needed up in the cemetery for makeup. I went up there, and Fiona asked me to finish hers because Jasmine was incompetent."

Tires crunched on the gravel outside, and I turned to see Carly step out of her deputy's vehicle. Rock met her there, and I turned my attention back to what unfolded in the kitchen.

"Did you use your own supplies or Jasmine's?" Dusty asked.

"Jasmine's, of course. My stash is for Daisy and is matched for her skin tone. She's much paler than Fiona. Plus Fiona's is much more expensive than Daisy's, a higher quality brand."

He pulled up a photo and showed her. "Is this her brand?"

Penny squinted at the photo, and her defiant look vanished. "No. That one's mine. That's my setting spray."

"Why did you replace Jasmine the morning Fiona died?" Dusty asked.

"Because Fiona asked me to," she said.

"But why would you do it? From what I've heard, she wasn't someone people bent over backward to do favors for, and you don't strike me as someone who bends over backward."

"I did it for Daisy. To keep the peace. To keep the production on schedule," she stammered.

Dusty looked at his notepad. "Why did you get fired from *Haunted Hollywood*?"

Penny narrowed her eyes. "How did you know that?"

"Please answer the question."

"Because I refused to do someone's makeup after they were rude to me."

"Who was it?" Dusty asked.

"You know who it was, or you wouldn't be asking." Penny crossed her arms over her chest.

Thoughts connected like puzzle pieces in my head. Dusty said it just as I thought it.

"Fiona."

"Hold up, you don't think I held a grudge all these years for that then offed her during the production that could completely change the trajectory of not only my career but Daisy's, do you?"

"Did you?"

"No, I made peace with that a long time ago. Fiona didn't even remember me. That was so long ago."

"Tell me about the setting spray. Did you use it on Fiona?"

"Fiona didn't have any, so I used mine," she said then added, "I've changed my mind about a lawyer. I'm not answering anything else."

"Understood." Dusty closed his notebook at the same time as his phone pinged. He cast a glance at it then announced, "I'll be right back."

"I can call my cousin Holly." Daisy shot a glare at Dusty.

Penny's eyebrows shot up. "The one who owns the diner?"

I nodded. "Yes, she doesn't practice but has the license. She helped me when I was in a jam a few months ago."

Scott spoke up for the first time since they'd all gathered in the kitchen. "No offense to your cousin—I'm sure she's great, D—but I have a feeling Penny will need someone a bit more experienced."

"I didn't do this," Penny said.

I watched through the window as Rock and Carly met Dusty in the driveway. Carly had evidence bags. *From the bus?*

"I believe you," Daisy said.

Penny stared at the table, her left leg bouncing. She looked like she might flee at any moment.

A couple of minutes later, both men returned, jaws working like they were training for the mouth Olympics. I dismissed that vision and looked to them, waiting for answers. I was almost as much in the dark as the people at my kitchen table. I was glad Kira and Teeny were upstairs, still in the attic, poring over Astra's old drawings.

Dusty laid a sealed evidence bag on the kitchen table.

"What are those?" Daisy asked.

"My deputy searched your bunks on the bus."

"You can't do that. You don't have a warrant!" Penny insisted.

"I don't need a warrant when the owner of said bus gave me permission," Dusty replied.

"I didn't!" Daisy insisted. Then the realization seemed to dawn on her. "Rock?"

The color drained from Penny's face as her gaze darted between Dusty and Rock and finally landed on Rock. If she could shoot fire from her eyes, he would be a pile of ash. "You had no right! My personal things are in there."

"What are you afraid we'll find, Ms. Sinclair?" Dusty asked.

"None of your damn business!" Penny stood so quickly her chair went screeching across the floor.

"Sit down," Dusty commanded.

I took a closer look at the evidence bag, thoughts coming together as my suspicions formed. Through the clear film, it appeared they'd gathered magazines, but they looked tattered.

"Are those...? No. They can't be." My cheeks flushed with anger as I saw the uneven edges of the pages where they'd been cut here and there.

"What is it?" Daisy stood and leaned over the table to get a closer look then sat back down with a thump as the realization hit her. "Those magazines have letters cut out of them. Like the ones pasted into the threats."

"Threats?" Scott asked.

"We found these in your bunk, Penny!" Rock roared as he stepped toward the table.

Dusty stopped him with an arm like the signs that come out on a school bus. "Let me handle this."

"This has been happening under my nose. On my crew. To Daisy." Rock huffed a breath and ran a hand roughly through his hair.

I got it. I was seething, too, that Daisy had been betrayed by someone on her crew, but it wasn't as personal to me as it was to Rock. He'd lived with Penny. He'd hired her.

"I'm good. Do your thing," he said.

"Can someone explain what the hell is going on?" Daisy's voice shook.

Dusty nodded to Carly, who grabbed her cuffs. "Ms. Sinclair, you have the right to remain silent."

seventeen

WE ALL STOOD on the porch, watching as Carly put Penny in the back seat of her cruiser. Not a single person on Daisy's crew was happy with Dusty or Rock.

Kelsey stepped off the porch. "I'm sure you tore the place up. I'll go work on getting everything back in its proper place."

"Rock, can we have a word?" Scott demanded through gritted teeth.

"And I'd like an explanation." Daisy stood toe to toe with Dusty, glaring up at him.

I didn't see how she needed it spelled out. It was plain to me. Penny had been the one sending the threatening letters.

Scott's and Rock's raised voices drifted through the walls, and their hand gestures through the window supported my supposition that they were arguing. From a phrase that penetrated the walls here and there, I could tell that Scott was mad about what he perceived as Rock's betrayal of Penny.

We went to the living room and sat. Daisy curled up on the end of the sofa, hugging a throw pillow.

Dusty sat in the recliner adjacent. "We found several magazines, glue, and scissors in the drawer under her bunk. Along with some illegal substances."

"Aconite?" I asked.

"Marijuana," he replied.

"Oh, please!" Daisy said. "That's legal in so many states."

"Not in Texas. And what's not legal in any state, Daisy, are death threats."

"Someone planted those in her bunk. I know Penny wouldn't do this." Daisy's fingers dug into the throw pillow.

"And the poison?" I asked. "The setting spray. I think it was meant for you."

"Exactly! That doesn't make sense. If she wanted me dead, why would she use it on Fiona instead? And why would she sign them TVW?" Daisy glared at Dusty.

"Does TVW mean something to you?"

"The Violet Witch. She was a fan who wanted to be on my crew."

"I'm still piecing the why together," Dusty said, answering her previous question. "But the physical evidence doesn't look great. The magazines and the other paraphernalia were in her bunk, and she admitted to using her setting spray on Fiona."

Daisy threw the pillow down and stalked down the hall to Aunt Mer's bedroom, slamming the door. Dusty exited the kitchen without saying goodbye.

That left me there alone. My own thoughts swirled in my head. Something didn't fit. Or maybe it fit too well. Penny had lived with Daisy on the bus for years. *Why now?* And I'd seen Penny in action. She was meticulous. She wouldn't be so sloppy as to use something meant for Daisy on Fiona.

"Oh, we thought we heard voices down here." Kira's voice penetrated my thoughts.

I turned to find both girls with arms full of what appeared to be Astra's sketches.

"Most everyone left." I didn't bother to explain the morning's happenings. They seemed so happy. I would find time for that later. "I'd almost forgotten you two were up there. What did you find?"

"Tons of my mother's old drawings." Teeny's face was as bright as the Christmas tree in the corner.

"Let's go into the kitchen and look at them."

"She was obsessed with drawing that tree," Kira said. "There are several more sketches of it. I doodle on the side of my notebook at school, but I do things like cats and funny faces. She doodled a whole freaking scene over and over."

"I wonder if that tree really exists somewhere," Teeny mused. "It seems too intricate to just be something she made up." She carefully placed the papers on the table and spread them.

My eyes roved over them. "You're right. That tree is the same in all the drawings. But I don't recognize it."

"Maybe Dad would know," Kira said. "But no, I don't want to ask him yet, because I have an idea for the perfect Christmas gift for him from me and you, Teeny!"

"She did more drawings besides the tree. But we left those in the attic for now. I wanted to keep them safe. How come you never told me about these?" She glanced at me through her eyelashes. "I mean, I know you gave me boxes of her stuff, but why weren't these in there?"

"I didn't know they were still around." I studied the sketches. Something about the repeated patterns was deliberate, as if Astra were trying to send a message—just like there was a message in the evidence against Penny. Too neat. Too convenient.

After the girls went back upstairs with the drawings, drinks, and snacks, my phone buzzed in my pocket. Aunt Willa Jo's number popped up on the screen.

"Hey, Aunt Will," I answered.

"Hey, honey! Listen, I'm sure you're all busy with the production, but I'm wondering if you have any time left to help prep for the Midwinter Ball. It's in two days, and there is still so much to do."

I glanced at the calendar on the wall. *Sheesh, how is it past the middle of December?* "Of course! What do you need?"

She filled me in on the to-do list as I wondered how much sleep people actually needed. I didn't think she or I would be getting much between now and the ball. "Sounds great! And I'll get Daisy, Teeny, and Kira on board as well."

"Get us on board for what?" Daisy asked when I disconnected the call.

"Wash your face and grab your coat, while I go upstairs and get the girls. We're headed to the town hall."

We all climbed into the Jeep and headed out, but as we neared the end of the driveway, Cal's vehicle pulled in. We both slowed to a stop and rolled down our windows.

"Where are you going?" he demanded. "We're supposed to be filming Daisy this morning." Bryan was in the car with him.

"Out to run errands for the Midwinter Ball. If you want to film us, you'll have to help with that." I put the car in drive and left.

"Dang, Star, you are cold!" Kira said.

"Party business is serious stuff," Teeny told her. "You

know Star. When she goes into focus mode, you'd better get out of her way."

"Amen to that," Daisy muttered. "But also, thank you. I'm not in the mood to be 'on' right now."

As we drove down the road toward town, I spotted Cal's vehicle behind us. I was tempted to take a detour and go the long way around, but Teeny was right. I was in focus mode. Plus, I felt guilty for not getting in touch with Aunt Willa Jo before now to check in with her on what I could do to help with the party, especially since Aunt Mer wasn't around to help.

"First on the list, we need to stop by the Merc because Granny is donating some gift baskets for the raffle. Plus, I want to check in on her," I said.

"Oh good, and we can run next door and see Dad," Kira said to Teeny. "That would be an awesome surprise!"

I glanced in the rearview mirror and saw Teeny nod, but she didn't seem excited.

As if Kira understood, she added, "I mean, I will for sure, but you don't have to. I'm respecting your boundaries."

I smiled to myself. Kira seemed to be getting the message, and Teeny seemed to be trying to set some boundaries.

"No, it's okay. We can go see him. We need to figure out his shirt size anyway, remember?" Teeny replied then explained to us in the front seat, "Kira came up with the idea of us making him a T-shirt for Christmas from us both."

Daisy grinned. "I would say he wears a large. He's filled out since I left town. And not in a dad bod kind of way, in a hot yoga instructor who lifts weights way."

"Eww! Don't talk about my dad like that!" Kira said.

"Yeah, we don't want to picture yoga moms with their hands on him!" Teeny said.

"Teeny, no! You made it even worse. Someone give me a fork to poke out my eyes!" Kira said.

"Why would we have forks in the Jeep?" Teeny asked. "And mentioning *adult fun time* isn't so great when our dad is concerned, is it? Payback, K!"

Kira groaned then said, "Hold up! You said *our*. Our dad."

"Yeah, he is. And no matter whose dad he is, he's ancient. I don't want to think of adults having... fun. Especially adults I *know*."

"And definitely not our dad!" Kira added. "Fun-time talk is forbidden when it concerns him."

All talk, fun or otherwise, ceased as we pulled into a parking space right in front of the Merc. I was glad to see Granny had new help. I smiled at her as she restocked candles but didn't introduce myself, as she would probably be gone by the end of the day.

Cal and Bryan weren't as lucky to find close parking and rushed through the doors breathlessly just as Granny handed over a large gift basket. Cal jogged over to us and introduced himself to Granny.

She looked him over. "I know who you are and what you're doing, but I want to know why you're filming my silly little store."

Cal looked around then and seemed to get the full picture of the store with the various items lining the walls from floor to ceiling and the rolling library ladders. "Little? This is an amazing space! How long did it take you to build this business?"

"Over a century, at least." Granny pushed her white curls off her forehead.

Cal laughed. "You look great for your age."

"Granny's parents owned it before she did, so it's been in the family for over a century," I explained.

"Oh, how interesting," Cal said. "Do you have a photo of them? That would be a great side segment, 'The Bell Family Witches.'"

"I do not," Granny replied.

"Not a single photo of your parents?" Cal remarked. "I'm sorry. Did they get lost somehow?"

He was trying to pull a concerned expression, but I saw beyond it into his investigative documentarian face. He was looking for a story. But there wasn't one. "All the family photos were lost in a fire."

Cal turned to me. "Oh, that must have been horrible for you to lose photos of your ancestors."

"It happened before I was born. Granny lost them years ago."

"I'm sorry to hear that. At least there are still the memories. I bet your mother and aunts have told you lots of stories about their grandparents." He glanced at me and Daisy.

"They died before Mamma was born," Daisy offered.

"I thought y'all were done filming." Granny narrowed her eyes at him. "Why are you following my granddaughters around? And asking impertinent questions?"

"We're doing a day-in-the-life segment, just to show what Daisy does on a normal day when she's not seeing ghosts."

"Mm," Granny said. "Well, I'll tell you what she doesn't do. She doesn't give people the third degree!"

"You raised four girls on your own without help from your husband or parents. What a strong woman you are! I can see where Daisy got a lot of her strength."

"She had Aunt Tatty," I said.

"Her sister," Daisy offered. She seemed to be glad the focus was mostly off her for a bit.

"Oh, where is she?" Cal glanced around as if Aunt Tatty would suddenly pop up from behind the crystal display.

No one spoke for a moment, and Cal added, "Oh dear, did she die too? I'm so sorry. That must have been a terrible loss. Losing someone who was your only lifeline to a far and distant past."

Granny snorted. "She'll turn up again like a bad penny."

Cal gave her a confused look, but she turned and hobbled toward the back, dismissing him.

"Aunt Tatty isn't dead," I explained. "She's off on a tour of Europe. And she and Granny don't quite get along."

"Like you two?" He'd laid the trap perfectly. The cameras had been rolling the minute they ran in the door, I had to assume.

"Those girls are best friends compared to Tatiana and me!" Granny hollered from the back.

"She has great hearing," Cal remarked.

"You have to understand, Astra and Star were born just four years apart and grew up together. I came along several years later, and they didn't even get to meet me until I was seven years old. But in that time, I feel like we became a family."

"You should have seen Astra with Daisy!" Granny returned. "You'd have thought she'd been handed a life-sized doll to play with. She loved to dress her up and braid her hair. If Daisy had been a bit smaller, I bet Astra would have put her in a carriage and pushed her around town. She loved kids."

I glanced at Teeny, who feigned interest in the gift baskets, but I could tell she was listening.

Granny shuffled back up to the front with a photograph in hand. I recognized it as the one that usually resided on the corkboard above her desk. It had been taken right before Astra went away.

"This photo contains everyone I love, minus those who weren't born yet. It's the only one I need."

Daisy looked over Cal's shoulder as he held the photo.

"I remember this. It was Granny's birthday. That's Astra there." Daisy continued to name the people in the photo, including Zeke.

"My dad is in it?" Kira's ears perked up.

"Your dad?" Cal questioned.

"Yeah, he's standing there, between Boone and Teeny's mom. Boone is his best friend, but he's out of town right now."

"Traveling for work or pleasure?" Cal asked.

"Not sure. He's in Europe somewhere."

"Europe again, huh?" He gave Granny a dubious look, as if she'd buried them in her backyard.

Granny glared right back at him. "There are much more interesting things for you to ask about than my family's whereabouts. What about the fact that your host's killer was caught?"

"What?" Cal asked. "Who?"

"You didn't know?" Daisy asked. "They arrested Penny this morning."

"Penny?" Cal's director-producer façade fell. "How do you know it's her? What evidence do the police have?"

I wasn't sure I should share any of that with him, especially on camera. It was an ongoing investigation, but before I could say that, Daisy launched in with, "The evidence for murder is so weak. Anyone on your team could've planted that there. And the stuff on my bus too!"

"Your bus? What?"

I laid a hand on Daisy's arm. "Should we really be talking about this?" My unsaid words were *To him. On camera.*

But the performer in Daisy had taken hold. She was on stage, and for whatever reason, she was spilling to Cal all about the letters she'd been desperate not to tell anyone about. "They found cutout magazines in Penny's bunk. But again, the property has been crawling with strangers. Anyone could've planted them there. So I'd take a closer look at my crew if I were you, Cal."

Cal stared at her for a long moment, and I saw his mind working. Then something else crossed his face. He seemed to shake himself out of it, and his director's mask slid back into place. He looked at his camera operator. "You got all that, right?"

As we were leaving, I hugged Granny goodbye.

She whispered in my ear, "Keep an eye on that one. He's hiding something."

Yes. Yes, he is.

TEENY AND KIRA stayed behind at Pub Dead with Zeke. They wanted to make a trip down the street to Which Craft? later for supplies for their secret project. It was the one punny name in town I kinda liked. And the owner, Laurisa, was an old friend. I told them to tell her hello from me. Then, after stashing the gift baskets in my car, we headed out. I wanted to tell Daisy what Granny had said, but Mourning Brew was a short walk away, and the crew wasn't far behind us, shooting more B-roll.

Soon, we arrived at Mourning Brew, and the door's bells jingled as we opened it. Holly looked up from the register and smiled when she saw us, then her look turned quizzical as the crew filed in behind us. The customers inside all turned to look as well. The café was much more crowded than Granny's store had been.

Holly came out from behind the register and greeted us. "What are y'all up to?"

"Your mom said you were donating some gift certificates for the raffle, and she sent us to taste the cake samples you prepared," I said.

"Oh, she said you were coming by for that, but I didn't know you were filming it."

"I hadn't planned to. They're just following us around to get some scenes of Daisy out in town and… oh my gosh! Fiona?" *Shoot, I didn't mean to say that aloud.* But I was shocked at seeing her there.

"Fiona?" Holly asked.

"She's here."

She stood at the doorway of the kitchen then disappeared through the door.

"Oh, this is perfect!" Cal said. "We can get more footage of Daisy talking to Fiona."

Daisy gave me a look that I imagined would mirror a drowning person's as they saw the last lifeboat sail away.

I picked up the mental life buoy. "Actually, Cal, I'm gonna handle this one. Daisy's been through a lot today. You said you wanted more Bell witches. Well, here you go!"

It looked like he was about to argue, when Holly spoke up. "Besides, Daisy can't go back there." Holly tapped on the sign to the back room that read Employees Only. "That's my kitchen back there. Star has been cleared by the health department. The rest of you haven't, so back up."

"Can we film from the door? I'll buy out the rest of your stock for the day if you say yes!" Cal all but batted his fabulous eyelashes.

"Sure, but if you step a toenail past the threshold of that door, you're out of here!"

I strode into the kitchen and found Fiona near the baking rack, sniffing pastries.

"What are you doing here?" I asked her. "I thought ghosts only went to places that held meaning for them."

Her head whipped up when I spoke. *"I don't know how ghost rules work, but I was thinking about those decadent biscuits we had one morning, and all of a sudden, I was here. I haven't left since. It smells wonderful here. And the coffee, have you ever smelled something so divine? What are you doing here? Have you found my killer yet?"*

"The police have arrested someone, but I don't think they've got the right person." I glanced over my shoulder to see if Cal was filming. Bryan had his camera pointed toward me, so something was happening at least.

"Who did they arrest?"

"Penny."

"Penny? The one who did my makeup? She confessed?"

"No, in fact, she's insisting she's innocent, but the police found evidence stacked against her. Her setting spray—the one she used on you—contained aconite. It's poisonous. They think that's what caused your death."

"Is that the only evidence against her?"

"There's more..." Thoughts swam through the murky water of my mind, trying to find each other and make a connection. But I needed more time to think about it, time when everyone wasn't staring at me, waiting for my next words. I shook my head to clear it. "They think she's been sending threatening letters to Daisy."

"Star, can you relay to us Fiona's side of the conversation as you go along?" Cal asked. "For narrative purposes?" I did, then he said, "Ask her about her getting Penny fired."

"I apologized to her about that," Fiona said. *"The day she did my makeup. I recognized her and asked her why she was helping me out when I'd been awful to her. She said she was helping Daisy, not me. And that she took her craft seriously and would give me the same care she would give anyone sitting in her makeup chair. I apologized, and she seemed appreciative. Tell the police they have the wrong person. You can tell them I said so."*

But that wouldn't hold up in court. I needed to find proof that she didn't do it.

I relayed all that to the camera, leaving out my own thoughts on the matter.

"Did she say anything about the threatening letters to Daisy?" he called from the doorway.

"Why would she know anything about those?"

"I mean, how does she explain the magazines in Penny's bunk if she's innocent?" he asked.

"Watch it. We're not putting Penny on trial on your show, Cal!" Daisy insisted.

"Why would I know anything about the magazines?"

I opened my mouth to tell everyone to shut up and let me think, but those swirly thoughts I'd been having swam together as if in a hurricane, and everything went dark.

I swore to Medusa I would strangle someone if I didn't get a break soon. Another hot flash shot up from my soul—or at least, that was what it felt like—and burned to the tips of my hair. What I needed was a cigarette, but the damn doctor had made me give those up because of my heart. I would rather be dead right now than here. Where the hell was Cal? I wanted to get this done so we could leave and I could dump a bucket of ice over my head. One would think, with it being December, I would get some relief outside, but no, we had to be filming in god forsaken Texas of all places. Why? Drusilla Von Leigh traveled everywhere. Why in the hell did she have to come back to Texas? Couldn't she have been in Alaska? Frostbite would be heaven compared to this hell called perimenopause.

I wiped my brow and continued to scan the landscape for Cal. Madison said she'd seen him go this direction.

There! Near the tour bus. Who was he with? Daisy's assistant? Kitty? Kelly?

They seemed to be having a heated argument. What did he just give her?

"Star? Are you okay?" Holly spoke above me.

The swirly thoughts dissipated, and the bright lights of Holly's kitchen brought me back to the present.

"You had another of your visions, didn't you?" Fiona asked.

I nodded, and Holly took that as her answer. Her shoulders relaxed.

"But I thought I had to touch you. I haven't moved from my spot."

"Sometimes, they're spontaneous."

"Was that another vision, Star? It looked pretty intense. What did Fiona show you this time?" Cal called from the doorway. He'd taken Holly's words to heart.

"She was having a hot flash." It was the truth, but I would keep the rest to myself for the time being. Until I could make sense of it. Right before I'd merged back into reality, I'd seen one more person in the scene. Penny.

"That's why you're drenched in sweat," Holly said. "Sheesh, your visions are getting more intense."

"Daisy," Cal said in his most documentarian voice. "Why do you think your powers didn't also manifest with visions? What makes Star's different?"

Daisy looked at the camera and turned on Drusilla to full wattage. "Because we're not factory made, love. I'm one of a kind!"

While that scene was happening, I whispered to Holly, "Can you get them back to the front? I need to ask Fiona one more question, alone."

She winked at me then stood. "Okay, the show is over, folks. If you want more time, you'll have to buy me out for a month." She walked toward them, waving her arms like a person who waved airplanes in.

Once the door closed behind me, I quickly relayed the vision to Fiona. "Do you remember that?"

"No, I don't. I mean, that sounds like me. One good thing about being dead, no more raging hormones and hot flashes."

"So, that helps me with the timing, because you'd remember anything that happened before you drank the herbal coffee. But it doesn't clear up the mystery completely. I need to talk to Penny. But I don't know how."

"What's the problem?" Fiona asked.

"She's in jail," I said.

"So? Is this jail Alcatraz? If not, then we can go there. Isn't your boyfriend a cop?"

"He's not my boyfriend, but yeah, Dusty is the one who arrested her."

"Even better!"

. . .

Back in the dining room of Mourning Brew, Cal swiped his card while Holly boxed up the remainder of the day's baked goods.

"What are you going to do with dozens of biscuits and pastries?" Daisy gave him a quizzical look. "Your crew isn't that big."

"I saw a sign on our way over about a food kitchen, so I thought I'd ask if they could use a donation." He shrugged.

"For real?" Holly asked. "You're not just saying that?"

"Why is that such a surprise? What do you do with your leftovers? Throw them away?" he asked as if it were the most impossible thing he'd ever heard.

"No, I mean, I have a few times. But I usually sell out, and other times, I've sent them home with my employees or given them to any regulars who are here at closing time." Holly reached behind her, grabbed one of the boxes she used for catering coffee, and filled it. "Take this too."

He nodded in approval and stuck a twenty in her tip jar, then turned to Daisy. "I think we have what we need from Star for today, but once you're good to go, I'd like to get a few more shots around town."

She started to argue, but I knew there was only one thing I could do right now. "Go with them, and I'll finish the errands."

I tried to give her a look that meant *Don't argue, I have a plan,* and it must have worked because she nodded. I was sure it helped that being the star of the show wasn't such a hardship for her.

"I'll be there in a minute," she said to Cal, and once he and his crew cleared out and Holly had me sitting in her office with a sausage biscuit and a glass of juice, Daisy launched into questions for me. "Was it Fiona? What did she say?"

"She doesn't believe Penny did it." I didn't tell them about the vision. Not yet. I wanted to do a bit more investigating on my own. I wasn't sure there was anything to what I'd seen. Cal seemed way too nice to be a bad guy. And I didn't want to freak out Daisy about Kelsey until I had reason. All she needed was to lose faith in yet another of her employees. "I want to talk to Penny and get her thoughts."

"And how will you do that?" Daisy asked. "It's not like you can just waltz into the jail."

"Sure, she can. It's all about who you know." Holly winked.

"Just because your boyfriend is the sheriff and—"

"He's not my boyfriend!" I insisted.

"I wasn't talking about her *boyfriend*." Holly put emphasis on the last word. "I was talking about her cousin, the lawyer."

chapter
nineteen

HOLLY LEFT MOURNING Brew in her staff's hands, and I left Daisy with the documentary crew. Holly drove me to her house, where she gave me a pantsuit to change into and donned one herself. Then we drove down to the county jail. Fiona followed us and kept silent for the most part.

When we arrived at the jail section on the backside of the county courthouse, Holly presented her credentials at the desk and asked to speak to Penny.

"She saw this on a TV show, didn't she?" Fiona scoffed. *"This doesn't actually work in real life, does it? She's a baker!"*

"She passed the bar," I said.

The clerk at the front desk looked up at me, and I realized I'd said that aloud.

"Pardon?"

"I, uh… I'm just her assistant. I haven't passed the bar. But Holly, um, Ms. Bell, here, has. She is completely licensed and legal."

Holly gave me a "shut up" look and said to the clerk, "Pay her no mind. This is her first time in a jail."

"They don't bite," the clerk said. "License?"

I realized she was looking at me when she said it, so I dug in my purse and pulled out my driver's license and handed it to her.

She examined it then looked at me then back at Holly. "Another Bell. Your assistant is related to you?"

"Yes. She's my cousin and works for me part-time," Holly said. It was the complete truth, but making biscuit dough was probably not what the clerk pictured me doing.

The clerk handed back my license and instructed me to sign the clipboard as well, then buzzed us through the door. A guard ushered us to a small room and, a few minutes later, brought in Penny.

Fiona and Holly began talking at once, and I couldn't hear both, so I held up a hand and said, "One at a time, please."

Holly and Penny stared at me, then Holly said, "Oh, Fiona is here too."

Penny raised her eyebrows. "Why is Fiona here?"

"She believes you're innocent."

"Well, that's one person," Penny said.

"Can you explain why you had those magazines in your bunk?"

"I don't know. Someone placed them there."

"Do you think it's anyone in your crew?"

"My crew?" she scoffed. "Are they really my crew now? Seems they've all turned against me. But no, no one would need a reason to. We all get—got—along great. We're a family."

"Fiona saw Kelsey and Cal arguing one day. I think she saw you nearby too. Do you remember that?" I asked.

Penny seemed to consider. "I don't think so. I can't imagine Kelsey arguing with anyone."

I glanced at Fiona, who shrugged. "*It was your vision.*"

I tried to remember more details. "They weren't far from the bus. And then you came out of it. I think you were wearing a gray sweater, and your hair was held back. Maybe with a white headband?"

"Oh! Could it have been a sweatband? And a gray sweatshirt?"

The vision snapped into focus in my mind. I didn't relive it, but it was like zooming in with a camera lens. "Yeah. I think that's right."

"I do remember that. I was going for a run. I only gave them a glance. I don't know if they were arguing, but Cal was not happy, and he handed Kelsey a paper or something, which she shoved into her jacket."

"Yes!"

"I figured it was just some papers for Daisy."

"When was this?"

"The first full day of the shoot, I believe."

"Before Daisy got the most recent letter. What if the letters are from Cal, and he bribed or—by the angry way Fiona says Kelsey snatched the letter—blackmailed her into sneaking them into Daisy's regular mail?"

"But what reason would Cal have?" Penny asked. "He didn't know Daisy before they arrived for the documentary."

I turned to Fiona. "Could it be for the documentary? To cause some drama so it's more exciting?"

"*Possibly?*" Fiona paced.

I turned over thoughts in my head, and Holly got down to business with Penny. "If they keep you, you'll need a better lawyer than me, but for now, retrace your steps the morning Fiona died. Who else had access to your gear?"

Penny scrunched her forehead. "Cal went through my stuff at one point. He said he was looking for eyeliner."

"Why was he looking for eyeliner in your stash? Isn't he from the other crew?" Holly asked.

"Yeah, but I told him about a brand I used on Daisy that stayed on so well, you almost needed an act of Congress to remove it." She smiled at the memory, then her smile faded. "You don't think...?"

I thought about Cal taking food to the food kitchen

on his own dime. *Could that be just for show? To make us think he's a good guy?*

"Anyone else?" Holly asked.

"Just Kelsey. She would sometimes come and get makeup wipes for Daisy." Penny ran a hand through her hair. "But she could never do anything like this. She cried once when the bus accidentally hit a squirrel, and she insisted the driver pull over so we could bury it. Plus—and I don't want to sound mean—I don't think she's clever enough to pull off something like this. If anyone on our crew did it, that would mean they looked Daisy in the eye daily, pretending to be part of the family we've made. Why wouldn't Kelsey have acted before now? She has more access to Daisy than anyone."

It was a rhetorical question none of us could answer, but before any of us could reply, a knock sounded at the door, and Dusty poked his head through. "Time's up!"

Dusty's jaw worked as he escorted us out. Holly tried in vain to fight him on it, claiming, as Penny's lawyer, she had a right to visit her client.

"Except you're not her lawyer." He stopped short in the middle of the hallway, and we both nearly ran into him.

"Says who?" Holly asked.

By that time, we'd reached the waiting room again, and he nodded at the clerk we'd given our licenses to. She called a name, and a slick-looking man stood and approached the desk.

Dusty opened the front doors and ushered us through. "Okay, now, what in the world were y'all doing?"

I explained the vision. "The only way for me to see Penny was for Holly to act as her lawyer."

"Which was perfectly legal in every way," Holly added. "I am allowed to consult with a potential client before I'm hired."

"Yes, you are," he said to her, but he didn't take his eyes off me. "The only way, huh? Is that what you really believe?"

"Are you telling me you'd just let me waltz in and talk to your suspect in jail? Wouldn't that have been unethical, especially since I intended to prove her innocence?" I crossed my arms over my chest.

"You two clearly have some things to work out. I'll leave you to it," Holly said. "I'll be in the car."

I nodded, continuing to stare Dusty down.

He blinked then ran a hand through his hair as he sat on a nearby bench. "If Penny were guilty, anything you got from her would be inadmissible. Because you went in there with her lawyer present, under false pretenses."

"I didn't think about that," I admitted.

"That's exactly why we work as a team." He sighed. Then, after a few moments, he asked, "So, did you get anything useful from her?"

"No." I took a seat as well. "I don't think she did it."

"I don't either."

"You don't?"

"No, things don't add up. Or perhaps they add up too well. We were about to cut her loose. So if you'd waited an hour or so, you wouldn't have had to put on that ridiculous outfit."

"Ridiculous? Excuse me?" I stood and glared at him.

"You look damn good in a pair of jeans and a T-shirt, great in a sundress, and adorable in a pair of Rugrats pajamas," he said, recalling the outfit I'd had on when we first met. "But that pantsuit makes you look like you're playing dress-up in your great aunt Gladys's clothes."

"Great Aunt Gladys? I don't have one of those." I smiled.

"I did, and the only thing you need to complete the look is *Eau de Mothball* and a pillbox hat." He smiled back.

"I'll let Holly know what you think of her clothes." I resumed my seat on the bench.

He turned to me. "You do that. But seriously, Star. Next time, don't keep me in the dark."

"I can't promise that." I held up a hand when he opened his mouth. "Because you will always be you. You uphold the law to the letter. But I feel like you might bend the rules for me, and I don't want you to."

He snorted.

"And while Penny was a dead end, there may be another lead." I filled him in on what Fiona and Penny had witnessed between Kelsey and Cal. "But what I can't figure out is why Cal would do that. Just to boost the production?"

"Let me do some digging."

chapter
twenty

AFTER HOLLY DROPPED me off at Mourning Brew, I headed back to my car at the Merc. It was usually a pleasant ten-minute walk, but unfortunately, I'd left my jacket at Holly's house. December in Texas wasn't like December in Minnesota, but it was a chilly day, and the pantsuit fabric was thin.

I rubbed my hands and blew on them as I realized Fiona wasn't following me. At least I would get a bit of peace. A car horn honked, and the peace was broken, but then I turned and found Aunt Willa Jo waving at me from behind the wheel.

Thank you, baby Jesus! I jogged to her and jumped into the passenger seat, then held my hands to the vents, which blew warm air.

"What in the world are you doing out here in the cold without a coat, and what are you wearing?" she asked.

I explained about the impromptu jail visit and the reason for the clothes. "I did get started on the errands. The gift cards from Holly are in my pocket, and the gift baskets from Granny are in my car back at the Merc."

"I'm not worried about that, but why didn't you get Holly to drive you back to the Merc?"

"Probably for the same reason I'm out here walking in"—I glanced at the display on her dash—"forty-eight-degree weather, looking like I decided to go as a senator for Halloween. I wasn't thinking."

She smiled. "Yeah, you're not a pantsuit person, sweetie. I'm not even a pantsuit person."

I glanced at her cute pink-polka-dot-and-navy flared skirt and matching soft-pink top and agreed. "Anyway, I've done a terrible job on the errands for the Midwinter Ball today, but I promise I'll finish the things on my list and anything else you want to add to it."

Aunt Willa Jo shook her head. "Thank you, honey. This Midwinter Ball might be the death of me."

"What's going on?"

"The florist doesn't have the flowers I ordered weeks ago, and the caterers backed out at the last minute, so I'm on my way to Zeke to see if he can help out."

"Oh my gosh, why did they cancel?" I asked.

"The florist said there was a mix-up with her supplier, and the caterer's excuse was that the staff all came down with the flu. But I suspect the real issue is that they are both close friends with the ex-mayor's wife. She blames me for her current status. And don't even get me started on the venue. I could cry." At the stoplight, she laid her head on the steering wheel for a moment.

I patted her back. "No worries. The Bell women have got you, and we'll put on the most magnificent Midwinter Ball in the history of the Midwinter Ball!"

She lifted her head, her eyes glistening. "Thank you, sweetie. So, why were you talking to Penny?"

I explained my vision and the letters.

"The Violet Witch? Sounds mysterious. What does she have against Daisy?" Aunt Willa Jo asked.

"Good question! Daisy won't say much. But..." A thought occurred to me, and I pulled my phone out of my pocket and clicked on a browser. "Google is my friend."

By the time we reached Pub Dead, I had answers. But I wasn't sure what to do with them.

We found a parking space right in front of Pub Dead, just a few spots down from my car. While Aunt Willa Jo went in to talk to Zeke, I transferred the gift baskets from my car to hers then joined her inside. As I walked in, Teeny and Kira looked up from the barstools where they perched.

Kira jogged over to the hostess stand and grabbed a

menu. In a formal voice, she said, "Would you like a booth or a table?"

"Your dad put you to work, huh?" I grinned.

"He's short-staffed today, so his usual front-of-the-house person is waiting tables and seating people." She glanced back toward a harried-looking woman refilling water glasses at a nearby booth. "Teeny and I are helping out."

That didn't bode well for Aunt Willa Jo and the favor she needed to ask Zeke. "Did Aunt Willa Jo find your dad?"

"Yeah, they're back in his office, I think. So, you aren't staying? Are you taking Teeny with you?"

"I'm good with her staying here if she wants to."

I glanced toward Teeny, who seemed to be in deep concentration, tapping a pen to her lips.

"Good, because we're working on something super-secret for Dad for Christmas." She slid the menu into the holder on the side of the stand and skipped back to Teeny.

I found Aunt Willa Jo in Zeke's office as Kira had promised. Really, it was my cousin Boone's office. He was off traveling somewhere and had left Zeke in charge. And we, in the family, all deferred to Zeke, which was why Willa Jo was asking for his help instead of calling Boone.

Zeke scribbled notes as Aunt Willa Jo spoke. "We've sold only forty tickets, but in the past, they had at least a hundred or more in attendance. I guess let's plan for sixty."

"And you want hors d'oeuvres?"

"Yes, at the last one, they served several different kinds, but I think we'll be okay with one or two since it's short notice."

Zeke wrote something. "And then a sit-down meal?"

"Yes, with five courses. I know you don't have enough plates for something like this. The caterer was supposed to provide all that, but I think I'll have to drive to a restaurant supply store in Austin and—"

Zeke put down his paper and took Aunt Willa Jo's hands. "Willa, I've known you all my life, and while you're a classy woman—and the mayor—I've never known you to be a several-course, formal-plated-dinner type of party person. Why are you trying to copy what they've done in the past? You are not the past. You're Willa Jo Bell, breaker of tradition, paver of her own road, scrunchie-wearing, hippy-dressing, magic mamma extraordinaire. What would you like to eat at the Midwinter Ball?"

I smiled at him over her head. Zeke Fry hadn't been born into our family, but we'd grabbed him up as soon as we could. He was as much a Bell as any of us.

He smiled back at me then to Aunt Willa Jo. "Aw, now, I didn't mean to make you cry. I shouldn't have overstepped. I will do whatever you decide. I just wanted—"

She waved away his words. "It's not sad tears, Zeke.

It's tears of relief. Of realizing you're right. I've been trying to be something I'm not with this Midwinter Ball, and you're so right. I just need to put my own touch on it."

I put a hand on her shoulder. "Despite my poor performance today, we will all help, and together we'll make this the best darn party this town has seen, and those who bailed this year will be begging to be a part of it next time."

"I like your optimism. Can you solve my staff problem?" She gave half a smile. "While Zeke is a whiz in the kitchen, he's short-staffed as it is. Where will we get all the servers?"

We put our heads together and decided that with the whole family pitching in, we would have enough to serve at the party. Instead of a seated dinner, hors d'oeuvres would be passed around on trays as the guests mingled, followed by a dessert bar, where they could serve themselves.

"I feel so much better." The words were no sooner out of Aunt Willa Jo's mouth when her phone rang, and she uttered a four-letter word that only came out when she was really upset. She tapped the screen and put the phone to her ear. "Yes? Oh. I see. Well, thank you for letting me know."

"What now?" I asked when she slid her phone into her pocket.

"The band has canceled." She pressed her lips together and stared at the ceiling.

Zeke scribbled on his pad. "Music. Got it."

"Got what?" Aunt Willa Jo asked.

"Just leave it to me."

"Zeke, you're doing so much as it is."

"As Granny always says, family does for family," he said. "And if the Bells, and Kira of course, aren't my family, I don't know who is."

chapter
twenty-one

AFTER THE THREE of us finalized the Midwinter Ball plans, I headed back home with Teeny, who planned to spend the night with Kira but needed clothes and a toothbrush. She insisted they had to finish the project they'd begun. They'd not yet decided if they were staying at Zeke's or Jessi-Lyn's, but Jessi-Lyn was taking them to a movie first and had been close behind us in the car. We found Daisy in the kitchen with Kelsey and Scott. Kelsey was crying, and Scott stood staring out the window.

"What's going on?" Teeny raced to the table. "Did someone die?"

It gnawed at me that my niece was beginning to think that anytime someone cried, a dead body must be involved. Our lives had to get more stable soon.

"No, we're just upset about Penny," Daisy said.

"Hello! Recently deceased right here," Fiona called from the window seat.

So, that was where she'd gotten off to. Though why she'd suddenly decided to haunt my house instead of the bakery, I had no clue, and I couldn't ask her at the moment. "What about Penny? Wasn't she released?"

Teeny, relieved no one was dead, raced off to her room.

"She was, and she came straight back here, packed her bags, and left," Scott said.

"She quit," Daisy said.

"This is all my fault." Kelsey sobbed into her hands.

Daisy rubbed her back. "No, it's not. You were worried about me."

"But I broke up the band. Just call me Yogi Obo."

"Do you mean Yoko Ono?" I asked. It was petty to point out her mistake when she was crying, but I couldn't be sure they weren't crocodile tears.

Kelsey sobbed harder. "See? I can't do anything right."

Daisy threw her arms around her and squeezed. "You're wonderful, you hear me?"

"Lord, if I were still alive, I'd find this girl an agent. She's a natural!" Fiona threw her head back. *"Such drama."*

"The thing that bothers me most is that if Penny is innocent, then someone broke into the bus and planted the magazines and is still out there! I don't feel safe at all." Kelsey wrapped her arms around herself.

"I won't let anything happen to you, Kelsey," Scott said. "Not to any of you. And honestly, I don't think anyone broke in. We left the door unlocked many times while we were over here eating. Anyone could've just walked in."

"Did you remember to lock the bus before we left?" Kelsey asked.

Scott nodded and patted his front pocket. "I did."

"Why don't y'all just move into the house for a bit? I'm sure Star wouldn't mind." Daisy shot a glance at me.

I minded very much. *Woo boy. But how to be diplomatic about it?* I was saved—at least temporarily—by the horn of Jessi-Lyn's car. Teeny came galloping down the stairs with a bag and shouted goodbye. That gave me a second to gather my thoughts.

"I, uh... sorry, y'all are great people, but it's not my house. I think we should ask Aunt Mer first. I'll send her a text, but it may take a while for her to get it, since she's only turning on her phone when they're in port."

I fully planned to pretend to ask Aunt Mer and have her say no. I didn't want anyone in the house other than Teeny, Daisy, and me. But Scott had been cooking for us for weeks. *How could I say, "I trust you to feed me but not to sleep under my roof"?* Plus, I hadn't made up my mind yet about Fiona's suspicions. What she'd seen between Kelsey and Cal could be completely innocent, but I wouldn't take chances.

I had to get Daisy away from her so I could tell her about their exchange.

"Daisy, I'm sorry about Penny. But I need to talk to you about the Midwinter Ball. Some stuff has happened, and I need to update you. I know this is a rough time, but Aunt Willa Jo needs all our help," I said.

She looked at me over Kelsey's head, and I tried to communicate with my eyes the urgency of the matter.

Kelsey lifted her head. "Help with the Midwinter Ball? I'd love to help."

Crap.

"What do you need? I can help too," Scott added. "You've all been so good about hosting us here for so long."

Kelsey wiped tears off her cheeks, and everyone gazed at me.

"*You handled that perfectly.*" Fiona rolled her eyes.

Scott pulled out a chair for me, and I had no choice but to sit and tell them about the Midwinter Ball.

"We need servers for the food and probably help setting up. Aunt Willa Jo is contacting everyone in the family to pitch in too. Zeke said he's handling the music. Not sure what that means, but—"

"I used to DJ for weddings and stuff. I can help with that," Scott offered.

"Good. You can go by Pub Dead and talk to him." I

pulled out my list to see what else we needed to do. My phone rang, and Aunt Willa Jo's face appeared on my screen.

"More bad news. The venue has now been canceled. I think I'll just have to call the whole thing off. If we can't have it at the community center, I don't know who would rent us space, especially with this short notice."

"Why did they cancel?"

"They say they have a rat problem, and the exterminator can't get there until next week."

"A rat problem? Sounds to me like it's an ex-mayor's-wife problem."

"I'd bet my life savings on it," she said.

"What's going on now?" Daisy whispered.

I held up a finger.

"Aunt Willa Jo, I'm putting you on speakerphone. Daisy is here with Kelsey and Scott." I added that last part quickly so she would know not to say anything about our conversation in the car. "They've all volunteered to help, and we'd just finished making our lists, so I want to tell them what's going on."

"Thank you, but I don't think help will be needed after all. With the venue canceling, there's nowhere else to have it. At least nothing we could get during the holiday party season on such short notice."

"Maybe there is," Daisy said. "When Cal was out

filming me today, he wanted to get some B-roll, and we were down on Raven Row, you know, where all those old Victorian houses are?"

"Yes?"

"Well, there's that big one that used to be a bed-and-breakfast but then sat empty for years. Someone has renovated it, and it's now for sale."

"Oh, really?" Aunt Willa Jo asked. "That's interesting, sweetie, but I'm not sure how that can help us."

"The realtor was there putting more flyers in the lockbox as we were walking by, and she recognized me. Apparently, her daughter is a huge fan, so she asked me for an autograph. We got to talking, and I mentioned how I'd always loved that old house. She said many people did but not enough to buy it. She asked if I wanted to see the inside. I suppose she was hoping I'd put in an offer, but my point is, the place is perfect for your Midwinter Ball. I'm wondering if they'd rent it out to us for the night if we promised to also pay a hefty cleaning fee so it would be show-worthy again after. She gave me her card, so I can give her a call if you'd like."

"Who was the realtor?" Aunt Willa Jo asked.

Daisy gave a name I didn't recognize, but Aunt Willa Jo said, "Oh, good! She's new in town. She won't be one of the ex-mayor's wife's friends. Sure, sweetie, give it a try. Can't hurt. I'll hold off on shutting it all down until I hear back from you."

Daisy was reaching for her phone before I even disconnected my call with Aunt Willa Jo.

Scott said, "Oh, and I'll call Cal. He'd probably help out too!"

"The more hands, the better!" It would give me a chance to observe him and Kelsey again to see if anything was going on.

As Scott picked up his phone and sauntered into the other room, Kelsey snorted. "Cal is Hollywood right down to his blond roots. He'll probably make this a razzle-dazzle spectacular."

"Blond roots? He's not a natural brunette? How do you know?" I asked.

She seemed to realize she'd spoken aloud and hesitated, then said, "You can see them if you look closely enough."

I made a mental note to look for myself the next time I saw him, but I had a weird feeling about those two. First, the apparent argument over the mysterious envelope Fiona and Penny had witnessed. Now, she was commenting on his hair.

Before I could consider it further, Daisy swirled back into the room. "We have a new venue!"

I didn't have a chance for the rest of the evening to get Daisy alone to let her know what I'd found out. After a bit more party planning, Scott had cooked dinner with little to nothing of what he'd found in the fridge and made us a yummy pasta dish. After that, Kelsey wanted to play Nerts. But when they finally got ready to leave, something occurred to me. I grabbed Scott in the kitchen while Daisy and Kelsey talked by the front door.

"Hey, was Cal ever a blond?" I thought about what Kelsey had said about his blond roots.

Scott laughed. "Cal? Not as long as I've known him. I can't picture him with anything other than his signature jet-black hair. Why?"

"Just something I heard."

Daisy hadn't even waited for the door to close before jumping into the shower—without helping to clean up. I extended mental forgiveness since she'd been through a lot the past few days and finished the kitchen myself. When I returned from my shower, I found her in my bed.

She looked so young and innocent with her hair wet and blankets up to her chin. Tears rolled down her cheeks, and I sat carefully on the side of the bed. "It'll be okay."

She shook her head and whispered, "It's all so much."

The floodgates opened, and it all came out. I sat beside her and listened, acknowledging her fears. I didn't give her platitudes of how everything would be okay. She didn't need reassurance at that moment. She needed release and validation.

In the end, I decided not to make it worse with Fiona's suppositions. I would wait until I had new information from Dusty. Meanwhile, I crawled into bed beside her, and once Daisy was softly snoozing, I picked up my phone and continued my online search.

chapter
twenty-two

I AWOKE with a start before sunrise. The security light streamed through an opening in the curtain, illuminating the empty spot where Daisy had been. Her side was still warm, so I thought maybe that was what had woken me— her slipping out of the bedroom. But my eyes caught movement near the bedroom door, and I reached for my glasses. When everything came into focus, I found Daisy there gripping an old baseball bat of Astra's that I'd kept, not for protection but to remember her by.

"What in the world are you doing?" I asked her.

She whirled and shushed me, then whispered, "I heard a noise downstairs."

I was about to mouth that it was probably Teeny then remembered she'd spent the night with Kira the night before. I climbed out of bed and tiptoed to the window. In the dim light, I saw there were no cars in the driveway.

But I also didn't hear noises downstairs. "Are you sure you heard someone? Maybe it was the wind."

"No, I heard it more than once too."

As if to support her point, a loud crash sounded then.

"Maybe it's Scott starting breakfast early?" I whispered.

"He doesn't have a key, and you locked the door last night, right?"

"Yes!" I'd locked it, checked it again, then had even gotten out of bed once Daisy was asleep to check it a third time. I was starting to get scared.

"Plus"—she sniffed the air—"there is absolutely no bacon smell."

I reached for my phone on the bedside table and tapped the contact card for Dusty.

He answered on the first ring. "What's wrong?"

"We think someone might have broken into the house."

"Where are you?"

"We're in my bedroom."

"All three of you?"

"Daisy and I. Teeny spent the night with Kira."

A car door slammed, and the Mustang's engine came to life.

"Is there a lock on your bedroom door?"

"No."

"Pull a dresser or something heavy in front of the door

and go get in your closet. I'll be there in a few minutes. Put your phone down while you do it, but don't disconnect the call."

I heard his siren go on. I did as he said and grabbed one end of the dresser. When Daisy saw what I was doing, she helped, and we slid it in front of the door. My TARDIS trinket box fell off and broke. I didn't have time for an emotional response just then because I was sure the intruder had heard the noise and would be bounding up the steps at any moment. Instead, I grabbed Daisy and my phone and sprinted to the closet. It was much too close to what had happened to me in the fall when I'd been kidnapped, and I couldn't stop shaking. Daisy squeezed my hand. I still clutched the phone in my other hand but had forgotten about Dusty until I realized he was shouting my name from the phone.

"I'm here. Sorry, we're in the closet now."

He didn't say anything for a moment then let out a breath. "Good. Stay put. I'm almost there."

After another few agonizing minutes, I heard the siren switch off. Dusty said, "I'm pulling into the driveway now. If I don't call you back in a few minutes, giving you the all-clear, call 911."

Then he disconnected. The next few minutes seemed to stretch on for hours. There was a bit of shouting below and footsteps on the stairs but no gunshots. Then my phone rang.

It was Dusty. "I'm outside your bedroom door, and you're safe."

I jumped up and flew to my bedroom door, Daisy close behind me. We moved the dresser, and I opened my bedroom door and threw myself into Dusty's arms.

He held me and whispered into my hair. "You're okay. I've got you."

I realized two things at once: Instead of my usual pajamas, I'd slept in a tank and underwear the night before, and Dusty also seemed to be wearing his pajamas. He seemed to figure that out at the same time. And if his eyes hadn't registered that, his body had. I pulled away and reached quickly for my robe on the back of the door. His cheeks flushed. He had nothing to hide behind.

"What happened?" Daisy asked.

"I did," Scott called from the bottom of the stairs.

Daisy pushed past us and skipped down the stairs. "What in the world? It's a bit early for breakfast."

That left Dusty and me momentarily alone. His face was still flushed and made mine flush again.

"I'm going to get dressed really quick." I shut my door and shoved the awkward moment out of my head as I slipped into some very chunky, unsexy sweats then padded down the stairs to join the others in the kitchen.

The full story came out soon after. Scott's face was tomato red the whole time he told it. The toilet on the bus had stopped working the night before, and he really needed to use the bathroom. Apparently, he knew where we hid the key, so he let himself in to use the bathroom.

Daisy stopped him there. "You're a guy. You can pee standing up."

"I didn't have to pee." His face went from tomato to grape.

The story continued. He'd left the lights off because he didn't want to wake us but had tripped over the chair in the living room. "I thought for sure I'd woken you up, but when I didn't hear anything from upstairs, I went to check the kitchen fridge in case I needed to make an early run for breakfast groceries and bumped into the kitchen table."

He showed proof of that by pointing to an angry welt on his thigh.

The screen door opened, and Kelsey rushed in. "What in the world is going on?"

Scott said, "You can tell her. I'm going to the bus to get dressed and hopefully salvage some of my dignity and goodwill by going to the grocery store, which should be open by now. I'll be back to make breakfast soon."

Daisy giggled. Now that the danger had passed and the adrenaline was gone, I felt exhausted. I started a pot of coffee while Daisy relayed the story to Kelsey—with a much more dramatic flair than what had actually happened.

I turned to Dusty. "I'm sorry we dragged you out of bed for this."

"Never be sorry for being safe. I'm only ever a phone call away."

I remembered then what I'd found the night before and knew it was time to tell him. "Hey, can we talk alone for a moment? In my bedroom?"

He squeezed the back of his neck. "I... uh... I think we need to wait until the case is over."

I laughed. "Love that confidence, but it's about the case."

His complexion did its own best grape impression. But then he was saved by the bell, or at least the dinging of his text message alert. He glanced at it and frowned. "After you."

When we were back in my bedroom, I pulled up the screenshots I'd taken from my search a few hours previously. I showed him the grainy photo. "Do you know who that is?"

He squinted. "It looks like Cal, but with blond hair?"

"It is." I zoomed out. "Do you know who the girl beside him is?"

"No, should I?"

"I mean, if you'd done the digging you said you would do after I saw you at the jail, you might." I raised an eyebrow at him.

"It's only been a day. My people are working on it."

"Okay, well, this person"—I pointed my thumb toward myself—"has already figured it out. The girl with Cal is the Violet Witch. Her sister went missing looking for clues during Daisy's scavenger hunt three years ago."

His whole face went from patient to interested. "The same scavenger hunt the clues in the letters are from?"

"The very same."

"How do you know that?"

"You can find almost anything online." I pulled up the video I'd bookmarked.

"Hello, my little witchlings," the Violet Witch said in a sad voice. She was in full makeup, including heavily done eyes with bright-purple eyeshadow and lipstick. After she went on another rant about Drusilla's scavenger hunt and her missing sister, she closed her eyes and took a deep breath. "I cannot live in a world where people like Dru can get away with leading a young girl to her death and no one seems to care. Her fans follow her like sheep, hanging on her every word. Some of you listened for a little while, but then, once Dru released a new video, that's all you could talk about. It's obvious none of you care about me or my sister. So, this is the last you will ever hear from the Violet Witch." The video faded to black.

"That's not all," I added, clicking on a different video and scrolling down. "Look at this comment from a Callum Covington."

Dusty's eyes scanned the screen, and he frowned. "So, she has a brother too?"

"Not just any brother. When I clicked on the profile, I found that Callum Covington is the same person as one Cal Roberts."

Dusty's eyes widened. "I think it's time I talk to Cal again."

"And Kelsey," I added. "The only reason I even looked into Cal was because of something she said." I told him about the Hollywood roots comment. "I think she either knew him from before or she's done her own research."

"What are you getting at?"

"The exchange Fiona witnessed. What if, instead of Cal blackmailing Kelsey, it was the other way around?"

chapter
twenty-three

"YOU WANT TO TALK TO ME?" Kelsey paled. "Why?"

"First, I need to ask if you want a lawyer."

With Cal not currently on the property, as Kelsey was, Dusty began his interrogation with her downstairs in my kitchen.

"A lawyer?" Daisy stepped in front of Kelsey as if she could shield her from Dusty's questions. "Are you arresting her?"

"No, but it's procedure, Daisy. You know that."

"I can call Holly," Daisy said, "if you want a lawyer present. Or we can ask her for someone else."

Kelsey shook her head and stared into Dusty's eyes. "I have nothing to hide. I've done nothing wrong."

"So, you're waiving your right to a lawyer?" Dusty asked.

"I am. What are your questions, Officer?" she asked.

"Sheriff," he corrected.

I had a sudden déjà vu from the autumn when he'd questioned Teeny. We'd stopped the questioning to get Holly. Teeny was innocent, but we hadn't taken any chances. She was a minor. Kelsey was an adult and not my relative, and I had my own suspicions about her, so I sat on the window seat, a safe distance from Fiona. *Has she been there all night? Did she meet Caroline?* I had so many questions I couldn't ask right now.

Dusty sat as well. He flipped through his notepad then looked at Kelsey, who sat across from him, with Daisy beside her. "What is your relationship to Callum Covington?"

"I have none," Kelsey stated. "I have never heard that name before.

The lie hit me like a slap, and the words burst forth before I could stop myself. "What about Cal Roberts? How did you know his hair was blond when he was younger?"

She gave me a blank stare.

"You said Cal was Hollywood down to his blond roots. You knew he was blond."

"It was a guess," she stammered. "He doesn't seem to do a great job at covering his roots. I noticed."

"But Scott has worked with him for years and never knew his hair was blond," I said.

"This is why I am being questioned?" Kelsey shot at me. "Because I was observant of someone's shoddy hair coloring attempt?"

Dusty regained control of the interrogation by shooting me a warning look. "A witness observed an altercation between you two a couple of weeks ago. They said he handed you an envelope, which you snatched from him and shoved into your coat pocket. Can you tell me more about this event?"

Damn, he was going for it. I noted that he didn't reveal it was Fiona who'd witnessed it.

Fiona rubbed her hands together in glee. "*Oh, now it's going to get real.*"

Kelsey stayed silent for a beat then slowly shook her head and whispered, "I can't."

"Are you denying it happened?"

"Sheriff Palmer, what exactly are you accusing my employee of?" Daisy asked.

"I'm not accusing her of anything at the moment. I'm just trying to find out if the witness is credible and, if so, what happened during the exchange."

"Is this true, Kelsey?" Concern, but also a little suspicion, tinged Daisy's voice, as if she were connecting the dots, as I had.

The tears came then, and for the next few minutes, we got nothing from Kelsey. Dusty stayed silent and let her cry.

Daisy rubbed her back and murmured reassurances like, "It'll be okay. We can work through this. Just tell us what happened."

"Those are real tears. Not from a bottle. She's either innocent, or she missed her calling. She should be in front of the camera instead of behind it," Fiona said.

Kelsey sniffed loudly then scrubbed her eyes. "I... I'm so sorry, Daisy. I would never hurt you intentionally, but I was scared. He threatened me."

The last words came out as a whisper, and I was starting to believe I'd misjudged her as well.

"He pulled me aside and told me that he'd been watching me and thought I had promise in the industry. He said, after this project, his studio would be working on a huge project and he could get me a job on it if I'd do him a favor." She turned to Daisy. "I hate to say it, but I was so tempted. I love working with you, but the way he talked about the project, it sounded like it could be a huge break for me. So, I asked him what he wanted me to do."

"That part is true. We're doing a partnership with a huge franchise, developing a new miniseries that will make a ton of money," Fiona interjected.

"What did he want you to do?" Dusty asked.

"He gave me a pink envelope and asked me to give it to Daisy. I asked him what was in it, and he said it was just something to spice up the documentary. He said it was all aboveboard."

Daisy stopped rubbing Kelsey's back and stared at her.

"But I told him I didn't feel comfortable doing that. I was on your team, not his." Kelsey sniffed again loudly. "He reminded me of the career move possibility, and I told him I would rather do your laundry forever and have a clear conscience than do his dirty work. Then he resorted to threats." The tears began falling again. "He said that he and Scott went way back and that Scott would believe him over me. He said he'd make up lies about me and make sure I never worked again. I snatched the letter from him and told him I would do it."

"That's totally what it looked like from my vantage point," Fiona said.

"I planned to take it to Rock, but Cal said he'd know if I didn't follow through, and I got scared, so I put it in Daisy's coat pocket, but I swear I didn't know what was inside. Daisy, I would never hurt you. And I completely understand if you have to fire me now."

"Cal was the one sending the letters? To make the documentary more exciting?" Daisy asked.

"That's what he told me," Kelsey said. "I felt icky about it, but I had no idea what was in the letter, or that you'd received others, until the night you had them spread out on the table."

"That's not all. I think he lied to Kelsey, or at least, it wasn't the full truth. I think he had other motives. Star found something." Dusty nodded to me.

I pulled up the photo on my phone and strode over to their side of the table. Claiming the chair on the other side of Daisy, I showed her the photo of the girl with short, spiky hair dyed purple. "Do you recognize her?"

Daisy shook her head. Whether in denial or disbelief, I wasn't sure. "It's the Violet Witch."

"Who is she, and what does she have to do with Cal?" Kelsey asked.

"Cal is her brother," Dusty said.

"I need some air." Daisy's chair scraped the floor as she stood abruptly. She was out the front door before Kelsey could say another word.

"I should go check on her." Kelsey stood, but Dusty held up a hand.

"I'm afraid you and I aren't done yet. I have more questions."

"I'll go," I said.

Daisy was vomiting near the corner of the house.

"You okay?" I rubbed her back.

She shook her head.

"Of course not. I saw the videos. The Violet Witch was nuts."

Daisy straightened and wiped her mouth with the back of her hand. "She was relentless. She begged to come intern for me, said she'd do anything. She was annoying, but I never feared her. And she eventually stopped sending messages. Then, a few days after the scavenger hunt, she posted a video about her sister."

"Cass. I saw the video. She accused you of purposely making the clues hard so no one could find the prize. And blamed you for her sister's disappearance."

"It all blew up, and I started getting hate mail from people who believed her. Then, after leaving a final video saying she couldn't live without her sister, she took her own life. And now, finding out that Cal is her brother? He's been taunting me for months."

Tires crunched on the gravel as Daisy's car pulled into the driveway.

"Crap, Scott's back. I don't want him to see me like this," she said.

I turned on the water spigot on the side of the house. "Here, splash some water on your face and rinse out your mouth."

She did as I said and was standing upright again by the time he opened the car door.

"I found that raisin bread you like, Daisy." He clicked the key fob, and the trunk lifted. I went to help him with the bags.

"Oh, thank you." Daisy joined us.

Scott stopped then set the bags in his hands back in the trunk. He strode over to hold Daisy by the shoulders. "What's wrong?"

Daisy opened her mouth, probably to make up an

excuse or lie, but instead, she broke into a sob and laid her head on his chest. I scooped up the bags he'd set down and left them to it.

Just as I stepped onto the porch, the screen door flew open, nearly hitting me. Kelsey stopped when she saw me, and I took a step back at the look of pure hatred in Kelsey's eyes. But it wasn't focused on me, as she barely paused to acknowledge me before stepping off the porch and heading toward the bus. I hoped Dusty got to Cal before she did. If looks could kill, the guy would be a pile of ash by lunchtime.

Dusty crossed the threshold to take a few of the bags from me and set them on the counter. "I need to get dressed and talk to Cal. I'll check in later, but just keep your doors locked, okay?"

I nodded.

He turned when he was almost to the door. "And no more hiding keys on the porch, Star."

chapter
twenty-four

AFTER ANOTHER WONDERFUL, but quiet, breakfast, where I ate way too much of Scott's delicious food, I made a list of the things I needed to do before the Midwinter Ball the next night. Daisy only pushed things around on her plate, which told me I couldn't count on her to help. Her mind was elsewhere. And Kelsey was literally elsewhere. She hadn't come back from the bus to eat, even when both Scott and Daisy texted her. So, it was up to me.

"Scott, I left Zeke's number on the fridge if you want to give him a call about DJing tomorrow night," I said. "Now that Cal is off the list of helpers, we'll be short. You still okay doing this?"

"Yeah, sure." Scott was much less peppy than usual.

"I totally understand if you're not. It must be a lot, finding out your friend is a creep," I said.

"That's just the thing. I don't think he is. I mean, this doesn't match the Cal I know. I didn't even know he had a sister. He never once mentioned her. There has to be some misunderstanding," he said.

"Kelsey wouldn't make up stuff. Especially not when it comes to my safety," Daisy said. "And you said yourself, the business changes people. Maybe Cal used to be the guy you knew, but it's been years."

I had my own thoughts on that, but it wasn't the time to talk about that. Besides, we had party business to take care of.

As if she'd read my mind, Daisy asked, "What's on your list for the party prep today, Star?"

She likely needed something to take her mind off things, but I didn't want her out of the house until I knew Cal was in custody. "Can you make some calls to Holly, Isaac, and the others and make sure everyone is lined up to help? Find out how many people we still need, and if we run out of family, start calling friends like Jessi-Lyn. Her number is on the side of the fridge. And find out if Aunt Mer and Gavin are coming back before the ball. If so, enlist them to help." I hoped I hadn't overwhelmed her, and if she missed a few people, I could follow up later.

For my part, I headed down to the real estate agent's office to get the key for the house on Raven Row so I could inspect it. I was crossing every digit I had, hoping it was in as good a shape as Daisy had said it was. We were putting on a Midwinter Ball, not a Halloween party.

I was pleasantly surprised to find that even the lawn was nicely manicured. Large pots of poinsettias lined the steps leading up to the expansive porch. If the inside was just as groomed, it would do nicely. The house, however, was filled with ghosts. Okay, so "filled" was a slight exaggeration. There were three total—an older gentleman with white hair, a young boy I judged to be about eight with curly blond hair, and a middle-aged woman with brown hair to her shoulders.

I didn't make eye contact with them, so they didn't approach me. I checked out the house and found another spirit upstairs looking out the window. I guessed it was a she because I could only see her back. Her clothing was bright and cheerful, which was a contrast to her long white hair. I couldn't judge her age, but with hair that white, she had to have been elderly when she died.

I called Aunt Willa Jo on my way down the stairs, "The location is perfect! I let the realtor know to send a bill to the mayor's office and that your secretary will pay her. I did double-check the fees, and it's less than half what you said you were paying for the nasty rat-infested community center."

Aunt Will Jo squealed with glee. "Have I told you lately how amazing you are, sweetie? Thank you so much!

Hey, how did everything go yesterday? With your suspicions?"

I filled her in on the latest and finished with "But we're letting Dusty handle it while we concentrate on having the best Midwinter Ball ever."

"Yes, we will!" she said.

We compared our lists and what each of us still had to do. And I took a couple of tasks off her hands, including going to check on Granny. She protested, but I said, "It's okay, I need to go by and pick up Teeny anyway. She texted earlier that she and Kira stayed at Zeke's last night instead of Jessi-Lyn's."

"Oh wow, that's progress."

"Yeah, but I hope it was fully her decision and she didn't feel pressured by Kira."

"Teeny is stronger than you sometimes give her credit for, Star. And there are worse things to be peer pressured into at their age than spending time with her biological father and half sister—people she's known her whole life but who now have different titles."

She had a point. Teeny wouldn't suddenly give in to Kira if she hadn't wanted to. She could be just as stubborn as Kira.

When I parked in front of the Merc, I texted Teeny that I was there and heading upstairs to see Granny and that she could come over when she was ready. If she'd felt pressured to be there, she would run over immediately. If not, she would take her time getting her things.

One of Granny's employees of the week stood at the register. I waved as I sauntered past and took the stairs in the back room up to Granny's apartment. I found Granny on the sofa with a TV tray in front of her, eating a piece of fish and broccoli.

"That looks tasty," I said.

"I'd rather have a cheeseburger, but Zeke said I need to eat something besides the greasy food they serve next door, so he cooked it himself. What's another cheeseburger gonna do at my age? I've earned my right to them. Lord knows, in my next life, they'll go straight to my thighs." She stabbed a piece of broccoli and examined it like a bug had crawled onto her plate.

"What if you come back as broccoli in your next life and kids hate you and so do grannies jonesing for a cheeseburger?"

She cocked an eyebrow at me then laughed. "You're something, my girl. So, what are you doing here?"

"I came by to get Teeny and visit my favorite grandmother," I said.

"Your only grandmother."

She said it as a joke, but in reality, she was. My father's parents were out of the picture long before I was born, and my grandfather, Granny's husband, had died decades ago. So, Granny was the only grandparent I'd ever known. I wondered then what my other grandmother looked like. I'd seen photos of Granny when she was younger, and she'd been stunning.

"How was Janet doing downstairs at the register?" She shoved the last bite of fish in her mouth and took a gulp of iced tea.

"Janet? I thought that was the girl you fired a few weeks ago."

"I can't keep up with all their names, so from now on, they're all Janet to me."

"Good, she was making mystery bags, I think."

She braced her arms on the sides of her chair to stand. But her arms wobbled, and she flopped back down.

"What do you need? I can get it."

"Can you speed up time so I can get rid of this useless husk?"

I looked at her plate and didn't see any husks on it, then realized she was talking about her body. "Granny! Don't talk like that. You're going to be with us for years yet."

"Not if I can help it. There's a small black wooden chest in Tatty's room. Can you get that for me?"

"Sure."

"I had Zeke move all the stuff from the storage closets into Tatty's room after she left. I figured I'd get some good use out of the space before she comes back and becomes a pain in my rear again."

Aunt Tatty had left suddenly in October, after we discovered she'd—inadvertently—helped cover up Astra's death, years ago. I still wasn't sure how she was managing to find her way around Europe by herself, but when I'd brought it up to Granny, she'd only said, "Before your mother and aunts came along, Tat and I traveled the world. She knows her way around."

I located the chest and brought it to Granny, and she said, "I need you to do me a favor, Star. Can you take this with you and keep it safe? And listen to me. Don't open it until I'm gone. Okay?" I opened my mouth to, again, reassure her she wasn't going anywhere, but she held up a hand. "Don't give me platitudes. You're the one I trust most with this. Just do as I say."

I nodded. I'd learned years ago that it didn't do any good to argue with Granny.

"Keep it in a safe place. You'll know what to do with it when the time comes. Now, if you wouldn't mind, I'd like to take a nap. Give Zeke my love."

I kissed her on the forehead. "I love you, Granny."

I didn't get a chance to call Dusty until later that evening. He'd texted me hours earlier that Cal was in custody, so I was able to relax about Daisy's safety. But I wanted to know the details—or at least the ones he could share in an ongoing investigation.

"He's not talking." Dusty sounded tired.

"He won't confess?" I asked.

"More than that. He won't say a word. He won't confirm or deny his guilt or even request a lawyer. He just sits there, starting straight ahead. His eyes flickered when I brought up the stepsister and asked if that's why he did what he did. But other than that, he's completely quiet. I figure I'll let him simmer in a cell overnight. He'll be ready to call a lawyer in the morning."

"You headed home now?" I asked.

"Just walked through the door. I want nothing more than a hot shower and a full night's sleep."

Thinking of him in a steamy shower distracted me, and I forgot what I was going to say. Instead, I said the lamest thing. "I'm too tired to even undress, much less shower right now."

His voice was husky when he said, "At least put on your Rugrats pj's." It called back the memory of that morning, when he'd shown up at my bedroom door, wearing nothing but pajama bottoms and a Captain America hoodie open at the front.

It was too much. So, I did what I usually did and deflected. "I can't. They're at the dry cleaners. I'm wearing them to the Midwinter Ball tomorrow night."

He laughed. "That I'd like to see."

"Will you be there?" *Why do I feel like a teenager asking a guy to a dance?* "If so, you should definitely wear your Captain America hoodie."

Before he could answer, Daisy burst into my room.

"Kelsey is missing!"

chapter
twenty-five

"MISSING?" I asked.

"She's been gone since this morning, and she's not answering her phone." Daisy entered my bedroom, pulling Scott and Rock behind her. "What if Cal took her?"

I was thankful I'd been too tired to get undressed—and too shy to say the things to Dusty I'd really wanted to say.

"Cal's in custody," I said.

"What's going on?" Dusty asked.

"Daisy says Kelsey is missing, and—"

"Missing? Who is missing?" Teeny joined them.

Meanwhile, Dusty lobbed more questions at me.

I put two fingers between my lips and whistled. "Everyone, take a breath. I'm talking to Dusty. Let me put him on speaker so I'm not trying to have two different conversations. Dusty, you're on speaker, and Daisy, Scott, Rock, and Teeny are in the room."

"Start from the top, Daisy. When did you last see Kelsey?" Dusty asked.

"This morning, when you were questioning her. Scott and I were busy with… with things and stuff and didn't notice the car was gone until this afternoon." She colored slightly when she said that last part.

"Are her things still on the bus?" I asked.

"I'll run and check." Rock dashed out of the room.

"I'm not sure I could deal with it if I lost another member of my crew. First Rock, then Penny, now Kelsey?" Daisy buried her face in her hands.

"Back up. Rock?" I asked. "How are you losing him?"

"He's tired of being on the road and said he misses home and Carly. It was one of the reasons he pushed so hard for the documentary—so I might get picked up by the network and he could quit as producer and move back here."

I wasn't sure how to feel about that. I let my brain try it out for a moment then found I didn't care one way or the other. Progress.

"Daisy, Cal is in custody, so I don't think Kelsey is in danger," Dusty said.

"But she left here earlier, looking like she wanted to murder Cal," Daisy insisted. "What if she found him before you arrested him and he hurt her?"

Rock returned then. "From what I can tell, all her stuff is still in her bunk."

Dusty asked more questions about the exact timing, and the three of us answered to the best of our memories. "I'll do some checking. Meanwhile, call the local hospitals to see if she was admitted." He didn't sound as confident as he had before.

Does he think there's something to Daisy's fears?

We disconnected, and Daisy and Scott left the room.

Teeny sidled up to Rock and wrapped her arms around his waist. "I'm glad you're staying in town."

"Thanks, kiddo!"

She left the room, leaving him and me alone.

"Sorry, I didn't get a chance to tell you. I wanted to make sure I could really come back before I said anything."

I shrugged. "You have no reason to inform me. I bet Carly is thrilled."

"And you?"

"I'm happy for Carly." I realized how that sounded and sighed. "Rock, I don't know how I feel. I'm exhausted. It's been a bit weird having you back. And yeah, I've been counting the days until you left again."

"Ouch."

"You wrecked me. It took years to get over that."

"I'm sorry."

"And now you're in my face all the time. So yeah, I've

been wanting things to go back to normal." I flopped back onto the bed and threw an arm over my eyes. "That being said, it hasn't been horrible having you back. I've forgotten how it was to be your friend. We were friends before we were more." I pulled my arm down to look up at him, and the room was empty.

Teeny stepped into my room with her toothbrush in her mouth. "He didn't hear any of that last bit by the way."

Awesome. He left thinking I still hate him.

I didn't get to sleep until after midnight. Daisy and Scott checked the hospitals with no luck. And Dusty never called back, so I left Daisy downstairs with Scott after reminding her three times to lock the door after he left. She said she would, but when I woke up around 3 a.m., I couldn't help but worry she'd forgotten, so I padded downstairs to check. It was secure. So the next morning, when I found Scott cooking breakfast and Daisy's bedroom door closed, I stood glaring at him with my hands on my hips.

"How did you get in? Is there another key?"

"I, uh..." His face flushed.

"*Leave him alone, Star!*" Caroline admonished. She sat lounging on the window seat. "*He never left last night.*"

"Oh, you never left."

"How did you know that?"

"Caroline."

"She was watching us?" He set down the spatula and leaned against the counter.

"*Oh, heavens no! I would never!*" Caroline said.

"No, she wasn't watching you. Sheesh, she's not a perv." I listened to the rest of what Caroline explained and relayed it to Scott. "She saw you and Daisy disappear into Daisy's room, then a few hours later, she poked her head in just to make sure Daisy was okay and found you both asleep."

"Who was watching me sleep?" A sleepy-looking Daisy came out of her bedroom wearing an oversized T-shirt.

"*Oh my stars, now she's going to think I'm a stalker. Tell her I was just watching over her. Y'all are my family,*" Caroline said.

"Caroline was. She was checking on you last night to make sure you were okay with me." Scott slung an arm around her to whisper something in her ear, and she giggled. He turned back to me. "Where is Caroline now?"

I looked at Daisy, giving her the chance to answer him.

But she also looked at me for the answer then laughed. "Oh, it's okay, he knows now. We talked last night."

"Oh, thank goodness! Keeping up the ruse was getting exhausting." I slumped into a chair.

"*I agree,*" Caroline chimed in.

"And you're okay with it?" I asked him.

"Oh yeah! Daisy's other power is even more interesting than seeing ghosts—no offense to either you or Caroline—but not having to get out of bed to retrieve my hoodie from the living room comes in handy on cold mornings." Scott placed a platter of bacon on the table.

"Good. I like you two together. And now that's settled and breakfast is ready, we need to eat so we can get to the venue to help decorate," I said.

Daisy nodded without looking up from her phone.

"Still no word from Kelsey?" I asked.

"No. Nothing more from Dusty?" she asked.

I'd left my phone upstairs, so I jogged up to get it and found a missed call from Dusty. I dialed him on my way back downstairs after knocking on Teeny's door and letting her know breakfast was almost ready. By the time I'd returned to the kitchen, he'd answered.

"Hey, are you okay?"

"Yeah, sorry, my phone was up in my bedroom. What's up?"

"We found Daisy's car. It was in a Walgreens parking lot over in Pflugerville."

"Let me put you on speaker," I said, then to Daisy and Scott, "They found the car abandoned."

"I'm headed over to interrogate Cal again but just wanted to check in with you. What are your plans today?"

I took him off speakerphone and went out onto the porch. "We're headed to the Raven Row house to decorate for the ball tonight. The whole family will be there."

"Good. Stay together. In pairs at the very least. No one is to go off alone."

"But Cal is in jail now. We should be safe, shouldn't we?" Even as I said it, something tingled in my head. I knew that wasn't right. I had a feeling Kelsey went missing after he was arrested. *Does he have a partner?* "Are you thinking Cal isn't working alone?"

Dusty hesitated.

"You're off speakerphone. It's just me."

"I'm thinking there's much more to this than any of us know, Star. I'm thinking I don't want you in a similar situation as October. I'm thinking I couldn't bear it if you were hurt again, or worse."

My heart sped up and not because of the danger he'd portended. "I'll be safe. And ditto."

chapter
twenty-six

SINCE DAISY'S car was being impounded, Daisy, Scott, Teeny, and I rode together in my car to the venue. Many of the other family vehicles were already parked on the street outside the house, and Aunt Willa Jo greeted us with open arms when we walked through the door.

"You two girls are the bomb-diggity! This location is fabulous—miles above the community center. I'm glad those old biddies made things difficult for me, because now we'll have the most memorable Midwinter Ball Dead End has ever seen!" She squealed and whirled away to direct Isaac on where to put the boxes he'd brought in behind us.

I couldn't help but smile. Aunt Willa Jo's joy was contagious.

Holly approached me with a clipboard. "Mamma has me directing things, so, Teeny, you'll be helping Kira make the gift bags in the room down the hall. She's not here yet, but I'll take you there in a moment and get you started."

Teeny nodded while taking off her coat.

"Oh, that reminds me. Scott, would you mind being on coat check duty tonight?" She pointed to a corner where a rolling rack stood along with a podium. "You'll be there. We'll have a ticket system. That reminds me, I have to find out which box those are in."

"I'll hunt those down for you, and I'll gladly be the coat check guy tonight." He smiled.

"They'll be in a box labeled Office or Organization, I think." Holly turned to me. "You and Daisy need to come with me to find a dress."

"Oh, I already have one picked out. I'm wearing a red satin—"

"Mamma didn't tell you?" Holly scrunched her nose.

"Tell us what?"

"You're both helping greet people when they come in, after they've cleared coat check. And you'll be dressed in period costumes."

Daisy clapped her hands. "Seriously? Like Victorian? That's fun!"

I didn't share in her glee but would do whatever I could to help out, so I said, "Lead the way."

"Isaac. Can you help Teeny take the boxes that say gift bags to the second room on the left, where the tables are set up?" Holly asked.

I pulled Holly aside. "Before you send us all off, you need to know something. Kelsey is missing, and Daisy's car was found in a parking lot. Cal is still in custody, but Dusty wants us to use the buddy system so no one is alone."

Holly's expression changed while I was talking, then she replaced the worry with a smile and nodded. She tapped the clipboard with her pen. "All right, Scott, instead of setting up the coat check station right now, can you help Teeny until Kira arrives?"

"Will do!" He and Teeny headed over to the stack of boxes, and the rest of us went up the stairs.

We stopped at the room where I'd seen the white-haired ghost staring out the window. She was still there, her back toward us. Opposite that wall stood a rack of dresses.

"Mamma rented a selection of period-appropriate gowns from a costume company, and Moira, from Cutthroat Salon, has volunteered to do our hair and makeup," Holly said. "She's going to set up in here, too, so this will be our dressing room."

I found a gorgeous sapphire-blue gown and settled on it, though the corset looked a bit snug. Daisy squealed the minute she saw a pink one and snatched it. And Holly found a red one for Aunt Willa Jo and an emerald one for herself. Once that was settled, we all returned downstairs to continue preparations.

The first thing I did was check on Teeny and Kira. They were tucked away safely in the gift bag room with Zeke, so I let them be. We worked for hours then took a break to eat pizza from Slashers, which Holly had delivered. It was set up in the kitchen, and when I went in to get a second piece, I found Rock sitting on the kitchen counter.

I jumped up to sit beside him and shoulder bumped him. "Hey."

He bumped me back. "Hey."

"You missed out on the best conversation last night."

"Did I?" He stared at his plate. "With who?"

"Me and you. Except you weren't there because you walked out while I was pouring my heart out."

He looked up at me then. "When I left, you were basically telling me I was in your face all the time."

I laughed because of the irony. We were sitting shoulder to shoulder, and our faces were inches from each other. "And here I am in your face again."

He smiled. "So, what else did we talk about after I left?"

"I told you that I'd forgotten how much I missed being your friend."

"And what did I say back?"

"You said, 'Star, I would very much like to be friends. I want to stay in town to be near my sister, and I don't want it to be weird between us, and I miss hanging out with you because you're the most awesome, bestest person in this town, besides Carly, of course, because I have to say that since she's my sister and—"

He shoulder bumped me again. "I said all that, did I? Man, I'm wordy. But also, again, I am truly sorry for what I put you through. If I could go back and change things, I would. I'd give anything to not have it end the way it did. But I don't have a TARDIS."

I snorted. "Even if you did, the Doctor wouldn't let you change history."

"Well, that depends on which doctor you're talking about. Number Twelve might have let me do it. But Ten? Not a chance." He smiled.

"Listen, I understand why you felt you had to choose between us—"

"I wasn't choosing her over you. I did it *for* you. I didn't want you to lose another sister. She was going on the road with or without your blessing, and I was the best one to protect her."

"But you went behind my back, to my mother, Rock."

"*Her* mother."

I opened my mouth to argue, but he spoke again quickly. "No, I get it, I do. I know what a betrayal that was. And I paid the highest price for it. I lost you."

I stared at him a beat. "You were right, though. It wasn't my decision to make. Mamma should've been consulted from the beginning. Thank you for being there for Daisy. I can't imagine what kind of life she'd have had if Mamma had hired someone else as her producer."

"I failed her. I'm the one who got her involved with Cal."

"No. Cal is the only one to blame for Cal."

We both sat in silence for a moment.

Then he shoulder bumped me again. "So we're good?"

"As long as you never make me play Hungry Hungry Hippos again." I returned the shoulder bump.

"Deal."

With everyone pitching in, including Carly and Grey, who showed up after lunch, we were done by three. We all went home to shower and rest a bit before we had to go back that evening.

On the drive home, I thought about my family, both born and acquired, and felt joy—not for the first time—in seeing us all work together. That was my family. When something needed to be done, everyone pitched in. Even Granny had been zooming around in her scooter, looking more energetic than she had in a while.

I thought about the wooden box she'd given me last night, tucked in a safe place at home, and hoped with everything I had that I wouldn't open it for a long time.

twenty-seven

TEENY WAS the first out of the car, springing toward the front door, claiming the upstairs shower on the way. But just as she reached the porch, she screamed. I dashed across the yard at the same time as Scott and Rock— who'd insisted on following us home—to find a disheveled figure sitting on the porch swing. Cal. I reached Teeny and pushed her behind me. Scott stood in front of us with Rock by his side.

I reached for my phone to call 911 and found my pocket empty. I swore. Leaving my phone lying around would be the death of me someday.

Cal held up his hands in front of him and took a step back. "You haven't talked to the detective?"

Rock strode toward Cal and punched, but Cal expertly ducked and jumped back. Rock lunged forward again, and they both tumbled to the porch floor, rolling down the steps.

"Stop!" Dusty bounded out of his car.

I hadn't even heard him drive up.

Daisy yelled, "He escaped and showed up here!"

"He didn't escape. He was released but was instructed to stay away from you." He gave Cal a look. "At least until I could reach you and explain."

Dusty pulled Cal up by his collar and righted him. "Were you trying to get yourself killed, man? These are the Bells. They will tear you apart with their teeth if they think you mean any of them harm."

"You released him?" I skipped down the steps. "Why? And why the hell didn't you call me?"

Frustration burned in Dusty's eyes, but his tone was calm. "Where's your phone?"

Color filled my face. "I don't know. Oh. You did call, didn't you?"

"Several times. Let's all go inside, and I'll explain. And can someone get him a wet cloth or something?" He cocked his head toward Cal, whose lip was bleeding.

Once we were settled at the kitchen table, the story unfolded.

"Cal, do you want to explain to them what you told me about your sister?"

Cal dabbed his chin with the damp dish towel I'd

given him. "I haven't been completely truthful with you all. My sister—"

"Is the Violet Witch. Yes, we know," I said. "I figured that out ages ago."

He gave me a sharp look. "You knew? How?"

"When Daisy got the last letter, I decided to do some research. I found her videos, including the last ones about her sister, who went missing during Daisy's scavenger hunt, along with the one where she said her final goodbye. Her account is still active, so I combed through every video and found a comment on one of her earliest ones from a Cal Covington saying, 'Hey, little sis, great video! Soon you'll be in Hollywood with your big bro.' When I clicked on the profile, I found Cal Covington was you. You've been using a fake name with us. Cal Roberts. And you dyed your hair black."

"Guilty as charged. Cal Covington sounds like a trust fund kid, especially with sandy-blond hair. So, I changed it to Cal Roberts years ago. The hair was because my first role was a bit part as a punk rocker. I dyed my hair black and had exactly one speaking line, but I liked the look and kept it."

"You told me you were an only child," Scott said.

"I am. My parents had one child. Then divorced. My mom remarried when I was sixteen, and my stepdad had a four-year-old daughter I got to see every other weekend and for two weeks in the summer. I never really went back home after college, and a few years later, my stepdad died, so Ella and I lost touch long before you and I started dating."

Scott and Cal had been a couple. I wondered if Daisy knew. I turned my head to catch Daisy's reaction to that news, but there was none.

"And Cass? Your sister who went missing? Why wouldn't you divulge that connection to Daisy?" I asked.

"She wasn't my sister. She was Ella's half sister. While my mom married Ella's dad, her mom married again and had another baby. Cass was two years younger than Ella. But I never really saw her except in her car seat through the window when their mom would pick up Ella from my house," Cal said. "And I didn't mention it because I didn't want you to think I'd be biased during the filming."

"And you didn't think to mention your stepsister was the Violet Witch? A fan obsessed with me for years? Is she the one who convinced you to do this documentary?"

"Of course not. Scott reached out to me. He told me you were the real deal. Like I said, I hadn't seen Ella for years. The comment on her video was just me trying to be supportive of her art. I had no idea she was your stalker, nor that she later blamed you for Cass's death."

"But you blamed me for Ella's death. Isn't that why you sent those letters?"

"Ella's not dead. And I wasn't the one sending you the letters."

"Ella's not... but the video... her farewell video as the Violet Witch," Daisy insisted.

"What video?" Cal asked.

I pulled it up and showed it to him.

When it finished playing, he sighed. "Always the drama queen. But I can assure you Ella is not dead."

"You said you lost touch with her. How would you know she's not dead?" Rock asked.

"Because I saw her the other day. And so have you all."

Then it hit me. Drama queen. *Cal is Hollywood right down to his blond roots.* She hadn't seen the pics of him online. She'd known him. "Kelsey?"

"Hold on, I don't understand," Daisy said. "What about Kelsey?"

"Kelsey is Ella? The Violet Witch?" I asked. "But I saw the videos. That's not possible. The Violet Witch was a plus-sized girl. Purple hair and—"

"Her last video was three years ago. In her farewell video, she was killing that persona. Wasn't she? Not herself," Daisy said.

"When I saw her on the video call, I almost didn't recognize her. She's lost a ton of weight, but I recognized her eyes. I didn't know why she was pretending not to know me, so I stayed silent until we could talk."

"Ella? What the actual—" Scott began but stopped himself after casting a glance at Teeny.

"Good grief, I'm fifteen. You can say 'hell' in front of me," Teeny said.

Except I didn't think hell was the word he'd intended. Honestly, I thought we all felt what he wanted to say. No one spoke for a moment. Then Dusty said, "I verified everything. Ella Jackson is Kelsey Wright."

"No. This cannot be happening." Daisy buried her face in her hands.

Scott wrapped his arms around her.

"So, if Kelsey was behind everything this whole time, what was going on when Fiona saw you giving an envelope to Kelsey?" I asked.

Cal snorted. "What Fiona saw was me confronting her. I found the letter in her things. I asked her what she was up to, and she told me to mind my own business and that she was just venting; she'd never actually give the letter to Daisy. Then she snatched it from me."

"Is that what you were arguing about with Fiona in her trailer? When you told Fiona to leave *her* alone?"

He nodded.

"Why did you two pretend not to know each other?" Rock asked.

"Why didn't you tell us about it? Or that Daisy's former stalker was now her assistant? Did you know what she was up to?" Betrayal burned in Scott's eyes.

Cal shook his head. "She said she didn't want anyone to know our connection because she didn't want me to be accused of being biased. And I had no idea Ella was a stalker, or even that she blamed Daisy for Cass's death."

"But the videos!" Rock insisted.

"I didn't see those later videos until Sheriff Palmer showed me. And I had no idea there were more letters. When I confronted her about the letter that fell out of her jacket pocket, she said it was just something to blow off steam. She had no intention of actually giving it to Daisy."

"And you believed that?" Scott asked.

"I guess I wanted to believe it for her sake, for the sake of the four-year-old girl who worshiped her stepbrother and cried every time she had to leave me." He let out a long breath.

"Hold on!" Scott said. "Kelsey was the one who first suggested Daisy send in a tape to *Truthbusters*. Was this all a setup?"

Cal sighed. "No, Drusilla wasn't on our radar until you sent in the tape. If it had been anyone but you, Scott, I would've thrown it in the trash."

Daisy kept her face neutral, but her hand moved ever so slightly, and his glass tipped over, spilling his water into his lap.

Cal gasped, swiped at his wrinkled linen pants, then stared at the glass. "How did that happen?"

"Guess you're clumsy," Daisy said.

He narrowed his eyes at her but continued. "Honestly, I took the job to be near Scott again, to see if there was still anything between us. But I could see from the first day that he was smitten with you, and you with him."

Daisy and Scott exchanged glances, and he reached for her hand.

"So, all this time, all this freaking time, she was living on my bus, working for me, and sending me those horrid letters before she tried to kill me," Daisy said. "How could I have been so blind?"

"What was her goal with the letters? Why not just kill Daisy if that's what she planned to do? Why send the letters first?" I asked.

Cal ran a hand over his five o'clock shadow. "I think, at that point, she'd lost all sense of reality, and in her mind, the riddles in her sadistic letters were her way of honoring her sister, Cass. Or maybe her way of making sure you never forgot your biggest fan."

Daisy stood and left the kitchen. Scott and I both stood to go after her, but she called from the hallway, "Sit down. I'm coming back!"

After a few moments, she returned with a small stack of papers. She placed them on the table side by side. "I never forgot Cass. And I never will."

The papers were copies of various articles about her, about her disappearance. They described her physical characteristics and what she'd been wearing—a purple top and a multicolored paisley skirt—when she went missing from the side of the road after she and Ella ran out of gas driving all over, trying to solve the clues Drusilla Von Leigh had dropped in videos. Something about that outfit seemed familiar. The fabric fell in folds, and the shades of purple, aqua, and pink swirled together.

Purple shirt. Paisley skirt. Pale-blond hair. The Midwinter Ball.

The final piece clicked into place. "I know where to find Cass."

chapter
twenty-eight

"I SAW HER. She's at Raven House," I said.

"At the venue for the Midwinter Ball?" Daisy asked. "Why would she be here? In Dead End? The articles said she and Ella ran out of gas near Waco."

"Searching for your scavenger hunt prize. The articles say she was also a big fan of yours. Spirits gravitate toward where they were happiest. Maybe she's trying to be near you?"

Daisy looked horrified. I didn't blame her. Having a stalker in life was bad enough, but having one she couldn't see... Oof.

"How do you know it's her?" Dusty asked me.

"The article described the clothes she had on when she went missing. The same clothes the spirit at Raven Row wore. It didn't click at first because I thought the ghost was an older woman since all I could see of her was long white hair. But the article also mentioned she had pale-blond hair, and sometimes, the palest blond can look almost white. It has to be her."

"I don't want to talk about this anymore. It's time to get dressed for the ball," Daisy said.

"You can't possibly be thinking of still attending," Scott said.

"Of course I'm going. I'm not going to let Kelsey… no, I'll refer to her as Ella from here on out, because the Kelsey I thought I knew is dead to me. Only Ella, the Violet Witch, exists now. And she won't keep me from living my life," she said.

"Daisy, quit being so flippant about your safety. She tried to kill you," I said.

"She's right, D. Your life isn't worth it," Scott said.

"My car was found a few counties away. I think she's long gone," Daisy said. "Right, Dusty?"

"That's how it looks, but to be safe, we'll put extra patrols at the Midwinter Ball."

"You can't be condoning this, Dusty! That house has so many rooms. Not just downstairs but upstairs," I said. "The car was found, not Kelsey."

"I told you, I don't want to hear that name again." Daisy stood.

"Fine, *Ella* is still out there. She could've left the car there and stolen another. She knows about the ball. She could show up there and try to finish what she started. She tried to kill you, Daisy."

"She did, Star. But that wasn't the worst thing she did. She pretended to be my friend, my right hand. I trusted her. She will not break me. She will not keep me from living my life, and I hope she does show up because I will scratch her fucking eyes out. It's too late to cancel, anyway," Daisy said. "It's going to start in less than two hours. We need to go shower and get back there. Unless you would rather she show up here at the farm."

"I hate to say it, but you're probably right, and if she didn't strike there, she would do it when you were alone somewhere. At least the ball will provide safety in numbers, and I'll put extra protection on site," Dusty said. "This way, we might actually catch her tonight."

I didn't like the idea one bit, but I knew I wouldn't change her mind. And she sure as hell wasn't going to the ball without me. "Fine."

"No one is to mention a word of this to Aunt Willa Jo. Not tonight. This is her night." Daisy glared at me.

"It's only because you know Aunt Willa Jo would cancel it," I said. "As she should."

"She needs this, Star. She's been working so hard."

"She needs you alive more. And I swear to god, Daisy, I will murder you if you get killed tonight. Please don't be reckless." My voice cracked, and I pulled her into a hug.

.   .   .

We arrived at the venue a few minutes late and rushed to the dressing room only to find it empty.

"Huh, I thought Aunt Willa Jo and Holly would be waiting here for us," Daisy said.

So did I, but it gave me a minute to talk to Cass at least. I motioned to the window, where she stood.

Daisy mouthed, "Is that where she is?"

I nodded and went to her.

"Hey, Cass?"

She didn't stir at first. But I said her name again, and she slowly turned. I wondered how long she'd stood in that same spot, staring out the window. Now she stared past me and opened her mouth, but nothing came out. She rushed toward me, and while I'd been prepared to dodge her, she was too quick. She passed right through me, and I was plunged into a vision.

It was different than the usual ones. Much more broken. Short flashes of memory that moved quickly.

"Ella, I know I'm right. The clues clearly point here. This is where the prize is hidden."

A flashlight beam cutting through darkness... searching empty rooms... a hidden closet... excitement turning to confusion...

"Someone found it in Concord, Massachusetts, Cass. I told you we should've gone there."

I came to with Daisy staring at me.

"You had a vision?" she asked.

I nodded.

Cass was back by the window as if none of it had happened—like a video starting at the beginning again.

"What did you see?"

Footsteps pounded into the room, and Dusty appeared as well.

"They were here, in this house, searching for Daisy's scavenger hunt prize," I said.

Daisy tapped her chin. "The clues were supposed to lead them to Sleepy Hollow Cemetery in Concord, Massachusetts. It's one of my favorite graveyards. 'Take a pilgrimage with me to sacred grounds for a transcendental meditation.' The literary authors buried there were known as transcendentalists," Daisy explained.

Cass turned around again with excitement in her eyes and said with Daisy, "'*Where the dead end up among tree-lined paths, sleeping in the bed for days.*'"

"Sleeping in the bed for days?" Dusty asked.

"You'd have to see the way I wrote it. I capitalized 'bed' and 'for' and the 'd' in days," Daisy explained.

"Bed... for... d... Bedford?" I asked.

"Yes! Sleepy Hollow Cemetery is on Bedford Street."

"Okay, but you'd also probably sleep in a bed for days if you were staying in Raven's Row Bed and Breakfast. In Dead End. Where fans of yours make pilgrimages. Daisy! No wonder no one found it," I said.

"One plus seven plus eight plus eight equals six. Number Six Raven Row," Cass said.

I repeated that.

"Yeah, 1788, the year Massachusetts became the sixth state. I know. It was a stretch. I told you it was too hard for anyone to solve." Daisy clapped a hand over her eyes. "No wonder she came here looking for me."

"We didn't come here looking for you." Cass crossed her arms over her chest. *"We were looking for Dru. Or rather, the clues she left."*

I glanced at Daisy and realized once again the stark contrast between her and her online persona. I wasn't sure if I should tell Cass that Daisy was Dru.

Just then, Holly showed up, and Aunt Willa Jo rushed in behind her. "Sorry we're late. Twins. Mud. And white shirts. That's all you probably need to know. But we do need to get dressed, Sheriff, so you'll have to say goodbye for now."

"What about my costume?" he asked.

Aunt Willa Jo said, "Go find the room downstairs off the kitchen. That's where the guys are."

"The guys have costumes?" I asked.

"We can't have our escorts wearing street clothes, can we?"

I couldn't wait to see the results.

The hairdresser worked on Aunt Willa Jo first while Daisy, Holly, and I began layering on the different garments that made up our ensembles. We took turns helping each other. I watched Cass at the window. I'd never seen a ghost stand so still for so long. Something wasn't quite right with her. Understandably. She'd come all this way just to get a chance to meet Daisy and had ended up dead. Now, she was face-to-face with her and didn't even recognize her. I thought that might be a small comfort because I couldn't imagine what it would do to her if she realized Daisy couldn't see ghosts at all.

When the hairdresser was done with Aunt Willa Jo, she started on me, pinning up my curls into a coif befitting my dress. Soon, she was done, and the torture of stuffing myself into a dress made for a woman who had to have survived on birdseed and willpower began.

The rest of the family stood at the bottom of the stairs, waiting as the four of us made our grand entrances. Dusty, Scott, Rock, and Zeke were dressed in similar male counterpart period costumes and seemed to be waiting to escort us. Daisy, of course, took Scott's arm. Aunt Willa Jo and Holly took Zeke and Rock's arms, respectively, and that left Dusty for me.

"How in the world did she talk you into this?"

"You can't honestly think I'd rather be anywhere but by your side?" He smiled. "I mean, with a killer on the loose."

"Right, but you, uh, that's not your usual attire." I nodded to his velvet waistcoat that just happened to perfectly match the shade of my dress. *Did Aunt Willa Jo plan that?*

"You don't like it?"

In fact, I adored it. Not that it was much of a change from his usual sharp attire. It was more that he was doing this to keep my sister safe. "It suits you. But where is your weapon?"

He pulled the jacket back to reveal a holster. "There's another in my boot."

"How will you do the elaborate period dance moves Aunt Willa Jo has planned for the big number?" I cocked an eyebrow at him.

His look of horror tickled me. "No one told me there would be dancing."

"You do know that a Midwinter Ball is not a festive sports match, right? Why else do we have a DJ?" I nodded to where Scott was positioned on stage.

"I mean, I know there will be dancing, but choreographed ballroom dancing?"

I burst out laughing. "I'm totally pulling your leg. I was trying to take it further and had planned a whole bit about costume changes. But I couldn't keep a straight face."

"You're the worst." He leveled his gaze at me, but his eyes twinkled.

It was nice to have a moment's reprieve from the gravity of recent events.

The mic crackled as Zeke adjusted some settings then handed it to Aunt Willa Jo.

"My little team of minions, I just want to say how much I love each and every one of you, and I appreciate your help. And if no one shows up besides us, then we will have a damn good party, right?"

We all shouted back in the affirmative.

"All right! So everyone knows your jobs, positions. The guests should start arriving soon, so let's do this!"

We all cheered and took our positions.

Aunt Willa Jo didn't have anything to worry about because guests started arriving right on time. They trickled in at first, and Daisy and I greeted them at the door.

"Oh my goodness, this feels like stepping into a Dickens novel!" one lady exclaimed.

I heard another say, "I wasn't so sure what our progressive lady mayor had planned for the evening, but this is so much better than any of those stuffy events at the community center."

Dusty helped Scott at the coat check station, not out of the goodness of his heart, I was sure, but to keep an eye on Daisy and me.

Eventually, Aunt Willa Jo pulled us from door duty to mingle, so I was finally able to get some food. I didn't like that Daisy wasn't by my side, but I spotted her with Scott in the corner once and on the dance floor another time. So long as I could spot her pink dress, I would be fine.

It wasn't until sometime after eleven, when the party was winding down, that I realized I hadn't seen Daisy for a while. I scanned the room for her and didn't see the flash of pink anywhere.

Before I could go look for her, Dusty was at my side, dipping into a low bow. "May I have this dance?"

I laughed from the shock of it but took the hand he'd offered. He whirled me onto the dance floor, where a few couples were still dancing.

"Great detective work this week," he said.

"I was just following the lead of the most dashing detective I know."

"Oh, you and Sherlock Holmes are personally acquainted?" he asked.

"Haha. You're hilarious," I said without a smile.

"I mean, you could at least try to be a little convincing."

I scanned the room, barely hearing him.

"Are you okay?" he asked.

"Sorry, I know we're trying to have some fun banter here, but I'm... I haven't seen Daisy recently. Have you?"

"Yeah, she and Scott went to the kitchen earlier." The corners of his mouth turned up slightly. I'd filled him in earlier on Scott spending the night, so he'd probably drawn the same conclusion I did now. They were getting in some alone time. "And don't worry, I've had a plain-clothes officer on her at all times. Between the two of them, she'll be safe."

I was about to relax and get back to our banter. Then I saw Scott across the room talking to Isaac.

I let go of Dusty's hands and rushed to him. "Where's Daisy?"

"She went upstairs to change clothes," he said. "Deputy Anderson went with her and is guarding the door. I poked my head up there a moment ago, and he gave me a thumbs-up. What's wrong?"

"How long has she been up there?"

He glanced at his wristwatch. "Actually, it's been a while. You don't think...?"

We both dashed toward the stairs with Dusty close on our heels.

The deputy lay on the floor outside the open door of the dressing room.

"Anderson!" Dusty knelt beside him, placing fingers on his neck. "He's alive."

Dusty asked Aunt Willa Jo to announce to the stragglers that the venue was closing and guests needed to clear out. After briefly filling her in on our concerns, he said, "Don't mention Daisy is missing. We don't want them to panic, or worse, for them to post about it on social media."

He located Carly, who was slow dancing with Grey,

and asked her to accompany me to the dressing room upstairs.

"See if Cass has seen Ella tonight," he instructed me. "Or if she knows anything more. Then I want you out of here." To Carly, he said, "Take her somewhere safe then report back to me."

He walked away, but I strode after him and grabbed his arm. "Wait, you can't just bark orders and leave."

"I wasn't aware I barked. I thought I spoke calmly."

"You know what I mean." I huffed a breath. I let go of his arm. "You can't order me around like I'm one of your deputies."

He squeezed his eyes shut then massaged his eyelids. When he opened them, he said, "Star, I don't want to go through this again. You've barely healed from the last time you were in danger."

"So have you!"

"It's my job."

"*My* job is to protect my family. My sister is missing, and I can't go through that again." My voice broke.

He pulled me into a hug, enveloping me in his arms, and I let him.

He murmured into my hair, "I will find her. But I need a clear head to do that, and if I'm worried that you're off somewhere in danger as well, my attention will be split. Please, just go with Carly. For Daisy's sake?"

The music stopped then, and Aunt Willa Jo made the

announcement thanking everyone for coming and telling them about the gift bags waiting for them on their way out. She'd stationed Teeny and Kira there to hand out the bags as people made their way to the doors. Zeke stood beside them with a watchful eye.

Dusty tipped my chin up, forcing me to look at him, and I thought perhaps he was about to kiss me. Instead, he said, "Call me when you get home. Or sooner if you learn anything from Cass."

Carly escorted me upstairs, but Cass was nowhere to be seen. With Carly's help, I changed out of the ball gown and back into my street clothes. When I hung the garment back neatly on the rack, I noticed something else. "Daisy's dress is here."

Carly appeared by my side. "Don't touch it."

"Carly. Look." I pointed a shaking finger at a slip of paper pinned to the inside of the collar with a smear of blood and a single line of text.

Where the dead end up.

chapter
twenty-nine

AFTER CARLY CALLED Dusty to update him, she said, "Hey, I need to get you home so I can get out there and help look for Daisy. You ready?"

"I can get myself home," I said. "I want to try talking to Cass again."

"Have you lost your mind? Kelsey, or Ella, has your sister. What do you think she would do to you if she found you alone?"

"She wouldn't hang around here. The note said, *Where the dead end up.* That sounds like a cemetery to me. You need to get out there and find Daisy. You can't waste precious time chauffeuring me around. Please, Carly."

"Absolutely not. In the first place, Dusty would demote me to street sweeper. Secondly, I know you. You wouldn't go home. You'd go out looking for her yourself. And three, I love you, and I need you to stay safe."

"Fine, let's go." I resigned myself to going home, but she was right about one thing. As soon as she left me there, I would head back out.

However, when we got downstairs, I realized that wasn't going to happen either.

Grey waited for us at the door. "Ella doesn't know where I live, and the farm is quite isolated. I think you'll be safer at my house."

"Brilliant suggestion, my love!" Carly said.

I mentally cursed whatever made the two of them fall in love. Once again, it was them against me.

"It's like you don't trust me," I said to Carly once we were on the road.

"It's like you forget that I actually know you," she said in a mocking tone.

"Sometimes, you're the worst best friend ever." I sighed. We both knew I didn't mean it. I laid my head against the door and watched the trees swim by until I got dizzy.

"He cares about you a lot, you know. He wouldn't be like this if he didn't," Carly said.

"He'd better not be changing my radio station back there." I looked over my shoulder at Grey behind us in my Jeep as if I could see him through the back window of Carly's cruiser.

"I'm not talking about Grey," she said. "But yeah, he's probably changing the station to something stupid like country music."

I knew who she was talking about, but I didn't want to discuss it.

Her radio crackled, and —speak of the devilishly handsome sheriff—Dusty spoke. "All clear at the lake. Report."

Other officers took turns reporting their location, then Carly picked up the radio. "On Route Four headed north."

"Why did he go to the lake?" I knew the answer but wanted to hear it from her.

She paused for a moment. "In case Ella has taken Daisy out to where Astra died."

Where the dead end up. It was clever. But she'd been fooling Daisy for months, and the rest of us for weeks. She wouldn't make it that easy.

We arrived at the darkened house, and Carly went around checking all the doors and windows and closets, turning lights on as she went. Then she came back to the car where she'd left me with Grey. "All clear."

They had a quick goodbye kiss, and she was gone.

"Look, I know you're not happy to be babysat and that you're worried about Daisy, but I'll do whatever you want while we wait. We can start on that soccer show you always rave about."

"*Ted Lasso* is too good for you. And it's football. Real football," I said.

Instead, we settled on some episodes of *Gilmore Girls* we'd already seen, and after the second episode, he fell sound asleep.

I realized then that I hadn't let Dusty know I'd made it to Grey's. I knew Carly had, so I wasn't worried that he didn't know I was safe, but after the way we left things, I didn't want him to think I was holding a grudge. Okay, well, a tiny one, but he'd waited long enough. I went to my bag to get my phone and found my charger, and other items, but no phone. *Not again.* It must have fallen out in Carly's cruiser.

Frustrated, I went out and sat on the porch. It was chilly, and I hadn't brought my coat, but the sky was gorgeous, and I didn't want to go in. I looked up at the stars, hoping that wherever Daisy was, she was safe. It was funny. I'd been mad at her for so long and definitely pissed off when she showed up on my birthday, but no matter how angry I'd been at her over the years, I'd never wanted any harm to come to her. I never should've left her side at the party.

Damn it. That was where my phone went. I'd taken it out of my pocket of the old dress and set it on the table in the dressing room, but I never put it back in my pocket once I'd changed clothes. I opened the front door, casting a glance at Grey, but his snores told me he was gone. Grabbing my keys and purse, I headed out.

The street around the house was empty, and the house was dark. I positioned my keys between my fingers to use as a weapon, like I'd seen on a self-defense video. With those in one hand and my pepper spray in the other, I was prepared. I refused to get kidnapped and put into danger again. And I'd seen enough scary movies to know people shouldn't creep through a dark house alone. So, I unlocked the front door with one of the keys I still had from the realtor and turned on every freaking light as I went.

I found my phone—and Cass—exactly where I'd last seen them. I checked my phone to find I had missed calls as well as a low battery—less than five percent left, according to the indicator—then pocketed it. First, I would try talking to Cass, since I was here, then I would return all the calls on the way back to Grey's while my phone was charging in the car.

I was prepared to try a few times, but just as I opened my mouth, Cass rushed toward me. "Dru's in danger."

"Where? Where is Dru?"

"She's there." She pointed to the opposite wall. She seemed a bit more aware than before.

I rushed out of the room to the one next door and

flipped on the lights but found it empty as well. When I returned to the dressing room, I said, "Cass, tell me where Dru is. Please."

She once again pointed to the wall. "She's there. Ella is going to hurt her. Ella is so mad. She won't even talk to me."

"You've seen Ella *here*? Tonight?"

Cass nodded.

"In this room?"

"Yes, she went through there." She once again pointed to the wall.

I really wished ghosts made sense. Fiona and Caroline were much more coherent. Another ghost I'd dealt with in October had been a little less so, but none I'd dealt with were as scattered as this one. Maybe it had something to do with the way they died, which made me wonder how exactly Cass had died. I was about to ask her when I heard something. It was so faint, I wondered if I'd imagined it. Then I heard it again.

"Did you hear that?" I asked her.

She only pointed to the wall. It was beginning to get frustrating. Then it hit me. In my visions from Cass, there had been a secret closet or a compartment of some type. I shoved the pepper spray and my keys into the pocket of my joggers and rushed to the wall where Cass had pointed, then felt along the paneling, my fingers searching the surface for anything out of the ordinary.

I found it—a small depression in the wood. I pushed, and the panel moved, swinging open. Behind it was Daisy curled into a ball. Her hands were tied behind her, and it looked like she was dressed as Drusilla. Black lipstick was smeared on and around her lips, and she wore a black wig. She was so pale. I couldn't tell if she was breathing. No, she had to be alive. I refused to accept any other circumstance.

I felt for a pulse. Weak, but there. I shook her. "Daisy, honey, wake up. We have to get out of here before Ella comes back."

Just then, my phone vibrated in my pocket. Carly's number glowed on the screen. Grey must have woken from his slumber on the sofa, found me missing, and called her. *Perfect timing.* I answered, and the power alert sounded, then my phone went black. *Damn it!*

Daisy moaned but didn't open her eyes. *Oh god, what if Ella poisoned her like she did Fiona?* I had to get her out of there. I pulled her up to a sitting position and lightly slapped her face. "Daisy! You have to wake up. I can't carry you."

I felt cold metal against my neck at the same time as I heard, "Good, because you're not going anywhere."

chapter
thirty

"STAND UP SLOWLY and back up to the wall," Ella said.

I didn't move, not because I was being difficult but because I was frozen with fear. The sharp jab from the knife point got me going. I would have thought, since I'd been in danger before, that I would have become a pro at being threatened with a weapon. It didn't get any easier, trust me.

Ella had me sit in the chair in which I'd had my makeup and hair done just a few hours previously. She backed toward Daisy, keeping an eye on me, and that was when I noticed she was dressed as the Violet Witch. Atop her head was a purple wig, and the makeup was hastily done but similar to what she'd worn in her videos.

"You're going to stay over there, and Daisy and I will sit right here."

The metal of the knife glinted in the light from the decorative sconces on the wall. She held it against Daisy's neck. If only I had figured out earlier what Cass had been pointing to, maybe I could've gotten Daisy out of here before Ella came back.

"What do you want with us?" I didn't care what the answer was. I knew from my experience in October that if I could keep the crazy murderers talking, it would give me time to formulate a plan.

"I didn't want anything from *you*. But you barged in here and ruined the show, so now you get to watch."

"Watch what?" I asked.

"Daisy telling her fans she's a fraud." She waved her phone at me. "She's going to confess, and I'm going to film it."

"I don't think Daisy could tell her fans her own name right now," I said.

Ella smirked. "We'll have to time it right. The drugs will wear off enough for her to talk but not enough for her to use her powers on me. Oh, don't look shocked. Of course, I know about her cheap magic tricks. Moving things through the air. That's how she convinced thousands of followers that she could see ghosts."

Maybe I could use that. "You're right. Daisy can't talk to ghosts. But I can. I've talked to Cass. She doesn't want you to hurt Daisy."

Ella scoffed.

"Yeah, well, even if I believed you, Cass gave up her right to make decisions the day she got herself strangled to death because she was devoted to a fraud." She positioned herself on the floor with Daisy leaning against her as if they were besties taking a selfie.

Got herself strangled to death? How did she know that?

"Hello, my little witchlings!" Ella said to the camera in a false singsong voice. "I'm back, and I've got none other than Drusilla herself here. She has some big news for you. Hold on to your gravestones because it's going to blow the lid off your coffin!"

"Are you recording that?" I asked.

"Yeah? And?"

"Why don't you go live? That will make a bigger impact. You'll be famous!"

"Do you think I'm stupid? I know what you're up to. Like I want the cops rushing in here and ruining the show. You'll have to be smarter than that to fool me."

"Like you fooled Daisy and her crew?" I remembered the story Daisy had told of how Kelsey had gotten a job. "You show up at a comic con pretending to be helpful just to worm your way onto her crew so you can prove she's a fraud?"

"I didn't know then that she was a fraud. I didn't find out until I overheard her and Rock talking one day a few weeks after I was hired. He was encouraging her to tell us that she couldn't really see ghosts because it was getting harder to fake it, the longer it went on. They thought they were alone, but I'm really good at blending into my surroundings."

"Yeah, you really are. You had us all believing you were Kelsey, the doormat, instead of Ella, the Violet Witch."

"That was my favorite part. Daisy and I have that in common. No one recognizes her when she's not in her black wig and makeup. Just like no one recognized me without my signature purple."

She slumped her shoulders and looked up timidly through her heavily done lashes. "Oh... I'm Kelsey, and I'm so helpless," she said in Kelsey's soft voice then straightened and, in the Violet Witch's voice, said, "See? Daisy's not the only one who can perform."

I thought of what Fiona had said about Kelsey being a drama queen and wished I'd put it together sooner. I prayed I could still save us both. "Is that why you want her dead? Because she lied?"

"You of all people should understand me. She's gotten famous on a power that she doesn't have, one that you do have. And you're working how many jobs and staying here in this town, taking care of everyone? Don't you want more?"

"Everything and everyone I need is here." I shrugged. "I don't need the spotlight like you and Daisy do. And you know, I'm starting to think Daisy doesn't really need it either. I think, with Scott and our family, she's found everything she needs."

Ella scoffed then held up the phone and started again. "We're here in Dead End, and believe me, it's aptly named. People come here and never leave."

I snorted. "Oh god, you sound lamer than Daisy."

She shot me a glance and continued speaking to the camera. "I've met Dru's whole family, and no wonder she ran away with her sister's fiancé."

"Oh yeah? Well, at least my brother didn't turn me in to the cops!" I hollered.

She picked up a chair and hurled it at me so quickly I barely had time to duck. It bounced off the wall inches from my head. "Next time, I won't miss. Now shut the hell up, or I'll duct tape your mouth, and maybe your nose, closed."

As I straightened, I registered what had poked my leg when I'd ducked. The pepper spray was in my pocket.

Daisy moaned again, and her eyes fluttered.

"Well, look who decided to join us, witchlings! Dru, what do you have to say to your fans?"

Daisy mumbled something incoherently.

"We can't hear you!" Ella said in a singsong voice. With one hand, she slid the knife under Daisy's chin and, moving her mouth like a puppet's, said, "I'm a fraud!"

If I used the pepper spray on her and disoriented her, making her drop the knife, maybe I could get to the chair and hit her over the head hard enough to knock her out. I would have to be quick, and I needed her to come closer to me. But for that, I had to make her mad.

"What did she ever do to you to make you hate her this much?" I asked. "I don't get it."

"Of course you don't get it. You've always hated Daisy. You never got caught up in her web of lies. I worshipped her. I wanted to be her. All I wanted was a little advice for my own channel, but could she bother to answer a single message? Not one."

"So, you're doing this because a loved celebrity was too busy to answer a message from a wannabe like you? Do you think you're that special? How would she ever get anything done if she answered every single message from thousands of fans?"

"They didn't love her like I did!" She slammed her fist on the wooden floor.

"Or was it because, even if Daisy gave you all the tips and tricks in the world, you could never get anyone to be as dedicated to you as her fans are to her? Not even your own stepbrother, who forgot you existed."

She dropped Daisy, letting her head flop to the floor. I winced at the thump she made against the hard wood. But it did the job I'd intended. Ella left Daisy and rushed toward me. But instead of getting near enough that I could put my plan into action, Ella kicked my chair over backward, sending me toppling.

"You leave Cal out of this."

Daisy moaned, drawing Ella's attention, and she returned to the other side of the room.

She pushed the black strands of wig hair out of Daisy's face and poked my sister's forehead. "And then this one did that stupid scavenger hunt, and Cass, on the pretense of coming to spend time with me at college in Austin, came there for an intervention. Our mom was worried I was failing out of college and sent Cass to talk some sense into me. She thought I was obsessed with Drusilla."

I laughed and sat up.

"What's so funny?"

"You obsessed with Daisy? Of course not! How absurd. If you were obsessed with Daisy, would you show up at a comic con after changing your name and your appearance and weasel your way onto her staff to attempt to destroy her life from the inside? Of course not. That's just crazy talk."

This time, her foot hit my head, and I stayed down.

"I didn't do it to destroy her. I did it to be like her. She wouldn't give me the advice I needed to go viral like she did, so I decided I'd study her from inside the petri dish."

"Which part of that scientific experiment included sending her cryptic letters from someone who'd faked her own death?" I closed my eyes, bracing myself for more physical abuse. As long as she was hurting me, she wasn't hurting Daisy, and if I could keep her talking,

Daisy would have more time to wake up and use her powers to save us. But when the pain didn't come, I opened my eyes and found she was by Daisy's side across the room.

"Maybe I should slice open her throat and let her fans watch as her blood pours out of her body just like her lies poured out of her mouth."

Ella flicked the tip of the knife into the hollow of Daisy's throat. It had the desired effect. I shut my mouth.

"*Leave her alone!*" Cass rushed through the wall and through me.

"*You got it wrong! I told you it didn't make sense!*" Ella yelled at me. "*I told you we should have looked in New England.*"

"*No, it's this house. The clues point to it. Where the dead end up. Sleeping in the bed for days. One plus seven plus eight plus eight. It's here. We just have to keep searching.*"

"*It's over. Someone found it!*"

"*How? We've been here and haven't seen anyone else.*"

She shoved her phone in my face.

I read the text, Found Drusilla's clue in Sleepy Hollow Cemetery in Concord, Massachusetts.

The girl held up a coffee can and a paper in the photo.

"*It's a fake.*"

"*No!*" *Ella yelled.* "*Dru just responded.*"

"*But...*" *I turned to face the window in confusion.*

"You were wrong. And once again, you wouldn't listen to me!"

In the glass's reflection, I saw Ella come at me like she was going to strangle me, hands held out. But she wouldn't. She was my sister.

"You've ruined everything! This was my chance to finally get Dru to notice me!"

I felt her hands around my neck. Squeezing. I couldn't speak. I couldn't breathe.

I came to, coughing so hard I almost threw up. I'd felt her betrayal as if it were my own. "You killed Cass," I whispered. "In this room."

Ella dropped the knife. Daisy's right hand made the smallest movement, but I couldn't be sure if Ella noticed.

"And tell her, I remember. I remember the end."

"She said to tell you she remembers the end."

Ella shook her head and grabbed the knife again. "You're lying," she said but didn't sound as confident as before.

"You were too much of a coward to face her while you killed her, but she saw your reflection in the window. I felt it. I felt her pain. The betrayal she felt. The confusion. How could someone she trusted take so much from her?" I turned to Cass. "I'm sorry Ella hurt you. Big sisters are supposed to protect you. Yours didn't. You didn't deserve what she did to you."

"El-bear, why did you do it?" Cass asked.

I relayed what she'd said, in the same small voice—not to add drama, as Ella had before with her singsong voice, but because it was all I had left.

She gripped the knife and stood, letting Daisy flop back on the floor. Daisy's eyes met mine then, and I knew she was awake, but Ella's actions drew my attention.

"Where is she? I want to face her when I talk to her."

"Over there," I lied, pointing to the corner farthest from Daisy.

"You ruined everything for me. We could've gotten to Concord before the other girls, and then I could've gone viral and become someone!"

She continued screaming at the wall, and Daisy flexed her hands.

"'You were already someone to me,'" I repeated the words Cass said. "'Why did you need strangers to love you?'"

"I didn't need everyone to love me. Just Cal. I wanted him to see I'd become just as big as he had. Then, maybe he would have come back." Her voice cracked.

As suddenly as Ella's tirade began, it stopped, and she whipped around, waving the knife at me. "Oh, you almost got me. You almost made me forget you were here. Well, guess what? I'm done. With both of you."

She picked up another chair and flung it at me faster than I could dodge. It hit, and I swayed. I could not lose consciousness. My head hurt. I had to stop the two Ellas lunging toward me. I blinked, and they became one, but she stopped mid-stride. Behind her, Daisy sat up, her hands out in front of her. She flicked one hand to the side, and the knife Ella held flew from her grasp and slid across the floor. Daisy wiped sweat from her brow, and that moment of broken concentration released Ella, who lunged forward and grabbed me around the neck.

I clawed at her hands, gasping for breath. *Just like Cass.* I'd felt it through her eyes. Now, I was experiencing it in my own body. Then I heard a crack. For a moment, I thought it was my neck, until Ella howled in pain. Several more cracks rang out simultaneously, and Ella withdrew her hands from my neck. Her fingers looked strange, bent backward at odd angles.

Daisy stood, arms outstretched. "Back away from my sister, or I'll break more than your fingers."

Ella wailed in rage and turned toward Daisy. Daisy's energy seemed to give out then as she slumped back to the floor. I scrambled up and hurled myself at Ella, jumping on her back like a rabid monkey, taking us both to the ground. She had a lot of strength and determination for someone who'd just had all of her fingers broken. We rolled back and forth, finally ending up with her on top of me. Her hands came toward my neck again, when suddenly, she flew back several feet and hit the wall behind us.

I scrambled up to find Daisy standing with her arms

out, holding Ella against the wall with her power. "You know, I could snap your neck with a flick of my wrist."

At last, Ella looked properly scared. I had to admit, I was a bit scared too. This wasn't like Daisy. She wasn't a murderer.

"I could throw you through that window and to the sidewalk below and convince everyone that you jumped."

Ella, still suspended in midair, drifted slowly toward the window.

"Daisy, don't," I whispered, my throat still hurting from nearly being strangled to death. "Just keep her pinned there while I get help."

I wasn't at all sure how I would do that. My phone was dead. Daisy didn't have hers. But I couldn't let Daisy kill Ella. She would never get over it. Once the adrenaline stopped pumping and she realized we were safe, it would crush her. I *knew* my sister. She wasn't a killer.

Daisy strode toward the window, moving Ella in front of her like she was walking a dog. I followed. I didn't know what to do. Then Ella flew through the window, shattering the glass.

Oh god. I didn't know if I thought it or if I whispered it. I rushed to the window expecting to see her body surrounded by glittering glass shards, but she was still suspended in midair. Daisy hadn't killed her.

There was still a chance. And I knew what I had to do. I wrapped my arms around Daisy from behind and rested my chin on her shoulder. "I am so sorry I've not been there for you all these years. I'm sorry I resented you when you came to live with us. You were just a little girl sent away from your mother, like Astra and I had been years before, and instead of bonding with you over that, I resented you because you'd had more time with Mamma and she'd cried when she left you with us. She never cried over us. But that wasn't your fault. I am so sorry that I didn't support you when you wanted to go out on the road to make your videos. I am so sorry I never told you how proud I am of the wonderful woman you've become. I love you, Daisy Lea."

With each sentence I spoke, Ella descended closer to the ground, slowly and safely. The moonlight that illuminated her suddenly grew brighter, and I realized it was car headlights. Footsteps pounded on the sidewalk, and Dusty stood gaping up at us as Daisy carefully lowered Ella the last few feet to the ground then dropped her when she was close enough to get only a few bumps and bruises instead of a cracked skull. I didn't think that part was an accident.

Daisy turned and sobbed into my arms—deep, gut-wrenching sobs. I held her and watched over her shoulder as Dusty cuffed Ella. Another cop car pulled up then, and Carly jumped out, taking the front porch steps two at a time.

I whispered to Daisy, "It's okay. We're safe."

chapter
thirty-one

"WE'RE STARTING to make a habit of these hospital family reunions," Holly said.

"I'm just glad you're both okay," Aunt Willa Jo cooed. "I would never forgive myself if something had happened to you girls because of my stupid Midwinter Ball."

"The ball was a smash, Aunt Willa Jo. Far from stupid," Daisy said. "And Ella was hell-bent on hurting me, one way or another. If it hadn't happened there, she'd have grabbed me somewhere else. Star was right. I should've been less flippant about my safety."

"And Star should've kept her phone charged and superglued to her arm at all times." Teeny tightened the grip she had on my hand. "I was so scared when it kept going to voicemail."

I enveloped her in a hug and said in a hoarse whisper, "I'm sorry, sweetie."

"You get better soon, because once you're both well, I have a bone to pick with you," Aunt Mer said.

"Go ahead and let it out. You look like you might burst otherwise," Daisy quipped.

"I leave for two weeks, and my nieces are in danger again?" Aunt Mer raged. "And what were you thinking, Star, going after Daisy by yourself?"

She went on a few moments more, then when she was done, Uncle Gavin said, "You feel better now, hon?"

"Marginally."

Uncle Gavin laughed. "She did nothing but rage the minute we disembarked and she saw the messages from Granny about what was happening."

I would have a word with Granny about tattling on us if I thought it would do any good.

"I think more than a few of us want to shake some sense into you," Dusty said from the doorway.

I whispered, "How did you know where to find us?"

"Grey woke up and found you gone and called Carly. She tracked you and called me."

"Even with my phone dead?"

"A dead phone will still show your last location. Thankfully, you were still there. Had she taken you, we might not have found you in time. Daisy, you were smart to use your powers to get Ella out of the house and hold her there until I arrived." His voice was even when he said it, but I wondered if he suspected what she'd really been up to.

Daisy and I glanced at each other. We hadn't told anyone what had transpired in the room. And if they wanted to assume that was what had happened, I wouldn't stop them.

"Did someone let Granny know we're okay?" Daisy asked.

"Someone did!" Granny said from the doorway. She zoomed in on her scooter with Zeke and Kira following. "When he came by to update me, I insisted he bring me here to see you both for myself."

"Oh, Granny, you didn't have to come. You could've called," I whispered.

"Or you could've FacedTimed us," Daisy said from the other bed.

"I am FaceTiming you. I am spending time seeing your face. In person. Now, tell me everything. Are they keeping you overnight?" Granny looked between the two of us. "Let Daisy tell me, and you rest your voice."

I nodded.

"I'm fine. The syringe Ella dosed me with was a sedative, not poison, thankfully. It will be fully out of my system in a couple of days. Star's vocal cords are bruised but will heal. They've instructed her not to talk, but she's not great at following directions."

"Do you remember any of it?" I whispered, proving

her point. "Of how she got you into that hidden compartment?"

"Bits and pieces. When I got into the dressing room and closed the door, I thought I saw a flash of something in my peripheral vision, but before I could react, I felt a sting on my neck."

"Oh, honey!" Granny murmured.

"But how did she get into the house in the middle of the party?" Aunt Willa Jo asked. "Weren't all the exits covered?"

"I am not sure she did," Daisy said. "I think she snuck in before the party and was waiting in the secret compartment she stuffed me in. It had an empty bottle and some snack wrappers in it."

A nurse came in then and shooed the family out. We'd been lucky the staff had let all of them in for so long, but our luck had run out.

Granny asked to stay a moment longer. "I just arrived, and I'm old. I may not last another day. Would you deprive me of what could be my final moments with my granddaughters?" she asked in an exaggeratedly frail voice.

"Granny!" Daisy admonished. "Bite your tongue! You're going to live forever."

Granny held her head and gave a moan I knew was fake, then looked up at the nurse through her fingers.

The nurse gave Granny a look and must have believed

her because she said, "Five minutes, ma'am, then they need to rest."

Daisy was already closing her eyes. It had been a long day, but I had a feeling Granny wasn't just checking on her grandchildren. So, I kept my eyes open.

For a bit, she made small talk, then when Daisy's soft snores drifted to us from her bed, Granny said, "When you came to live here, you were a lost little girl. Now you're a strong woman who helps both the living and the dead. I'm so proud of you, honey."

I opened my mouth to thank her, and she held up a finger.

"Save your voice. I know what you want to say. I can see it in your eyes. Just listen to me for a moment. Changes are coming, Star. Big ones. But just you remember that endings are often just beginnings wearing a different coat. You'll understand what I mean when the time comes."

Christmas Morning

THE SUNLIGHT STREAMED through my window, and I stretched. Daisy's arm flopped onto my side of the bed, and I pushed it away. Then I remembered what day it was.

It's Christmas!

We had a tradition going back for years that we slept in the same room on Christmas Eve. It began when she first came to live with us and said she was scared of Santa because she'd once seen him punch Mamma's guitarist. She'd scream anytime Aunt Mer tried to get her to sit in Santa's lap. Even as an annoying teenager, she'd had an unnatural fear of Santa and still came and crawled into bed with me and Astra. Now, as an adult, I didn't want her anywhere else but here. Teeny had joined us, so the bed was quite crowded.

I leaned over and whispered in Daisy's ear, "Ho ho ho!"

She sat bolt upright then flopped down again. "I'll get you back for that, you beast of a sister."

A smell wafting from downstairs made me assume a similar posture, but I stayed upright. "Bacon!"

"Scott!" Daisy sat up again.

"For the love of all things holy, will you two shut up?" Teeny mumbled. Then she also sat up. "Christmas!"

She squealed and jumped out of bed, and Daisy and I joined her, having donned matching pajamas the night before that Daisy had provided. We galloped downstairs to find Aunt Mer and Uncle Gavin cuddled on the sofa in front of the tree, holding steaming mugs.

Scott poked his head through the doorway from the kitchen. "Oh, it's just y'all. Sounded like a herd of horses."

"I'm as hungry as a horse!" I whispered.

"A hoarse horse." Teeny giggled.

"Breakfast will be done soon. Hope the rest show up before it gets cold," Scott said.

Our usual tradition was to celebrate Christmas Eve with the whole family at Pub Dead then spend Christmas morning at our houses—which, for our house, usually meant me, Teeny, and Aunt Mer. And depending on the year—and their relationship status—sometimes Uncle

Gavin. But this year, we had a houseful on Christmas morning.

The front door opened, and Carly, Grey, and Rock came in, arms piled high. I knew it had to be a bittersweet occasion for Carly, who'd spent the past few Christmases with her godfather. She'd mentioned she and Rock would go visit him in prison later that day.

No sooner had we gotten them settled and unloaded than in came Kira and Zeke. Teeny squealed and ran to Kira. We'd invited and expected Zeke, but Kira usually spent Christmas with her mother.

"Mamma and I did our Christmas last night so I could spend Christmas morning with my Bester!"

Teeny threw her arms around Kira then released her and did the same to Zeke. After a moment, she ran off with Kira to find another chair to bring to the table.

I strode over to Zeke and gave him a hoarse hello and a hug. "Glad y'all could make it."

"I wouldn't want to be anywhere but here." He touched the photo of Astra hanging on the wall. It was her graduation photo—not the official one they did at the beginning of the year, but one of her on graduation night that I'd snapped. "I wonder what she would think of all this?"

I smiled. "She'd love every minute of it. Christmas was her favorite."

"Y'all hurry up and come eat! We can't wait all day for

presents. We have an amazing one for Star and our dad," Kira hollered from the kitchen.

"It better not be a puppy," Daisy said.

I laughed. *Was it less than two months ago she'd come back to town and was my surprise, and I'd worried it was a puppy?* Now, I couldn't imagine her not here. We still had some things to work out, like her not bringing up—daily —that I should make peace with Mamma. And her using all the hot water for her showers. But we would get there.

We sat down, and I filled myself with bacon, cinnamon chip pancakes, and hash brown casserole. There were many more options, but those were my favorites. *As are the people at the table,* I thought as I glanced around. We were missing a few—like Granny, who was spending the day with Aunt Willa Jo and her family, and Dusty, who was working the morning shift so those with kids could spend time with their families—but I was quite content to be surrounded by this motley crew.

And not just the living ones. I glanced at Fiona and Caroline, who seemed to be having an animated discussion. I caught phrases like *"a horrid, giant, hairy creature"* and *"a whole show about cakes?"* I had a feeling we might have a new resident besides Daisy. As a ghost, Fiona was a bit less *spirited* and seemed to be good company for Caroline. I was beginning to understand why Madison and Greta had made excuses for her. I might have been wrong about her, but I was not wrong about my mother. Who, by the way, hadn't even called to wish her daughters and her only grandchild a Merry Christmas. And when Daisy called her, it went to voicemail. She was probably sleeping off her Christmas Eve celebrations.

Once we were full, Kira and Teeny promised to do all the dishes later if we would leave them to come open presents. I had no argument with letting them do things, but Aunt Mer said we would all help now, and it wouldn't take ten minutes.

Daisy said, "Or I could do it in half that time."

Kira rubbed her hands together. "Yes, please. I want to see this. I've only heard about your superpower."

Daisy flicked her wrist, and the orange juice pitcher lifted from the table, but Aunt Mer intercepted it. "We have talents, not superpowers. We use them when needed, not to get out of chores."

When needed. Like when Daisy saved my life by using her power to keep Ella from choking me, and how I'd used mine to get Cass to show me where Daisy was being kept. Maybe this talent of mine wasn't such a curse after all.

The dishes were done, the old-fashioned way—a new dishwasher from Uncle Gavin—in record time with everyone doing their part. Then, once we were settled in the living room, Kira and Daisy passed out presents.

My presents were the usual assortment of books, fun T-shirts, and coffee mugs with pop-culture sayings, along with a replacement TARDIS trinket box from Rock.

Then, as Aunt Mer was gathering up the wrapping paper strewn about, Teeny handed me a small box. "This is from me, Aunt Mer, and Daisy."

I carefully removed the paper to find a white box with a familiar logo. Sometimes, we recycled boxes, so I never could be sure it held the actual contents. But the security tape was still in place. "You got me a smart watch? Guys, that's too much!"

Teeny pointed to it. "This will never leave your arm unless you are showering or charging it. Got it? We opted for the plan that lets you call from it even when your phone is missing."

"Yes, ma'am!" I laughed and threw my arms around her, then mouthed a thank-you to Aunt Mer and Daisy across the room.

As people filed out of the living room to various spots in the house, Kira sidled up to me. "My mom has one of these, and you can change the watch face. I think you can even put your own photos on it."

"Oh, that would be cool."

Kira handed me another package. "This is from Teeny and me."

I glanced up to see Teeny watching me with bright eyes and anticipation. "Oh, is this the super special gift you two were working on, like your dad's?"

"Yeah, but open yours first." Teeny glanced over her shoulder, where Zeke was showing Uncle Gavin the Creedence Clearwater Revival albums Daisy had given him. "Then you can watch him open his."

I unwrapped a framed drawing. One of Astra's. "It's you and your mom. I love it."

Teeny said, "I think it's you. See the hair?"

"But that baby is definitely you. See the chin dimple?" She nodded.

"Your mom never saw me with you. I didn't know you existed until after she died."

"I know. But I think she drew what she wanted to happen. She didn't die being mad at you. I think she missed you."

Tears filled my eyes and spilled over. I could no longer see the drawing or Teeny, but she threw her arms around me.

I whispered into her hair, "I love you so much, kiddo."

"I love you too," she replied.

"Dad!" Kira called. "We have something else for you!"

I dabbed my eyes with the tissues Teeny handed me and saw that her eyes were misty too.

Zeke made his way over to the sofa and sat beside Teeny. Kira positioned herself on his other side. I stood and grabbed my phone to get a photo of the three of them.

When Teeny handed him the package, he said, "Another one? You already gave me my presents."

"We saved the best for last," Kira replied. "And in case

it made you emotional, we wanted to do it when everyone wasn't watching."

Zeke glanced up at me, and I shrugged. He carefully pulled back the dancing-reindeer wrapping paper and found a T-shirt. He unfolded it and stared, his mouth open. It was the tree drawing that Astra had done in his yearbook with the words Don't Stop Be-Leafing. But they'd added something to the trunks of the trees. On one tree was the name Fry, Zeke's last name, and on the other Bell.

"How did you...?" His voice broke, and he scrubbed a hand over his eyes.

Kira pulled a Dead End High School yearbook out from under the sofa, where she must have hidden it earlier. "Mamma had your yearbook, and we found this in the back, so we—"

"My yearbook?"

Kira opened the book and showed him.

"We weren't together then. She didn't know about this place."

"Wait. So, it is a real place?" Kira bounced in her seat.

Teeny touched his hand. "Are you okay? We didn't mean to upset you."

Zeke snapped out of wherever his mind had gone, and he put his arm around Teeny. "Oh, baby girl, you didn't upset me. Not at all. I love it! I just haven't seen this in years."

"And see? We added something to the drawing. See the names? It shows that our families are connected as one, just like the trees. That was Teeny's idea." Kira smiled.

"And Kira knew you'd love the pun. Since you like dad jokes," Teeny added.

"I adore it. I'm going to go change into it right now. This is the best gift, girls. I love it!" He stood and headed down the hallway.

Kira bounced on the sofa and threw her arms around Teeny. "He loved it! Did you hear that! We win Christmas!"

I left them there to celebrate while I went to check on Zeke. I found him in the bathroom with the door open and the shirt still in his hands. "You okay?"

"What was Astra's talent?" he asked.

"She didn't have one. I mean, of the magical kind. She was talented in many other ways, but—"

"She never saw this tree before we found it together years after she drew this. We were exploring one day, a few days before she left for Nashville, and found this in the woods. I think... do you think... could she somehow have seen the future?"

I thought about that for a moment. "No, she would've told me. Or at least Aunt Mer."

"What if she didn't know that's what it was? What if she was just drawing what was in her head?"

I remembered the print Teeny and Kira had given me.

Astra had drawn me holding Teeny long before she was pregnant. "I think you're right."

He pulled his shirt over his head and replaced it with the new one. "It's like she's here with us."

I nodded. I really wished she were. Sometime soon, I would have to dig out the rest of her sketches to see what else she'd drawn.

Later that night, when our company had gone, I found myself alone in the house. Dusty had said he would come by if he could get away from the station, but other than a couple of apology texts that popped up on my watch, there'd been no updates. Teeny had gone home with Zeke and Kira. Aunt Mer was at Gavin's, and Daisy and Scott went out to the tour bus. Even Caroline and Fiona were absent.

I sat in the dark with only the Christmas tree and a fire roaring in the fireplace to light up the room. I took a sip of my cocoa. There was no one to take care of, no one who needed me, and nothing to clean. I exhaled a contented sigh and snuggled down to watch my favorite Christmas movies.

I was halfway through *The Muppet Christmas Carol* when someone knocked on the door.

I refused to get up from my comfy spot and hollered, "Come in!"

Heavy footsteps sounded in the hall. Soon after, Dusty appeared.

"Merry Christmas!" I sat up in the recliner and got a closer look at him.

He held a thermos, a paper bag, and a blanket. "Merry Christmas. I figured you'd be worn out after a long day of taking care of everyone and probably tired of Christmas leftovers. So, I brought takeout and hot cocoa."

"Oh, nice! And the blanket? Were you afraid the heater was broken?" I laughed.

"No, it's a clear night, and the stars are out. I thought once we ate, we could finally have that date I promised you."

I reached for his hand. "Stars, cocoa, and you on Christmas night? Sounds magical to me."

epilogue

New Year's Day

"Nerts!" Daisy hollered and threw her arms in the air.

"Again?" Scott covered his eyes. "How? I still have almost all the cards left in my Nerts pile."

"I warned you," Aunt Mer told Scott. "You sure you don't want to play that game with all the birds and colorful wooden eggs that the others are playing in the living room?"

"Yeah," Zeke called. "Come play Wingspan with us, Scott."

Carly chimed in with "Save yourself while you still can!"

"No," he said decidedly. "I'll stay here until the game is over. How much longer?"

I picked up the pencil and added the latest scores to

the tally. "Well, how about now? With the latest numbers, you reached a score of two hundred, which means it's over."

His protests were interrupted by a knock on the door. I couldn't imagine who it could be, as the whole gang was here at the farmhouse for New Year's Day. Most of us were playing games or watching the football game on television, except the girls, who were entertaining the twins outside with a scavenger hunt, and Granny, who snoozed in the recliner.

"Come in!" Uncle Gavin called from the living room.

Our mystery guest entered and closed the door behind him. All conversation in the other room ceased, and I leaned back in my chair to get a look.

"Cal," I said.

"Hey! Sorry, I don't meant to interrupt. Looks like you're having a party."

"I thought you'd left town already," Daisy said.

"I did. I went home for Christmas, but I had to come back to... take care of some business."

"Come in. Take off your coat." Aunt Mer stood, ever the gracious host. "Can I get you a plate? We have a ton of food."

He shook his head. "I can't stay. I just wanted to come by and, well, formally apologize to you all."

She ignored him and grabbed a plate.

"Man, this was all Ella. You aren't responsible for her

actions," Scott said then added, "I mean, yeah, should you have been honest from the beginning about your connection to Daisy's past? Yes, and well... I'm going to shut up and let you make your apology."

"No, you're right. I should've been upfront. And I should've reached out to you or the police when I found that first letter of Ella's. For that, I'm truly sorry. I can't erase anything that happened, but I am glad you both came out unscathed."

"I just hate that Cass wasn't as lucky. I had this one here to protect me." Daisy nodded to me. "Cass was killed by the big sister who was supposed to protect her. Because of me. The only comfort I have in any of this is that Star thinks Cass may have crossed over."

"Really?" Cal looked at me.

"Yeah, we've been at the house a few times this week, and there's no sign of her," I explained.

"I hope she's found peace. Wait, why were you back at the house? I'd think you would want to stay far away from it. Both of you. Was it just to check on Cass?"

"No." I smiled and jabbed a thumb toward Daisy. "This weirdo wants to buy it and turn it into the Bell Witches Bed and Breakfast."

Daisy shrugged. "I figure if Dead End is going to make tourist dollars off my name, I may as well collect some myself. And despite the fact that I got kidnapped and drugged there, I kinda love that house. Besides, the only way to get rid of bad memories is to remake them into good ones."

"So you're staying in town?" Cal asked.

"I am. I have no crew and—"

"Excuse me, you do still have a director of photography." Scott winked at her.

"Yes, I have one camera guy who I can't seem to shake." She leaned in and brushed her lips against his. "And my producer is going back to school to get his degree so he can teach."

"Good for Rock!" Cal said.

"And you've snatched up Penny, apparently." She raised an eyebrow at him.

"Looks like I owe you more apologies," Cal said.

"No, I think it will be good for her, and we talked a few days ago and parted on good terms. It's all good. When is my *Truthbusters* episode airing? I want to come clean to my fans about my ghost-seeing powers, or lack thereof," she said. "I owe them the truth before it comes out publicly."

Scott rubbed her back.

Cal smiled. "The *Truthbusters* episode won't be aired."

Daisy gave him an incredulous look.

"It won't?" I asked.

"That's the other reason I'm here. The studio—in light of recent events and to avoid any legal difficulties

—has decided not to air it. All footage is to be destroyed."

"Are you serious?" Daisy put her hands over her mouth.

"We didn't get enough footage to cobble together a whole episode. But for the record, I wouldn't have exposed you as a fraud. The title of the show is *Supernatural Truthbusters: Fact or Fraud*, right? And, honey, you put the super in supernatural!" He winked at her. "Scott is a lucky man."

"Hell yeah, I am!" Scott beamed.

"I made you a plate, Cal, but are you sure you won't stay?" Aunt Mer stood with a plate—containing so much food it could feed Cal for a week—in one hand and tinfoil in the other.

"I can't. I have things to take care of. But I have one more reason for coming by." Cal reached into his leather sling bag and brought out an envelope. "I made you something. Merry Christmas and Happy New Year, my lovely Bell witches."

"What is it?" Daisy held up what looked like a memory card.

Cal took the foil-wrapped plate Aunt Mer handed him. "Scott will know what to do with it. All of the other footage has been destroyed, and this is the only copy of any of it."

Scott took the card from Daisy and left the room.

Cal blew us a kiss. "You Bells have something beautiful here. Take care of each other."

After Cal left and we talked Uncle Gavin and Rock into turning off the game for a bit to let us use the living room TV, Scott hooked up a device, and soon a picture came up on the screen.

"The Bell Witches," a short film by Cal Covington Roberts.

"It's footage from the documentary," Scott said.

We sat mesmerized for the next few minutes as images flew across the screen. I had been right that the cameras had always been rolling, and it seemed Cal had saved all the best parts: Teeny and Kira with their heads together and Zeke watching them both with a father's smile, a close-up of Granny's hands, Daisy throwing her head back and laughing about something, me bringing bottled water and a sandwich to Daisy, and more. I watched the people in the room watch the faces on the screen and felt so much love for every single one of them. I thought about how different New Year's Day was from Thanksgiving. My heart felt lighter.

I met Daisy's eyes across the room, and she mouthed, "Kitchen?"

She was waiting by the sink for me and grabbed my hands. "I'm sorry I was a bratty kid and brought up all the things Mamma did for me that she never did for you and Astra, like Disney World and trips to London."

I opened my mouth to tell her I didn't really hold a grudge, but she shushed me, and I realized this was her version of what I'd done for her the night of the Midwinter Ball.

She continued, "I'm sorry about the way I went viral and that I used Astra's memory to do that. I'm sorry I asked Mamma to hire Rock to go with me on the road. I'm sorry I rarely came back to visit—especially after you almost died in October. I'm sorry that when I did come back, I wasn't honest with you about why I was here. I'm sorry my shenanigans put you in danger. Thank you for saving me from Ella that night, but mostly, thank you for saving me from myself. I know why you did what you did. I love you, Star Otillie. You are the only big sister I have left, and I couldn't imagine my life without you."

With tears streaming down my face, I pulled her into a hug. "I love you too."

When all the snot and tears were done, she said, "You remember that favor Aunt Mer told you I wanted to ask you the day after Thanksgiving?"

I nodded. "Yeah, about staying in Dead End?"

"No... That's what you thought I was going to ask? If I could stay here?"

"Well, not exactly. I mean, you don't need my permission to stay here. It's your home too. I guess I don't know what you were going to ask. Scott came in and announced the thing about SupeTV, and I jumped to conclusions. But I guess I never really thought it out."

"If you don't let me ask, I'm gonna lose my nerve again."

"Sweetie, you can ask anything. Anything! Except for me to go see Mamma. That, I won't do. Not yet at least."

"What about Daddy?"

"Daddy?"

"Mine, I mean. I want you to help me talk to him."

"Geoffrey?"

She nodded. "Remember when I wouldn't tell Fiona how I found out about my powers? I couldn't because they are so tied up in my memories of him, and I was afraid that if I spoke the story, my memories would fade. I can't remember what his voice sounds like anymore. And I know I won't be able to hear him, even if you do find him, but I want him to hear me."

I enveloped her in a hug. "You've got it."

Later that night, as I sat on the porch, wrapped in a blanket, Uncle Gavin, Rock, and Zeke argued over the best way to do the fireworks, and Zeke paced the yard, mumbling about how someone was going to lose a finger if they weren't careful. Daisy, Kira, and Teeny wrote their names in the air with sparklers the way Astra, Daisy, and I used to do. I thought about how Daisy's request to help her find and talk to her dad, and my acceptance, had shown our growth. We shared the same pain. We'd both lost our fathers young and were abandoned by our mother. We'd both dealt with that shared pain in different ways—her by becoming an attention hog and me by making myself smaller, trying to do things for everyone but myself.

Astra shared that same pain, but instead of letting it turn her into something else, she'd always stayed the same wonderful Astra—the one who could brighten anyone's day just by being in it. God, how I missed her. I wished she could see how my and Daisy's apologies to each other had healed something broken in us. We would both be okay.

Headlights shone on the proceedings in the driveway, and I recognized Dusty's Mustang. My heart fluttered. I didn't know where things were headed between us, but I couldn't wait to find out now that we didn't have any ghosts to deal with.

After he greeted the fireworks committee and the others sitting in lawn chairs, he found me on the porch swing. "I have something for you." He handed me an envelope.

"You already gave me this beautiful necklace!" I touched the hollow between my collarbones, where the silver star rested. It had been too extravagant, but I didn't say that. "You can't possibly give me more."

His eyes twinkled, but his face remained blank. "Oh, I think you'll like this much better than a necklace."

I took the envelope from him. It was thick. I unfolded the stack of stapled papers inside while he shone his phone's flashlight on them.

I scanned the first page. "Dusty! No. You're kidding me. Is this for real?"

He nodded.

"How?"

"The papers came through yesterday. A crew will be there Monday."

Tears filled my eyes as I read it again to make sure I wasn't dreaming. *A warrant to excavate the well on the property at...*

"Astra," I said as the tears spilled over. "We're finally going to find her."

As the fireworks exploded overhead, for the first time in over a decade, I had hope.

The End

For all the latest news, sign up for my newsletter!

afterword

Oh my goodness, y'all! Finally! Another book is done! This is almost as big for me as my debut. And it was a hard-won battle because while I knew I wanted Daisy back in Dead End, I wasn't really sure what to do with her once I got her there. I had a rough sketch in my head and some words on paper, but I just couldn't get the story to come out.

And honestly, it was rough going there for a bit. I questioned if I should even continue with this series. And worse, I doubted my abilities as a writer. But when it came down to it, I couldn't abandon this story, because I couldn't bear the thought of leaving Astra out there in limbo. I couldn't do that to her, and I couldn't do that to Star. I need for them to be reunited.

Then a friend helped me realize a big part of my block was because I didn't *know* Daisy. I'd spent years with the other characters, but she was a stranger. So I did what I usually do to get to know characters, I crawled inside her head by writing from her perspective.

What I saw was what her life was like when she still lived with her mom before she came to Dead End. At some point I may share in my newsletter what I wrote, but mostly it was just for me. And it served the purpose. It helped me to understand her. As I kept writing, she became part of the story, instead of an obstacle I had to overcome to get through the story. And by the end, she became my people.

Around this same time, I realized the only way I would get this book written was with some type of external pressure. So I set a pre-order date with Amazon. They have strict rules. If you cancel, you are banned from doing pre-orders for a year. But more than that, hanging over my head, was the thought of having to disappoint my readers.

And to help me make that goal, in January of 25 my amazing friend, and fellow author, Patti, suggested we try something different; daily, early morning, Zoom writing sessions. We'd previously met in person on Wednesdays but ended up talking more than writing many days.* ;)

So with Patti as my daily support, and November 29th as my goal, I churned out a draft in five months, revised it in two months, and over the following several weeks left it in the capable hands of my beta readers, editors, and proofreaders.

I can't make any promises for when book 3 might arrive, and I don't think I will do another pre-order until the book is mostly done, but I am hoping, with these new routines I have in place I can have it out sometime in 2026.

I also want to add, that another huge part of what helped me to get book two done, was YOU! Yes, you! The one still reading this even though the book is done. The one who left a review, signed up for my newsletter, and/or left encouraging comments on social media. As well as those of you who asked when book 2 was coming. You don't know how much it means that people enjoy what I write and want more. Thank you, thank you, thank you! From the bottom of my witchy little heart, a thousand times thank you! I hope that you enjoyed this book as much, or more than the first one!

We both acknowledge our chattiness, but we also both deeply understand in these sessions we have helped each other navigate the challenges that life tends to throw at women, especially those of a "certain age." I am not sure how I would have made it through the intense emotions of perimenopause without Patti.

P.S. We still chat during our early morning sessions, but

usually *keep it under 15 minutes.* And by usually, I mean
sometimes. 😉

acknowledgments

I continue to be amazed and extremely grateful for all the support I have in my life

And for *The Drama of Death* in no particular order, I want to thank the following people:

To my **Ocean's 6** peeps, Alli, Brittany, C, Kristin, and Scarlett. You've been in my life for over a decade and I couldn't imagine being an author without you all along for the journey. Especially these last few years with our yearly retreats.

We've had more adventures since book 1. So...thank you for Vegas and attempting to "set fire" to my problems. Thank you for Austin 2.0 and letting me lock myself in the focus cave to get those revisions done! And thanks for all the Swiftie convos, the "damning" of innocent Lindas, and witchy memes that happen in between the retreats. :D And an extra shout out to C for once again being an amazing beta reader.

To **Annette** for sending supportive memes, sharing in my obsession of Dreamlight Valley, and making sure I get my vitamin D(isney) often enough to make regular every day life bearable. And for knowing when I need space and when I don't. You are the goat! But not the screaming Muppet Haunted Mansion kind. ;)

To **Patti**! Holy cow! What a rollercoaster these past 2 years have been in both our lives. Even though I sometimes miss our Panera Wednesdays, we get so much more done with this new writing routine we've established! I don't think I could've gotten this book done as "quickly" as I did, without you! Nor could I have survived without your emotional support. :)

Thank you to **Lisa C.** for helping with the industry lingo, for the many memes and chats, the awesome swag, and for keeping me entertained with the various crustacean antics! Can't wait to hold your book in my hands!

To my sisters, **Lisa** and **Laura** for the care packages of Almond Joy, Peanut Butter M&Ms, and fun witchy office decor. And for always putting up with this bratty little sister.

I am thankful for **ALL my family and friends** both far and near! Whether you are mentioned by name or not. Or whether you read my book or not, you know I love you! <3

Thank you to **Alex** for the gentle nudges in bookstores when I'm nervous about speaking to the purchasing manager. You make me want to be brave all the time! And thank you for making our little family of 3 into a family of 4. Love you Paigey!

And as always, to **Tor** for being my biggest cheerleader. For always being proud of me, even when I don't believe in myself. And for understanding me in all my moods, especially when I'm doing my best impersonation of Ennui from *Inside Out*. And for reading aloud to me and doing all the voices. Thank you for your love, companionship, support, and board games. ;) Infinity.

about the author

Leslie Gail's debut novel first hit the market in 1979 with her riveting three-page illustrated novel, *The "Chrismas" Book.* It was not only a financial success—earning her a total of $2.50—it was also critically acclaimed by all the ladies in her mother's break-room group. ;)

These days Leslie's books are slightly wordier and no longer illustrated—which is probably for the best since she never could draw a proper "babby" Jesus. And are filled with magic, mystery, and big Southern families.

Leslie lives in Austin, Texas and is proudly doing her part to Keep It Weird. When she's not plotting murder, or working the day job, you might find her removing cat hair from every surface in her house, playing board games with her husband*, enjoying Saturday Brunch and bookstores with her family, singing along loudly to Disney songs**, or haunting local graveyards wherever she travels.

*Swedish husband. He wanted to make sure y'all knew his nationality. 😉 In case you mistakenly conjured up an image of Matthew McConaughey at a Longhorns game.

The cats wanted to make sure you knew Leslie cannot sing and that they've made more pleasant sounds while coughing up hairballs.*

***Leslie wants you to know that at least her singing never ruins the handmade Swedish rugs. So there!